Reviews of *Stickleback*

"Keep tight hold of your sanity when you plunge into the maelstrom of filth that churns between the covers of this brilliant debut novel. It is a book that grabs you by the throat and shakes you."

Tim Ellis

"There's a reason you won't find many Alans in the literary annals; sensible authors don't take on a challenge like this – it's too bloody hard to pull off. Connors may be as mad as his creation."

David Williams

"This is such a brilliant debut novel. The main character is vulgar but vulnerable and Mark Connors manages to depict him warts and all yet at the same time creating empathy in the reader. You really want him to get the girl and you can't help laughing along with him at times. Funny, insightful – and harrowing. I romped through this book."

Rachel Kerr

"Mark Connors has uncovered some of the complexities of mental illness and exposed them for people to get to grips with. Sticking with Alan Siddall throughout the experience of reading this book is like a window on the ups-and-downs of having a friend or family member with a mental illness."

MW Leeming

"Alan Siddall is one of the best comic creations I've read in a long time. I think this book is very perceptive about the modern mental health system, where 'service users' have achieved some limited powers and are prepared to use and abuse them, but ultimately are no more in control of their destiny than they ever were."

Terry Simpson

"A really good read and, from my own experience, horribly authentic. *Stickleback* is not just a diatribe against the mental health system or the people who work in it – it's much more nuanced than that. Thoughtful stuff."

Adrian Sinclair

Stickleback

Mark Connors

Published by Armley Press 2016

About the author

Mark Connors is an award winning writer from Horsforth near Leeds. He has won prizes and received commendations at various Literature Festivals. His poetry and short fiction has been published widely in the UK and overseas. His debut poetry pamphlet, *Life is a Long Song*, was published by Otley Word Feast Press in 2015. *Stickleback* is his first novel. For more information about Mark Connors, please visit his website at www.markconnors.co.uk.

Also by Mark Connors
Poetry:
Life is a Long Song (Otley Word Feast Press, 2015)

Acknowledgements

Copy editing: John Lake
Layout: Ian Dobson
Cover: Mick Lake
Author photo: Joanna Sedgwick © 2015
Production: Mick McCann

Stickleback © Mark Connors 2016

I give special thanks to the following people for their guidance and feedback during the writing of *Stickleback*: Lesley Connors, Rachel Kerr, Margit van der Zwan, John Lake and Barrie Sherwood.

I'd also like to thank the following people for their continued support: George Batty, Joanna Sedgwick, Aran Johnson, Faz, Mick Jaques, Kate Darley, Tim Ellis, the Connors/O'Connor clan in the UK and elsewhere and Armley Press for making this particular dream come true.

To Lesley and George

ISBN 978-0-9934811-2-3

Part One

The One That Got Away

1. Cassandra

When I heard that Dr Dofuckall had arranged a Care Programme Approach meeting for yours truly, I knew I had outstayed me welcome at Murton Croft. As me Uncle Bob used to say: *Times they are a changin'.*

There's a sign in the reception of Ward B: *Should you be having this conversation here?* It's for the benefit of the so-called mental health professionals. It tells them, in a subtle way, not to discuss ward business in an area where service users (the new posh word for nutters) may hear something they shouldn't. But it's amazing what they let slip on me quiet days.

You'll usually catch me in one of two states. I'm either as quiet as a mute mouse in the British Library or I'm reeling off every little thought that clutters up me noggin. At times, the staff could be forgiven for assuming I'm in Catatonia Central, barely functioning enough to swallow a slurp of tea without it decorating me beard. But if they saw me eyes, they'd think again. The eyes of the mad never lie. I wear me sunglasses from dusk till dawn and back again - have done for donkey's years – and me eyes are always working – even when the rest of me isn't; so are me lugs. So, when I'm sitting in reception, saying nowt and hearing all, tongue lolling lazily on me bottom lip, I might as well be fuckin' invisible. I hear all sorts. It's amazing what you can find out when you look like you've just had a lobotomy. And I'm not just talking about hospital business. I could tell you a thing or two about the staff as well.

*

It's the morning of me Care Programme Approach meeting, CPA for short (or, for those who speak English, the "What shall we do with this mad old fucker?" discussion), and I'm in one of me more flamboyant moods. I ask Pat, a fellow lifer, to crash me a fag.

"Menthols are for the chosen few," she croaks.

"If that's the case love then I'm glad I'm a fallen

angel," I say. Then she's back in the land of nod, as if someone's just twatted her with a lump hammer.

I'm in the TV lounge, finishing me cuppa after breakfast. A few of the patients are watching a property programme but it's a little bit late for them to be entering the buy-to-let market. Geoff still has most of his brekkie on his chin. I think he's saving it for later.

Beth, the new nurse, comes in to remind me of me date with Dofuckall and his foot soldiers. You can always rely on the staff to be predictable.

"Hi Alan. Dr Bell should be in about half-ten if that's okay."

"That's fine love but I've run out of smokes and nobody's crashin', are they Pat?"

"Yer what?" Pat wakes up from her power nap.

"Never mind, love. You pop off back to Kansas." I put me leather on.

"Are you going now?" Beth asks. "Can't you wait until you've seen Dr Bell?"

"Sorry love. No baccy, no CPA meeting. If they hadn't closed down the hospital shop we wouldn't be having this conversation. Take it up with management."

"But Alan, Dr Bell asked me to make sure you were around. It won't take long."

"That's what they all say love. I'll look like Moses by the time he's finished with me."

"But..."

"Listen, I've got a free diary till me heart packs up so he can always pop back tomorrow. Anyways, if I'm running a bit late you can tell Dr Bell that I'll be back before he can say lithium." That really throws her and I take pity on the poor girl. "Don't you worry, love. I'll be back before he gets here. Scout's honour. Dib dib dib, dob dob dob." I give her me old scout salute.

I've got a whole bloody hour. I don't know why she's getting her panties in a knot, that's if she's wearing any. I hope not. It's nice to have new wanking material. I may not be the schoolboy I was once, but I can still crack one off with the

9

best of 'em when the mood takes me.

On the way down to the shop, I start thinking about something that happened in Germany. It must be something to do with the weather. It's a bit foggy, like God's playing with his dry ice machine.

I was at the gate one day, playing hangman with Alfie Turner, when this bloke from Newcastle limped up and told us he'd been shot in the arse by a German baker.

"It's peacetime!" I said.

"Not for the baker," said the Geordie.

I thought I saw Hitler once in Stuttgart but he was long dead. Still, Saddam had look-a-likes to stop the Yanks getting him so I suppose one of Hitler's henchmen could have stepped in. Hitler did it himself once when he convinced Hollywood he was Charlie Chaplin. It worked like a treat till he started talking.

Maybe Hitler was the baker. I've heard he made a mean sausage roll. He wanted the Lake District to be his own personal playground. He must have liked gingerbread and read Beatrix Potter when he was a nipper. He once wandered lonely as a cloud until it pissed it down. He went back to his hotel for his brolly. He never saw the daffodils.

I pass a policeman who's walking the beat in a Day-Glo yellow jacket. He looks like a fuckin' lollypop man.

"Morning, officer."

"Morning," he says, not knowing what to make of me shades. I know what he's thinking: I'm either a blind bastard that's lost me stick, me golden retriever's fucked off to bang a bitch in heat, or I'm as mad as a March hare in the spring sunshine, only it's foggy as fuck. I can tell by his eyes he's gone for the latter. He'll make a fine Detective Superintendent one day.

I get to the shop and give Mrs Patel a big smile. I'm one of her best customers since they shut the nutters' tuck shop. I try engaging her in conversation but she doesn't like what she's hearing. I'm not at me coherent best so I won't hold it against her.

I see a woman over by the fridge. I see her profile. I

10

put a name to the face. But I've been wrong before and, in my condition, errors of mistaken identity can lead to all sorts of problems. I don't trust mesen just yet so I go over and take a closer look. This is quite a moment if she's who I think she is, a genuine big deal, and the only moments I get like this these days are when I'm twisting with the lithium pixies.

I walk over to her and decide to say the first thing that comes into me head. As usual, I'm not quite sure what that's going to be but out it pops anyway.

"Sausages are bad for the soul."

"Sorry?" She turns around and if she isn't who I think she is, then she's either got a twin sister or I'm up lithium creek without a soddin' paddle.

"You don't have to apologise love but I'd go for the bacon. I used to eat sausages and I've been on lithium for twenty-five years. Did you know that the legal requirement for meat content in a sausage is only forty-two per cent? And only fifty per cent of the meat has to be lean? Think about it."

She's already decided she's dealing with a Dundee cake but then I see something in her eyes that tells me there's a hint of recognition. I know it's not from the way I look. Must be me voice.

"Do I know you?"

"Well there's a question and it would take a better man than me to answer it. Picture me without me shades, whip me beard off, give me a short back and sides and take a couple of decades off me ol' boat race. You haven't changed much, apart from a bit of extra timber."

She looks like I've just slapped her in the face but she's curious enough not to let an unintended insult get in the way; not that she'd know I didn't intend to insult her. I'm fucked if I know.

"No, sorry. You'll have to give me a clue."

She didn't have much of her South African accent left, but Leeds has a way of dragging the sophistication out of you over the years. "No clues love. I don't have time for game shows. Dr Doolittle's waiting."

"Hang on a minute. Take your sunglasses off."

"I can't do that, love. You'll look into me eyes and see what the sausages did."

"But it's... are you blind?"

"No, love. I can see you all right. They keep the rain off me pupils."

She laughs and me stomach ties itself a reef knot.

Suddenly, I want to get the fuck out of Dodge but she's still playing and she'll probably make a run for it anyway when she figures out who I am so I throw her a bone or two.

"Twenty-six bus, long walk home in the snow, Kirkstall Abbey, kissy kissy, feely feely, Bob's yer uncle, Joan's yer auntie."

"Oh my God!" Now she looks like she's just walked in front of a bus and made eye contact with the driver before impact. I feel like puking, like I've got butterflies, only there's hundreds of the fluttering little fuckers.

"Wow. It's the leather jacket and your long hair – well, it's everything really. You used to be so..."

"Normal?"

"I was going for smart actually. Do you ride a motorbike now?"

"No love. Not in my condition. But I was born to be wild."

I'm surprised how well this is going after the last time I bumped into her.

"I'm sorry. I can't remember your name."

Maybe it's not going as well as I thought.

"Alan. Alan Siddall. Second-hand Sid. Siddall the know all, who does fuck all and knows jack shit."

She frowns. I don't think she likes the swearing.

"Of course. How are you, Alan?"

I feel a stir in me jockeys. "Not ten bad, Cassandra. Not ten bad. But tomorrow could be a different story. Like Lena Martell said, 'One day at a time sweet Jesus,' but what the fuck did she know?"

She frowns again. She definitely doesn't like the swearing.

12

"Are you still painting?" I ask.

"Not so much these days. I taught for years and it zapped me of any creative energy I had."

"Well, nice to bump into you again. The last time we met you ran away screaming."

"Sorry?"

"In Morrison's, Merrion Centre. Must be ten years back. I tried to hug you but you had other ideas. I wasn't a well man at the time."

"Sorry Alan. Not me. I lived in Birmingham ten years ago and I'm pretty sure I haven't seen you since that night you walked me home."

"Oh." That explained a lot. No wonder that woman screamed in Morrison's. Must have frightened the shite out of her, poor lass.

"Do you live around here?" she asks.

"Not far. Local nuthouse up the road, but this grey squirrel's outstayed his welcome."

She tries her best to look surprised. "Well, nice to see you again after all these years and thanks for the tip about the sausages. Didn't you used to be a butcher?"

"I still am, love, but only in spirit." It's awkward silence time but I'm ready to fill it. "Do you live around here then?"

"No, I've just started work around the corner."

She doesn't tell me where. I don't think she's up for an unannounced visit, not that I could blame her. There was a time when I wouldn't have wanted her turning up at my work either; but I had the wrath of Babs to worry about in those days.

*

Cassandra and I used to catch the 26 bus into Leeds. She'd get on about halfway through me journey. One time, the bus was full and she sat next to me. We got talking, and, before long, we were sitting next to each other out of choice rather than necessity.

Cassandra was from South Africa. She had moved over here with her British father who had moved back from

South Africa when her mother died. She was an art student then, back in the day when artists actually painted instead of bleeding or shitting on canvas. She'd sometimes show me her stuff. I thought they were bloody good but I knew as much about quantum physics as I did about art. She did self-portraits sometimes, which showed her inner demons. I did one once in the 80s, during creative therapy at High Royds. I looked like the Yorkshire Ripper. It scared the shit out of the nurses.

Cassandra was always having trouble with her boyfriends and she used to moan about her fellas that would come and go. Then one day, she didn't get on the bus and I assumed she'd gone back to Cape Town. I missed her. I fancied the pants off young Cassandra but I had a few years on her and I moved in very different circles: she worked with paint, I worked with offal. Besides, I was well into Babs as well. More fuckin' fool me.

I was a late starter with the ladies. After me national service, I couldn't get it together with women for a good few years. I'd been with prostitutes in Germany but I could never get the hang of the old chatting up business. Dip yer wick, shoot yer muck and off you toddle was my motto, not that I could dip mine without a pocketful of deutschmarks. It was a bit of a shock when I met Babs. She could talk the British out of Belfast and, like I said, I was a quiet bloke back then.

You wouldn't believe how many times I've thought about Cassandra over the years: the *what ifs,* the *if onlys*, the *why the fuck didn't I turn up for that date with her?* My life could have turned out very differently indeed. I often wonder if madness is more to do with personal happiness than any other contributing factor. You don't often meet a happy bunny inside the walls of a nuthouse; I can tell you that for nothing, not unless they're as high as a balloon in a hurricane.

I'll remember the night I walked Cassandra home for as long as I can still piss me name in the snow. I'd just helped Dad wash the floors down in our butcher's shop in Leeds market, and, as usual, I went to wash the blood off me hands in the reeking gents. By the end of the day, the sink in the shop was filthy with blood. After a day of swimming in it, I preferred the market lavs. I always a carried a bar of soap in a polythene bag I kept in me coat pocket. I've always been meticulously clean, even when I'm off me rocker.

Dad had left early that day to take me mam shopping. I walked down to the Duck 'n' Drake for a pint. The snow was already laying but I was desperate for ale and a bit of company so I decided to risk it, hoping they wouldn't stop the buses. By the time I'd finished me pint and left the pub, the whole of Leeds was like one of them plastic Christmas domes that you shake to make it snow. As beautiful as Leeds looked, I knew I was in for a long walk home.

When I got to the bus stop, the queue was long enough to tell me there'd be no more buses that night, so I decided to go back to the pub and get mesen tanked up. I'd worry about how to get home later.

It was then I spotted Cassandra trudging up from the Parish Church in her green wellingtons. Her beige duffel coat was done up to the neck, her hood was down and her long brown hair was flecked white with snow. She was walking lopsided due to the huge art satchel hanging over her left shoulder.

"Alan!"

"Now then. I thought you'd buggered off back to Cape Town?"

"No. I moved in with some of the girls from college. I had to get away from Dad. He was driving me up the wall. Are you going for the bus? I'm staying at Dad's for Christmas."

"I don't think they're running, love. I thought I'd sit it out in the pub and see if it calms down a bit. I don't suppose you fancy a drink?"

"Sounds wonderful but..."

"Fair enough, nice seeing you again."

I turned.

"Hang on, Alan. Go on then. Why not?"

We sat by the fire and dried off and she showed me her latest work. She showed me a landscape she'd done of Ilkley Moor from the Cow and Calf. It was brilliant. I can still picture it now.

One drink led to another and before long, she'd dragged out her art pad and was sketching me. The beer loosened me tongue and I told her a few yarns from me time in Germany and working at the shop with Dad. I didn't mention Babs though. I never told her about Babs.

By kicking-out time, we were four sheets to the wind and the wind wasn't dropping. We linked arms and started the long walk back home. The snow was deep and it took us about an hour and a half to trudge up to Kirkstall Abbey.

Cassandra, pissed as a rat on a stag night, thought we should have a look around the abbey and dry off a bit.

We went inside. The next thing I knew she was kissing me. I tried to undo her coat but she was having none of it. I was rock hard and me balls were hanging like wet sandbags. It doesn't matter now, I suppose. I've replayed that scene so many times and fucked her every which way till Sunday.

We reached the end of her dad's street at about one in the morning. She gave me a long lingering kiss and asked me to meet her at the Duck 'n' Drake the Saturday after Christmas, at seven. She told me she'd have put the finishing touches to her sketch of me by then.

I never saw it.

*

"Right then, love. I best be off," I say to Cassandra.

"Okay. Nice seeing you again. Maybe I will..."

I had already started walking out of the shop before she got to finish her sentence.

Me mind is racing, flitting from one thought to another. I start thinking about Dad. I start thinking about blood and pork. Then I recall a story from the paper the other day.

This woman, a grandmother no less, stabbed her bloke in the leg for eating her supper. She'd left a pork chop dinner in the fridge that she'd cooked the day before, so she could warm it up when she got home from work. When she got home that night, she opened the fridge and it wasn't there. She went berserk. He was sitting on the couch. She took her choice of weapon from the kitchen drawer, went over towards where he was sitting, bent down in front of him, screamed "Eat my pork then feel my fork" and stabbed the poor fucker in the leg. He forgave her, the stupid bastard. When Babs tried to stab me I locked her out of the house. She went to her mam's. I got a letter a few days later telling me she'd met a bus conductor called Derek.

I wasn't ready for my CPA meeting with Dofuckall so I walked into town and tried to calm mesen down.

2. For Whom Dr Bell Tolls

It's brightened up a bit by the time I get to town. I stopped mesen mid-rant halfway up The Headrow and I'm reasonably calm by the time I reach Dortmund Square. I keep trying to get me head around what's going to happen. The only thing I do know is that I'm up for the fight. They're not shoving me in some godforsaken shithole to rot me final days away.

I hear a loud Glasgow accent and for a minute I think it's Kenny. Kenny prowled the streets of Leeds almost daily for nearly 30 years, waxing hysterical to anyone who'd listen. The demise of our industrial base was his chief concern. While my enduring mental health problems are fairly complex and accumulative, Kenny was a different kettle of perch. He lost his job of 20 years in the tailoring trade in the early 80s, his wife and kid fucked off and he went barmy. Simple as. Cause and effect. He's been ranting about Thatcher and her merry men ever since. And he knows his stuff. He knows the tale of the Westland Affair better than Heseltine himself. Try and steer him clear of the miners' strike – fuck me – you just don't want to go there. But ask him about the Night of the Long Knives. He loves that one – the night they all stabbed that ginger bitch in the back – that image of her little teary face through the window of her car as the flash bulbs flashed outside Number 10. Kenny loved that. Me too.

This particular Scottish bloke is having a go at fresh air and the air is turning as blue as the Med on a summer's afternoon. He can't be a day over 30. He'll be staying at the crypt but I'd bet a pair of me best Y-fronts that he'll be sectioned by teatime. The cops will pick him up pretty soon, he'll be carted off down to the station, assessed, and he'll be with us in time for *EastEnders*. There'll be no booze at Murton Croft either and he'll be none too happy cooped up with the likes of us. I hope the loud bastard ends up on another ward. I think he and I would clash a tad, and he's a big bastard. I'd have a word but I've got me own shit to deal with.

I can't get Cassandra out of me noggin. I mean, today

of all days. Dofuckall will be doing his nut by now. They'll ring the boys in blue, tell them I've absconded and they'll be looking for me by now. One of the nurses will tell them me likely route. It's not that I'm not allowed to play out on me own but it's fairly obvious that today I'm in no mood for the circle shenanigans. This will be logged as a disappearance and I will be deemed a danger to meself once more.

If there's one thing that I'd change about mental health care, apart from being drugged up to me ball sack for the best part of me fuckin' life, then it's the abject humiliation of the Circle Game. It's something I'll never get used to, and I can handle meself. Imagine what it's like for the old ladies who've been admitted for the first time, all confused and disorientated, up in front of the interrogators. It's all very cordial and pleasant but that makes it worse. You are being quietly judged. The questions come at you in much the same way as an inquisition, only the tones are gentle and there are no thumb screws to look forward to. Just drugs. Lots and lots of drugs. And not the kind you can enjoy while listening to Black Sabbath's *Volume 4* or *The Dark Side of the Moon.* When you're a bit doolally, getting on a bit and more likely to burn your flat down when you leave the chip pan on, Murton Croft is your halfway house. It's your fucking purgatory. The thing is, as purgatory goes, it's not a bad old place compared to the alternatives. Hell is only a Care Programme Approach meeting away.

The chairs will have been laid out in the main meeting room by one of the support workers about 30 minutes ago. The circle's occupants will arrive in dribs and drabs: Barry Fowler, my far from charismatic social worker, Jenny, my primary nurse, my occupational therapist, the esteemed Dr Bell, and a support worker or three to make up the numbers. There will be no tea and biscuits. Dr Bell will do most of the talking. He'll start by divulging the reason for the meeting and then we'll get down to it.

The meeting is arranged to decide what to do with me but it's all a fuckin' farce. That decision has been made already and I for one had fuck all to do with the process.

I wander down towards the market. The sun has gone back in and there's a real chill in the air. I could do with a scarf. I've only got a fiver on me but I might pick one up cheap if I'm lucky. But the real reason I'm heading for the market is to take a trip down Butcher's Row. That's my version of Memory Lane. I haven't been down old blood street for a few years, unless I'm skipping down its slippery surfaces in me dreams, and boy do I dream of Butcher's Row. Always have done. We all have a place we like to return to again and again in our dreams and nightmares. Mind you, such places are not usually bespattered in pig's blood.

I wonder if I'll see any old faces. Butchers are usually butchers for life unless they go fuckin' mad like yours truly or they've been driven out of business by a supermarket or a fuckin' Tesco Express. If I'm lucky, I might still get a warm pork pie.

I cross the top of Briggate and a copper stops me.

"Mr Siddall?" It's hardly a surprise. I've been here before.

"That's me, officer. You'll have to be quick. There's a pork pie with my name on it on Butcher's Row and I want it in me mush before the jelly goes cold."

There's another cop on the other side of me and he tells his walkie-talkie that they've found me.

"Can I call you Alan?"

"You can call me Calamity Jane as long as I get me pie."

"Well, Alan, they're a bit worried about you up at Murton Croft and they've asked us to pop you back up there if that's okay."

"How much is he paying yer?"

"Sorry?"

"Doctor Dofuckall."

They both chuckle.

"Come on, Alan, let's get you back."

"I've got a fiver. I'll treat you both to a growler."

You try and be civil and it gets you fuckin' nowhere. We have a bit of a tussle but I look a lot fiercer than I am.

20

*

I'm practically walking across the ceiling when I get back to the nuthouse. I'm ushered straight into the meeting room and the circle is formed and waiting impatiently for me.

"Alan. What happened to you?" says Dr Bell.

"Sorry, Doctor. I got distracted."

"I've had to cancel three appointments and the rest of the staff have a lot on."

"I got delayed by the parade."

"What parade?"

"It's Pride of Pork Day. The butchers are everywhere. They're handing out free pork pies. Even the vegetarians are snappin' 'em up but they're spitting out the jelly. It's the best bit, Doctor. I should know. I was weaned on it."

The occupational therapist is trying not to laugh but the smiley muscles don't lie.

"Alan, I'm due over at the day centre so I'll have to be brief now. They're cutting down the bed numbers so we're going to have to make some changes." Dr Bell always refers to the bed managers and pencil pushers as *they* or *them* as though *they* or *them* were on the opposite side of the battlefield to his good self. Maybe they are sometimes but not today. Today it's moi versus the whole fuckin' lot of them. "We want you to take a look at a place that we" – see how quickly he changed to "we" – "think will be more suitable for your needs. It's over in Bingley."

"A care home, is it?"

"Yes. You need somewhere permanent."

"I'm okay here."

"That's just not possible anymore, Alan. We have to at least try and find you somewhere appropriate and Barry thinks he's identified a couple of viable options, and there's one place in particular that we..."

"I know I'm getting on, Doc, but can you honestly see me in an old folks' home? Have you ever seen me in the Reminiscence Club? It's all bloody *Oklahoma*, *My Fair Lady*, or *Barbara the Bleedin' Bolshevik Belly Dancer*! I might be sixty-eight but I'll take me Sabbath albums over that dippy shit any day of the week. I'll go back to me flat."

"Alan, that's just not possible. You need to be somewhere safe and we need to keep an eye on you when you're not feeling too good."

"I can top mesen in a fuckin' death camp just as easily as back at the flat. All I need is a sharp knife or the belt that keeps me britches up." I look around the circle and me eyes rest on Jenny. "Back us up, someone?" Jenny is me primary nurse. We go back a long way, me and Jenny Wren.

"Alan, why don't you have a look at the place Barry has picked out? If you like it, or you prefer one of the others on his shortlist, you could maybe go on a trial period and take it from there," says Jenny.

"I think that's the best course of action, Alan," concurs Barry.

"It's nice of you to join in, Barry. I thought you'd dropped off for a minute. Fuckin' cowboy."

"There's no need for that, Alan," says Dr Bell, although he would probably agree that Barry didn't really give a flying fuck about any of us anymore. He's just waiting for his pension to kick in so he can spend the rest of his days pullin' his pud over Fern Britten.

"Just have a look, Alan. See how it goes," says Jenny.

"I know how it'll go, sweetheart. I like it here. You all know how to handle me. I don't want to live with a bunch of walking corpses and nurses that don't know me from Ozzy Osbourne." The occupational therapist nearly laughs again. "If something's funny, love, do share it with the group 'cos I'm not bleedin' laughin'. Did my sister put you all up to this?"

"No," said Dr Bell. "Alison would prefer it if you stayed here. The home is in Bingley so it will be a bit of a trek for her."

"I don't care if it's in bloody Basra, I'm not going."

"The thing is Alan, this is an acute ward, whereas your needs are more long term now. You're sixty-eight."

"I know how old I am, Doc. I've got me date of birth on me bus pass."

This time, a couple of them laugh, but again, I don't.

22

There's fuck all to laugh about in this sorry state of affairs. I feel like giving Dr Bell me definition of acute by snatching the biro from his clipboard and ramming it into me left eye.

"And what happens if I go batshit again?"

"Well, you'd probably go to an acute ward nearer the home for a few weeks until you were better," says Dr Bell.

"What about me flat? Finances and all that?"

"You'll be under a section 118 so your flat and money are irrelevant. You'll have to talk to your sister about what to do with it. Alan, all we're asking at this stage is that you at least visit Willowbeck Gardens."

"Willowbeck? Sounds like sommat from a bloody Enid Blyton book. I bet it sounds a lot better than it looks, or bloody smells for that matter."

"Just visit and see what you think. Like Jenny said, you could go for a trial period and if it doesn't work out, we could look at other options."

"I'll think about it, Doc. Can I go for a smoke now?"

"Okay," he says. "Sleep on it and I'll pop back tomorrow and we'll have another chat."

"Can't wait, Doc."

I rise and leave the circle of indignity. I give Jenny a wink and me occupational therapist the finger.

*

They never fuckin' get it right, the so-called mental health professionals. I go back to me room and tell meself a story. I do this a lot when I'm agitated. I imagine I'm in me own documentary with that Louis Theroux. He did a programme on Jimmy Savile once. If ever there was a bloke born to be sectioned, it was that cigar-smokin' lunatic.

I first met Jenny in the late 70s when I was a relative newcomer to crazy town. And back then we did live in our own self-contained little Trumpton, tucked away from the rest of the world. It was called High Royds. Back in the day, it had its own shops, a bank, a chemist, a chapel, a cricket pitch and tennis courts. Go back far enough and it had an upholsterer, a butcher, a dairy, a tailor, a baker, a fuckin' candlestick maker. It had its own soddin' railway station, not to mention acres of maintained gardens, fallow fields, tree-lined avenues and a huge pond. In the summer, you'd be forgiven for thinking its location was positively idyllic, with moorland above it and Otley Chevin in the distance. Let's not forget its clock tower with lightning rods that loomed over the main building like something out of a fuckin' Hammer horror film. And while we're on it, High Royds has been in loads of films since it closed its doors to its fucked-up patrons. I've seen the morgue that is our TV lounge liven up suddenly when High Royds has featured in some TV programme or other. Even fuckin' David Dimbleby waxed lyrical about it on *How We Built Britain.*

But inside the walls of that fuckin' hell hole was a very different story, and Jenny, like meself and a handful of lifers at Murton Croft, have lived to tell the tale. Well, we're all a part of the same yarn.

If I had a quid for every sad bastard who told me they were going to write a book about their life in High Royds, I'd be on a plane to Timbukfuckintu by now. You wouldn't believe some of the shit that went down. It was stranger than fiction could ever fuckin' be.

Me point is, they don't realise I've become what they were trying to stop by closing down High Royds. They closed down shitholes like that because there was a culture of institutionalisation that had blighted mental health care for nearly a century. There were people on wards in that place that went in at 21 and never came out again. But I never settled in that fuckin' dump. We slept thirty to a room and when you woke up on a morning, some other fucker would be wearing your trousers. The long white corridors echoed with the screams and cries of the chronics, trudging around that colossal Victorian dump like zombies. Institutionalised? You've got to be fuckin' kidding. Every time I got put in there, I couldn't wait to get the fuck out.

So what do the powers that be do? They build smaller, newer units that are more like hospitals, without the acres of grounds and the clock tower; just functional red-brick buildings that are seemingly fit for purpose. But they make a huge fuckin' mistake. They give everybody their own little room, their own fuckin' bedsit, and the beds are not like those squeaking morgue slabs you got in High Royds, no siree. This is sleep easy time. Got me own little wardrobe. I can shut the door and listen to me CDs on me ghetto blaster. I can read me books. I can be alone or I can join the catatonics in the lounge for a spot of *Bargain Hunt*. I have a nice little nutter's bedsit to see out me days, nurses to look after me; me own little pad within walking distance of the city centre. Institutionalized? Of course I fuckin' am. They'll have to drag me out of here kicking and screaming.

3. Arthur's Return

I don't know whether it was the walk into Leeds, seeing Cassandra or the fear of the impending doom of Willowbeck Gardens, but I wasn't mesen for the rest of the day. I took a nap in the afternoon and missed me dinner. Jenny saved me a couple of ham sarnies and a bun and I ate them in me favourite spot for reflection: the seating area near the reception desk.

Bev tries engaging me in conversation but I'm not playing. Bev's an alarmingly obese support worker who doesn't like me at all. She was born with a growler in her pie hole.

She natters to Beth instead. Beth has been here since 7.45 this morning. She's very keen at the moment is that one. Bev's apathy will soon rub off on her. She usually wears a look of abject boredom and indifference across her ugly mush from the minute she puts her knickers on till the minute she peels them off. It's contagious, like the worst kind of stomach bug. Her smile is chilling at best. But I'd still give her one. I'd do her from behind with her head in a vice so she couldn't turn around. Me and Beverley will never see eye to eye.

Beth comes out from behind the desk, where Bev's ample arse will be glued to her chair until she needs her midnight dump.

"Do you fancy a cup of tea, Alan?" She's so sweet I almost break me silence. "Alan?"

"You won't get owt out of him tonight. He's in a world of his own," says Bev.

She walks back towards that colossus of disdain.

"Does he always wear sunglasses?" asks Beth.

"I can't remember the last time he didn't."

"Why?"

"You'll have to ask him that. Are you making that bloody tea or what?"

I watch Beth's tight little bum cheeks slyly wiggle beneath her black trousers as she walks into the staff kitchen.

What I wouldn't give just to see her naked. I feel mesen spring to life. It's nice to be reminded that I'm not dead below me belly just yet.

After me knob goes back to sleep, I nod off. I'm awoken by a familiar face a couple of hours later. He's accompanied by two paramedics. Their faces tell the story. You'll never get old Arthur in here without a fight. Arthur is six foot two and built like an air raid shelter. He has swept-back, nicotine-white hair, a 'tache to match and a rhubarb complexion. Arthur knows how to make an entrance.

"My word, Beverley," he says. "You look as cheerful as ever. Were you recently left at the altar, my darling? And who is this pretty young thing?"

"This is Beth. Beth, meet Arthur," says Bev.

"Hello, Beth," he says. *"Welcome to my world, won't you come on in?"* he sings. Arthur lets out a belly laugh, followed by a coughing fit, which is accompanied by a couple of hearty farts. "I beg your pardon, ladies. That last rascal nearly passed the nipper-offer. We'd have been in a right old mess then, wouldn't we?" He laughs again. The girls don't get the joke. He coughs again. His face goes a dark crimson, which, through me shades, looks life-threatening.

"Well if it is isn't Mr Siddall," he wheezes, and bends a little to catch his breath. "Ah. Not talking today? Makes a change, old boy."

Then he starts singing some opera bollocks. I fuckin' hate opera. Arthur's in the mood to perform and he's expecting an audience. There's no one sleeping tonight.

The paramedics lead him into the meeting room and Bev goes to get Big Roy from the TV lounge. Roy's a lazy bastard but he can pin down most of us without breaking a sweat. They like to have a big bugger around when admitting patients in case things get nasty. But Arthur wouldn't hurt a gnat unless he had a good reason. He's a gentleman with an intellect and a half. He's got more brains in one of his stools than half of the staff in this place. He's a retired university lecturer, a man of books, a doctor no less. But Arthur's most redeeming feature is that he loves to take the piss and, as he's more eloquent and erudite than most, he's hilarious with it. He makes the mouse run up the clock that much faster.

Me mind starts racing and I take a trip back to Butcher's Row. It's just like time travel only without the Tardis. I'm putting out the ox liver and tripe in the window with a sprig of parsley between each third cut of offal. When we were kids, me and Alison daubed pig's blood on our faces and put sprigs of parsley in our hair. She looked like Maid Marian after the crows had got to her. I looked like a crazy Errol Flynn. Me dad went barmy and tanned our arses for our trouble. They'd have locked him up for child abuse these days. He was a mean bastard, me old man. He treated me mother just as bad. She once told me that she knew how things were going to go two days into their marriage. He chucked his roast beef dinner at the wall as soon as it was laid in front of him. "I said rare, yer dozy mare." She never overcooked it again mind. The last time I saw him raise his hands to her I was big enough to stop him. We had a right old brawl. I wouldn't say I came out best exactly but I never saw him hit her again. I'd have taken a meat mallet to him if he had. I might be capable of a lot of bad things but I'd never hit a woman. I told a fellow patient in High Royds called Annie the very same thing back in 1979. She thought I was the Ripper. I was doing an impression of a Geordie at the time so fair dos. No one knew he was a Bradford lad till they caught the evil fucker. I shaved me beard off back then. Any bloke with a beard was a suspect in them days, even Noel Edmonds and Dave Lee fuckin' Travis.

I manage to get mesen up and I trudge down towards me boudoir to the sound of Arthur singing the Cornetto song in Italian. You know the one:

Just one Cornetto
Give it to me
You must me joking
They're ninety pee

I break me silence. "Alright, Pavarotti. Give it a fuckin' rest."

"And hello to you, Mr Siddall." Arthur laughs again.

28

Arthur coughs again. Arthur doesn't sound well at all.

*

I shoot bolt upright from a nightmare. I was in the shop again. Babs was pricking the pork pies but not in the centre. She was just picking random spots on the pastry top, the evil bint. Me dad was in his wheelchair, just like he was when he had his stroke. He was swivelling in a circular motion, mopping the blood off the floor, but it was too thick and congealed and the more he moved, the more his wheels left fresh tracks. He was carrying on, telling us that foot and mouth was on its way back and that blue tongue was rife in Airedale. To prove his point, he put out his own tongue which looked like he'd been chewing a leaking biro. Babs told me to kill him before we all got it. I threw a meat mallet at him but he ducked. Then Alison went over and beat him to death with a lamb shank.

You get some smashing dreams on lithium.

It's too early for breakfast so I make mesen a coffee and go out for a smoke. I've never seen such a dramatic reaction to government policy than when me and me fellow lifers heard about the smoking ban. It made the poll tax look like the introduction of winter fuel payments. We were fuckin' livid. At first, lifers over 65 were fuckin' queuing up to go into homes. You can still spark up in residential homes and for that reason alone, some chronic smokers have been happily shipped off to the death camps so they can smoke themselves into their coffins. When your nuts have disappeared into your stomach in the depths of winter, I have to say that smoking in a warm room does sound heavenly. But not heavenly enough to get me into a fuckin' home.

It's funny how when an old git like meself talks about a "home" the word automatically changes its meaning. "A home" couldn't be more different than "home" without the *A*. *Home is where your heart is;* or if it isn't, *Home is where your heart should be; Home Sweet Home; Wherever you lay your hat, that's your home,* unless of course you lay your hat on a coat stand in some old mansion that's way past its former glory, a place that once smelled of Pimms and cucumber sandwiches instead of that heady fusion of disinfectant, school

29

dinners, shit, puke and piss. "Home" is where the Oxo lady serves her family dinner; "Home" is where the Labrador puppy fucks off with the bog roll while you're struggling with the *Guardian* crossword with your scruds around your ankles. The idea of home is central to life itself, whether you live in a council house, a nice flat or a fuckoff mansion. "A home" is all about the other end, a reeking purgatory before you enter hell; your final, miserable days on this fucked-up planet.

I shiver throughout me smoke. Zahid on the main entrance reception tries another *hello* again as I walk back towards the lifts but I'm in no mood for pleasantries. I can't help but look forward to spending a bit of time with old Arthur though. If ever you could consider the notion that bi-polar disorder actually suits some people, then Dr Arthur Spencer would be a class example. He's never more animated than when he's riding the crest of a manic episode. He positively glows with the energy it gives him. His euphoria doesn't last though, and he soon stops singing and waxing lyrical about the Romantics and quoting chunks of Tennyson, Coleridge and Wordsworth. On his comedowns he reads his broadsheet irritably, muttering obscenities to himself. But he's a good bloke, one of the best. The staff love him. I love him although I wouldn't tell the old fucker. He's a joy to have around and there'll be no one of his stature at Guantanamo fuckin' Gardens, that's for sure.

I go back to bed for a bit when I get back to the ward and I wake a few hours later to a knock at me door. It's Jenny with me Weetabix. I've missed brekkie. "What time is it, love?"

"It's just after ten. Dr Bell's coming in around eleven-thirty. How are you feeling about it all?"

I sit up. She looms above me, raises me head and pulls up the pillows to encourage me to sit up. She pulls a chair over.

"I don't know, love. I don't want to go but I guess he has other ideas. I'd do a runner if I could trust meself to take me tablets. Come with me if you like. I'll sell the flat and we can head off into the sunset. What do yer say?"

"I don't think Brian would be too pleased about that, do you?"

"He's daft enough to cook his own fry-ups. Anyway, you'd soon get fed up of me." She takes my hand.

"Never," she says and gives me smoking hand a squeeze. "Right. I'd better go see to our friend Arthur. He'll be expecting his breakfast in bed just like you. Shall I get Beth to run you a bath?"

"Only if she gets in it wi' me."

"Behave, you randy old sod. Come on. Up yer get and get yourself bathed."

She gives me a big warm smile and leaves the room.

After I'm spruced up, I join Arthur in one of the quiet rooms, not that he knows the meaning of the word.

"Mr Siddall. How are we this fine morning? Ah, it's like that, is it? Don't let the bastards grind you down, old son. We can grind ourselves down without any help from those that hide in the shadows."

"It's good to see you, Arthur," I manage.

"Well, well. It speaks. I am privileged. Must be serious. We don't usually get a peep out of you when you're in your quiet mode."

"Dr Bell wants me to move on."

"Where the hell to? The Marriot? The Hilton?"

"Willowbeck Gardens."

"Oh my. Sounds ghastly. What about your sister?"

"What about her?"

"Won't she look after you?"

"You must be fuckin' joking. No fear. We'd kill each other. No, it's the knacker's yard for me."

"Just get some money out of the bank and bugger off somewhere. You must have a bit stashed away, Siddall. Get out there man. See the world. Have you ever been north of Kirkstall Abbey?"

"Sod off," I say. "I'm off for a slash."

"Five shakes and it's a felony!" he shrieks, then laughs, then turns purple.

"Fuckin' 'ell, Arthur. I'd lay off the pipe for a bit.

That's a bit of a rasper you've got there."

"Just a tickle," he says, grinning. "Talk to Advocacy, Alan. Get yourself some advice. That will put a few fireworks up their arses." He laughs again. He coughs again. He turns purple again.

After me slash, I go back to me room and get me leather. Philippa, the ward manager is behind the desk as I head for the door. "Hi, Alan," she says, just before I reach it.

"Morning, Philippa. Good holiday?"

"Lovely, thank you. Can I have a quick word?"

"I was just popping out for a wander. Nice tan."

"Thank you. It won't take a minute." She's all business these days, is our Philippa. We go into the meeting room. "So, how are you feeling about going to Willowbeck?" she asks, before I even park me arse.

"I haven't agreed to go anywhere yet, love."

"I know but are you thinking about it?"

"I'd rather stay here."

"I know you would but that's just not possible."

"I think it is."

She smiles. "Have a look at it, that's all we're asking."

"And what if I say no?"

"Go up there with Barry and if you don't like it there are other places."

"Can I go now?"

"I'd prefer it if you didn't," she says. "Dr Bell is on his way and we don't want a repeat performance of what happened yesterday."

"You heard about that, did you?"

"Oh yes."

"I'll just nip out for a smoke, if it's not too much trouble. You can keep an eye on me through the CCTV. I'll go and see if Arthur wants to keep me company." I get up.

"Alan? Do you mind if you don't?"

"What?"

"Ask Arthur?"

"Why?"

"Have you heard his chest?"

"You want it all your own way, Philippa. I bet you keep that husband of yours on a tight leash."

"Like you wouldn't believe," she says, smiling. And she means it.

Barry and Dr Bell arrive in the same car. I should sack Barry and trade him in for a social worker who is vaguely impartial. They're deep in conversation as they walk towards me. Then they look ahead and notice me, and they both put on their *Sorry, but time's up for you, fucker* smiles.

And the word is about to fall from me lips, a word that just might wipe the shine off their shit-eating grins. ADVOCACY. But I don't say it; I'll keep it up me sleeve like a joker, and play it when all me options have run out. *Advocacy* has always just been a word on a leaflet, with a drawing pin stuck in it on the patients' board near the dining room. But today the word has gravitas. I smile at the pair of them.

"Morning, gents," I say.

"Morning, Alan," they reply.

"I'll have a look at that place, er, what they call it?"

"Willowbeck Gardens," says Barry, as if he's selling a fuckin' time share in the shithole.

"Willowbeck, yes. Fix it up and I'll have a look. Let our Alison know will yer?"

"Of course," says Dr Bell.

"Am I dismissed?"

"Sorry?"

"Can I fuck off for an hour or so?"

"I suppose so, yes. Okay. Not too far though, Alan," says Dr Bell, reluctantly.

"I'm just off to pick up a bird at the off licence. You get some right crackers hanging about near the sausages."

They both laugh nervously. They think I'm joking. I'm hoping to bump into Cassandra again. I can't think of anyone else I would rather bump into right now.

4. The Milk Tray Controversy

I bet the fate fairies are laughing their little tits off. I loiter around Mrs Patel's for as long as I can without arousing suspicion. I don't loiter for long. A couple of chatting mothers walk by and grab their toddlers when they clock me. Even a couple of nasty-looking hoodies give me a wide berth as I hang around outside the shop in the gentle drizzle, like some nonce outside the school gates. I give up and go and buy some baccy.

Mrs Patel isn't in the mood for a chat. She never is with me. She seems chatty enough with every other fuckin' regular that graces her establishment. I'm a bit peckish so I buy a couple of veggie samosas and a bottle of water to wash them down. Mrs P might not like talking to mad bastards but she makes a mean samosa.

Babs used to like curries. We used to go to Iqbal's near the university now and again, back in the day when there were no bog standard takeaways; Jack of all cuisines and master of fuck all, peddling pizzas, curries, burgers, chicken, or any other fast food shite that people trough at will these days.

Babs liked them hot. I should have heeded the warning signs. Any bird who eats vindaloos on occasion is either tapped or as hard as fuckin' nails. Babs was both. I always stuck to the bhunas or I'd be shitting like a baby on pureed sprouts the morning after. Anyway, enough about that bitch. But that's not how it works. The minute Babs pops into me head, she's in it until some other thread leads me elsewhere. I start eating me samosas and zone out.

*

I first met Babs in the market. She used to help her mam run a clothes stall between Butcher's Row and the market lavs. I'd flash her the odd smile when I passed. She was a right looker but a tease if ever there was one. She could charm any pink cobra out of its basket. She was always done up like a fuckin' clown's mistress though. I'd never been keen on women who thought they were Mae soddin' West on a bad day – they were usually trouble, or so me dad said – but there was just something about her that made her an exception to me rule. It wasn't her *fuck me* eyes. Her sultry glances did me more harm than good. I always had to give it a minute once I got to the urinals. I can't piss through a stank-on any more than the next man, and I'd dread to think what would have happened to me face if I'd been caught with a stiffy in the gents back in them days. There were some mean, hard bastards in the market and any queer would have been hung up by his nads from the nearest roof joist and used for archery practice.

It was nothing to do with sex to be honest. The sex stuff put me off. I'd always gone for understated lasses. I'd porked a few prozzies in Germany but if I was asking anyone out, it was the plainer, more interesting girls I went for, like Cassandra. I'd always figured that if you were going to spend so much time with someone, it may as well be somebody who engaged your brain as well as your sausage. Babs didn't engage me brain but Christ did she make me laugh. She was funny. She wasn't just one of the lads – she was one of the lads who could blow like Satchmo after a pint or six in the Market Tavern, and like Louis Armstrong himself, she showed me what a wonderful world this could be. She was a mate you could shag without being arrested for sodomy and I fell in love with the bitch. It nearly killed me. They say it's better to have loved and lost than never to have loved at all. In Babs's case that couldn't be further from the fuckin' truth. Looking back, I would have rather stayed in love with me right hand and wanked mesen down the aisle.

We'd only been going out six months before I popped the question and I was as happy as an Irishman in a pork butcher's. It was after closing time at the Market Tavern. We'd just finished our fish 'n' chips. I took a little red box from me pocket with me hands still greasy from fish batter, fell to me knees, said "Will you marry me?" like a ventriloquist's dummy pretending to be pissed, and put me cheap ring on her slimy wedding finger.

Babs was from an Irish family up in East End Park. Unlike most Irish families in those days, she only had the one brother. Her parents' version of birth control was pretty effective. They couldn't fuckin' stand each other but like the good Catholics they were, they'd rather spend a long life of bitterness and resentment together than have a sinful shag with anyone else. Babs probably never had a chance.

They didn't warm to me at first until I literally started bringing home the bacon. And the chops. And the sausages. And the joints of pork and the black and white pudding that made them feel at home. I know the way to a Paddy's heart. Pig, pig and more fuckin' pig. Me dad helped her dad with the wedding costs and because they were both tight fuckers we had a shoestring wedding reception at an Irish pub called the Galway Shawl after getting married at St Patrick's Church on York Road. Me dad had no objections. We were hardly practising Catholics and our local priest hadn't seen us in church since our next door neighbour snuffed it. It was a good day though, one of the best, even though Babs drank twice her body weight and threw up during our wedding nookie. I wouldn't have minded but I was on me vinegar strokes at the time. It wasn't a good sign in retrospect.

If only I'd shown up that night at the parish church and met Cassandra. But Babs had me under her dirty spell. I was addicted to her. I was blinded to any possibility that I would be happier with Cassandra. Besides, Cassandra was still young then and probably didn't have a clue what she wanted or where she'd end up. Babs was more like me. She'd never leave Leeds. I'd bet she's still in Leeds now with fuckin' Derek if he hasn't knifed the bitch. There was no contest. Despite that night in the Duck 'n' Drake – Cassandra's face lit up by firelight; anything seeming possible – I chose to stay with Babs. I was the envy of every man I knew. I had a sexy wife who loved sex and nearly shagged me to an early grave. But even back then, some part of me was screaming *"Get away from her"* before we were married. I knew I'd be better off with a nice girl like Cassandra in the long run. Me dad told me to never marry a girl who everybody wanted because you'd never get a wink's sleep worrying about her pissing off with someone better looking than you. "Never punch above yer weight lad," he said. I knew he was talking shite. You can't choose the ones you love any more than you can choose your family but I still think it was more lust than love I had for Babs. And Cassandra just didn't do it for me like Babs did. Nobody did. Babs frightened the shite out of me. She was everything I wasn't. She was streetwise, she'd been around the block a few times, riding bareback like Lady Godiva on heat, and I didn't know what had fuckin' hit me.

It wasn't till one January night some five years later that I realised I might have made a terrible mistake. It wasn't our first row but it was my first trip to casualty as a result of a row with Babs. I had five stitches above me left eye. She threw one of her shoes at me and it split me noggin' open. It was all over an argument about where we were going to spend Christmas, and Babs won. Babs always won.

It's a weird thing being abused by your spouse when you're a bloke, and it was particularly difficult back then. You can't talk to anyone about it. I still don't like talking about it all these years later when shrinks bring me past up. You'd be a fuckin' laughingstock back in the day and I never laid a finger on her until the night she tried to stab me in the leg before she fucked off with Derek the bus conductor. But I put up with her for years and even though I've admittedly spent most of my life since as mad as a mad bastard can be, I'd be amazed if Babs hadn't been diagnosed at some point as being the crazy fucked-up scum queen I always knew she was. She needed help. Apart from being a hopeless alcoholic, she needed *real* help and I'd have probably tried to get her the help she needed eventually, if a certain bus conductor hadn't approached her for her bus fare on the way into town one fateful Saturday. I took some solace in the fact that Derek will have probably ridden the Hades express to hell and back a couple of hundred times with Babs and I'm certain he'll have a few tasty scars to show for it. I just hope he gave that bitch as good as he got. He did me a big fuckin' favour. I'm pretty sure either me or Babs would have ended up dead if we had stayed together and you'd have got good odds on it being yours truly. I just couldn't handle her. I don't think any bloke could, certainly not a fuckin' bus conductor. Derek might have had to deal with the odd pissed-up thug on the trams and buses during his modest career but a she-devil like Babs was a different kettle of perch. To handle a woman like that you need specialist training, the kind of training you need to tame fuckin' tigers, lions or mountain gorillas. I must have loved her though. I wouldn't be still ranting about her all these years later if I hadn't. Maybe I still do, the evil cunt.

*

I snap out of me harrowing gallop down Memory Lane and I'm standing by the bread. I've finished me samosas and could eat two more without any trouble. Mrs P is talking to another lady and they are both clearly talking about me. I realise I've outstayed me welcome and I fuck off out of it before they call the pigs. Any more trouble and they'll keep me locked up until it's time to pack me bags, put on me orange suit and get shipped off to Guantanamo Gardens with all the other illegal combatants.

"I'll just roll a cig and I'll be on me way, ladies."

Mrs P gives me her best attempt at a smile, which is almost pleasant under the circumstances. I'm not entirely sure but I think I'd been thinking aloud when I was on me internal Babs rant. I should phone ahead and get them to order something nice from the pharmacy. I'm going to need a little extra something. I know mesen well enough to know that lithium alone just won't cut it today. If Mrs P sold haloperidol I'd purchase some here and now and I'd be as happy as a bee with its head in a tulip before I got back to Murton Croft.

"It's been a pleasure, ladies," I say as I head outside. It's teeming down now but it won't make me lungs let me go any faster. I spark up, take a deep drag and start me long trudge up the hill.

I take cover in a bus shelter about halfway up the road. I get the usual look from an old bloke waiting for a bus, namely the "Is he blind or is he mad?" look, on account of me shades.

"I got them from Boots. These are prescription. I'd never go back to normal readers. Me eyes are too sensitive and it's true what they say about the eyes being the window to the soul, my friend. No bastard's looking into me soul, no matter how many lithium smarties they give me." He smiles nervously and breathes out a barely audible sigh when a bus appears just below Mrs Patel's.

"Take it easy, mate. I'm not here to hurt you. I'm here to help. Get yourself to Boots. You'll get another pair free if there's a sale on." He looks back at me and shakes his head, showing his pass and paying the driver.

"It's alright mate, move along." I say to the driver. "If I get on, I'll never get off."

I finish me fag and decide to look for Cassandra again. I need to see her. I've got so much to say to her. It's probably not a good idea but I do like to get more than phlegm off me chest. I've got a few decades of regret to talk through and I can think of no better person to share it with. I'll show those fuckin' fate fairies. This is going to happen whether those little fluttering fuckwits like it or not.

I stumble back down towards Mrs Patel's. It's still pissing it down and I'm fuckin' freezing so I select an appropriate Black Sabbath classic from me internal jukebox to help me on me merry way. I should really get mesen one of those iPod things. I sing "Fairies Wear Boots".

I stop singing. I start crying. I stop walking. I try rolling another cig but it's just not happening in the rain. I check me pockets for cash. I've got enough for ten cigs, a box of chocolates for Cassandra and a bag of chips if I'm lucky. I get the feeling I'm going to miss lunch, unless the fuzz show up for me again. It's always a surprise when the boys in blue appear from nowhere but I suppose I am a creature of habit. Well not today. Today, I'm going to get the girl and get someone else to bash me bishop for me for a change. I'm in the mood for love. It may take more than a box of Milk Tray but I'm going to take Cassandra in me arms and hope I don't get five years for me trouble. I'm going to win her heart and live happily ever after. Okay, that's the lithium talking but he who dares wins and all that jazz. I'm a man on a mission. It's time to get pro-active. I ain't going in no fuckin' home, no fuckin' way, José. Cassandra can live in me flat with me. I do realise that she might have something to say about it but if she saves a few bob in rent it just might tip the scales in me favour. Anything is possible, even for old Alan. I'm still Hank Marvin so I might have to eat the nut ones. But no one likes the nuts, do they? Not even nut jobs like me. Deluded? Me? Fuck off. Change is gonna come, whether change likes it or not. Second-hand Siddall is back and he means fuckin' business.

Mrs P is not happy to see me again. I check me reflection in the cold-drinks fridge and understand why. I even give meself a bit of a fright.

"Hello again, love. I've forgot a couple of things. Don't worry, Mrs P. I know I'm not looking me best but you've got no reason to be afraid. I haven't attacked you yet and I've been coming here for the best part of four years."

I soon realise that mentioning attacking her hasn't helped her feel less threatened so I decide not to try and explain things any more.

"Give us ten Mayfair and a box of Milk Tray."

"I don't have Milk Tray."

"You don't do Milk Tray?"

"No."

"I was a bit of a Milk Tray man in me time, love. Like James Bond. I'd abseil down the Cow 'n' Calf in me underpants if Cassandra would have me. You don't do Milk Tray?"

"No."

"That is a shame. I bet the lady loves Milk Tray. What about Terry's All Gold? *See the face you love light up with Terry's All Gold*," I croon. I don't get so much as a smirk.

"We don't do those either," she says.

"Well, something similar then. I've got a lady to impress," I say with a grin. Mrs P looks like she's about to scream.

"I have Celebrations," she says, with little conviction.

40

"If I wanted fuckin' chocolate bars for Ken Dodd's Diddymen I'd have fuckin' asked you for them. I want proper chocolates."

"There is no need to swear at me. Please pay for your cigarettes and go."

"Sorry, love, I didn't mean to..." I drop three pound coins on her counter, take me cigs and leave without me change. "Bye, Mrs Patel. I'll take me custom elsewhere in future. Take care, love. Fuckin' Celebrations. I ask yer," I mutter to myself.

Things are going from bad to fuckin' horrible. The fate fairies are pissing all over me plans. I decide to cut me losses and head back before I keel over from exhaustion or get meself arrested. Then I realise I'm struggling to walk. Then I realise I'm struggling to breathe. I reach the bus shelter. Then I fall onto the seat, arse first. Then everything goes as dark as a box of fuckin' Black Magic.

*

I come to and I haven't got a clue how long I've been out. I'm lucky I didn't crack me skull open. I'm a bit shook up. I have a little cry and then I spark up a fag. I don't know where the tears are coming from. I thought me tear ducts had been blocked up since JR got shot. Until today, I don't remember crying since the last time I tried to top meself two years ago. I didn't really try that hard. I tried hard enough to leave a nasty scar but I knew someone would find me and I knew who it would be. I remember the look on Jenny's face when she walked into me room. It wasn't just shock or general concern. It was fear that I'd finally managed it, after all these years. Fear she'd lose a friend. I've known scores of nurses, doctors, support workers, cleaners over the years who had spent as much time with me as they did with their own families, and although I'd met some decent professional people, there were only a couple who I could safely call friends without being utterly deluded. Jenny was a dear friend and I've no doubt at all, when I end up in me orange suit in Guantanamo Gardens, Jenny will visit me.

For the first time in me life, I wish I had a mobile

phone. I need to get back to Murton Croft as soon as I can. I need shelter. I need a cup of tea. I need a long sleep. I decide to get a phone. I might be a mad old bastard but I can still learn a thing or two. I've got fuck all to spend me brass on other than baccy and the odd CD. I can't even buy the chocolates I want without a big fuckin' drama.

I pull mesen together and start walking. It's stopped raining at least. I should get meself a proper coat as well and start acting me age, not me cock size.

*

Beth makes me a cup of tea while Jenny helps me get out of me wet things.

"You have to slow down a bit, Alan. You're getting a bit old for traipsing about in the rain." She unties me boots and helps me peel off me wet jeans as if I was five, not sixty-eight. She walks over towards me washing-basket and gets a pair of trackie bottoms and me Ozzy Osbourne shirt from the *Talk of the Devil* tour. I've been wearing it since 1982. It's like a security blanket. I'd fuckin' freak if I lost it. It's a miracle I haven't, to be honest. I've inadvertently traded garments with half the nutters in the western hemisphere in me time. I've swapped thousands of socks, undies and vests with fellow inmates in varying states of confusion but I'd never seen another man in me *Talk of the Devil* tour shirt.

What a gig that was. Leeds Queens Hall, 1982. Leeds Council nearly managed to get the show cancelled for indecency. Ozzy wanted to stage a fake hanging of a little midget called Ronnie Allen. He had to forego his morbid theatrics and just had the little fucker running around the stage occasionally throughout the set, like something from your worst nightmare. He was dressed in a cloak, with fucked-up makeup and frighteningly real-looking fake blood dripping from his mouth.

I only saw Sabbath the once back in 1973. Babs came with me. She was never really into music apart from Top 40 fodder. But she didn't mind a bit of Sabbath. She liked to fuck to "Symptom of the Universe" but who didn't. I never saw them again. Babs always put a stop to it, once she finally realised what Sabbath meant to me. It was either over money or just plain meanness but she always managed to scupper me plans. When she found out I'd bought us both tickets for the *Never Say Die!* tour, she ripped them to shreds and gave me a shiner that a pack of frozen peas did fuck all to shift. I lost interest when they hired Ronnie James Dio from Rainbow. He had a good set of pipes but he wasn't Ozzy. Ozzy brought out a live album of Sabbath covers after Randy Rhodes's tragic death and I bought mesen a ticket behind Babs's back. I expected Ozzy to play nothing but Sabbath tunes as per the live album, but he only played a couple and filled his set with stuff off his solo albums. It was fine by me. I've cherished Ozzy's early stuff ever since but lost interest after *The Ultimate Sin* in the mid-80s. I prefer to remember him as the rock god he once was, rather than the geriatric has-been rocker who can't put a sentence together without stuttering like a bullied school boy. It breaks me heart to watch him with his fame-obsessed wife and fucked-up kids on those fuckin' reality shows. He should have killed Sharon when he tried to strangle her years ago. He'd have done us all a fuckin' favour.

I change me undies as well and Jenny turns her back. She's seen it all before but she never crosses the line, not that I've got anything worth crossing it for. Jenny's a true pro. I wouldn't do her the dishonour of associating her with anything even vaguely sexual. I owe her that much.

When I'm decent Beth comes in with me tea and when they've both gone I put *Diary of a Madman* on. It's Ozzy's finest hour as far as I'm concerned. I haven't got the strength to mimic Randy's solo on "Over the Mountain" and by the time "Flying High Again" has reached the first chorus, I'm sinking into a deep sleep. Before I'm out, I remind meself to ask Jenny to track me down a box of Milk Tray.

5. Live from Murton Croft

I wake up feeling as bright and bushy tailed as a red fuckin' squirrel. I'm full of beans, full of life and ready to rock. I reach for me shades, get out of bed and stick *Blizzard of Ozz* on me mental-health-unit blaster.

A lot of heavy rock and metal bands have been accused of all sorts over the years. AC/DC were partly blamed by the police and the American right for Richard Ramirez, the serial killer who came to be known as "The Night Stalker". Ramirez left an AC/DC hat at one of the crime scenes and later the police found out that an AC/DC track, "The Night Prowler", was Ramirez's favourite song. The song is actually about a teenage boy sneaking into his bird's bedroom to play rudies without waking up her mum and dad, not about a man sneaking into women's bedrooms and slaughtering them in their beds.

Judas Priest were accused of putting hidden messages on their albums, designed to coax their fans to commit suicide. It went to court after a suicide victim was revealed as a Judas Priest fan. Jurors were forced to listen to some tool for the prosecution as he dragged a Priest album anti-clockwise against the stylus. It needed a real fuckin' leap of imagination to decipher the words *DO IT* from the racket that they heard. The jury were not convinced. As the late, great Bill Hicks once commented, and I'm paraphrasing: What kind of band would want its audience fuckin' dead? Commanding your fans to top themselves is probably not the best way of ensuring that your next album goes platinum.

Ozzy got into trouble for "Suicide Solution", the very song I'm listening to now. Ozzy got the blame for some kid who topped himself to his infamous track. I do have to admit, when I was in one of me more troubled periods, I did play nothing else but this song for quite a while and it certainly helped put me in the right frame of mind to top mesen. But why should poor old Ozzy get into bother for that? I was going to try and top mesen anyway, whether I'd listened to the song or not. You have to have some pretty fuckin' good reasons to commit the old hari kari and listening to a song just doesn't cut the mustard. But if you're going to slit your wrists, pop your pills, drink yersen to death, or chuck yersen off a fuckin' tower block, you might as well have a rockin' good tune with some serious guitar work by Randy Rhodes to go out to. Not that I'm planning to jump off the mouse wheel just yet. I'm just rockin' out in me room at two in the morning, standing in nowt but me Y-fronts, getting ready to mimic some tasty shreddin' on me invisible Flying V. I don't think Guantanamo Gardens is ready for me just yet.

Big Roy and Bev burst into me room as if I've just kidnapped one of the corpses from the TV lounge. There have been rumours about these two sneaking off for a quick fuck in the activity room on a night shift when all is quiet. They'd make a lovely couple, if your definition of lovely was very fuckin' off the wall indeed.

Roy edges around me warily, as if he's expecting me to throw a couple of punches. I'm lost in music, man. I'm in no mood for a tussle. I reach out to grab Bev for a dance and that's when he turns off Ozzy, bear-hugs me from behind and shuffles me away from her. If he wants a go at me Navy Rum, all he has to do is ask.

He asks me to calm down while Bev goes and gets me a little something and I'm guessing it won't be Ovaltine. She's not the fastest mover at Murton Croft. She'll be a while.

"If yer gonna keep holding me, old love, then at least sing us a lullaby. Go on Roy, give us a song. You know yer want to." I laugh hard. Roy doesn't laugh. Roy is getting a bit angry.

Bev eventually returns with me sweetie and a plastic shot glass. Roy lets me go and I sit up.

"Thanking you, young man. That was very nice." I look at the plastic shot glass on me bedside table and say to Bev, "Stick a shot of voddy in that, love, and I might even pork yer." I know it's not good to appreciate your own jokes but I nearly shit mesen laughing. Bev gives me one of her best joyless smiles that hide a thousand resentments. This woman needs help. She's worked the night shift far too long. "It is haloperidol, isn't it? I don't want to spend the rest of me days in a coma because you can't fuckin' read properly."

"Pick up the tablet, Alan, or stick out your tongue and I'll pop it in for you."

"We don't know each other well enough for cunnilingus love but I'll suck your tits for a tenner." Roy grabs hold of me again. "Alright tiger, calm down. I can't swallow me tablet with yer treatin' me ribs like a bloody squeeze-box."

I could have their jobs for this. Support workers are not permitted to administer medication. I should write it down for later and stick them up when I feel like it, fuckin' amateurs.

Roy lets go of me again. I put me hand out. Bev puts the tablet on me palm. I pop it in me mush and down the shot of water. I lie back down in bed and realise I've got a stiffy to attend to but I'll let them leave the room first. Roy tucks me in, bless him. "Pass us some of that roll before you go. I might need to blow me nose." She shakes her head and passes me three sheets of the stiff blue paper roll. "I'll let yer yank me sausage if I can milk yer udders," I say to Bev.

They do their best to ignore me farewell shot but I see the corners of Roy's mouth twitching up a little before he turns to leave. When they close the door behind them, I hear him laughing and I hear Bev telling Roy to fuck off. The joke's on me though. Those fat fuckers have confiscated me CD player and me cock's no longer pointing north.

I close me eyes. I see loads of coloured dancing dots. I start counting them.

*

I dress mesen and walk towards the dining room. Roy and Bev are both parked behind the reception desk. They've got that worn and jaded end-of-night-shift look. Roy sighs, whispers something to Bev, gets up off his arse and comes around the front to escort me. After the shenanigans of a few hours ago, it looks like I'm on close observation for the day but they'll get no trouble from me this morning. I'm still jet-lagged from me flight of fancy. Roy walks me into an empty dining room. It's only seven.

I point to me desired items and the big black bruiser behind the counter (who looks like she's on community service) plates up me bacon, scrambled eggs and tomato. Big Roy gets me tea and orange juice.

I'm joined by a couple of spooks in wheelchairs who usually frequent the TV lounge from dusk till dawn. They greet me with a "Good morning" but I fail to see what's fuckin' good about it.

Breakfast is a struggle. Me paws are shaking like Jimmy Cagney at the end of *Angels With Dirty Faces*. The way I'm feeling this morning, I'd be happily strapped in to ol' sparky and lit up like a soddin' Jumping Jack. Roy takes pity on me and guides me grub to me mush. All that's missing is the *open wide for the choo choo train* song. He's not a bad old brute. It's his bone-idle fuck-buddy that I can't stomach. She's got a right nasty side.

Arthur is usually first in for brekkie but he always takes a couple of days to adjust to his new surroundings. Like me good self, he was probably a bit lively last night so they'll have put a little extra something in his cocoa. Then, in a few days, he'll begin his slow downer. I won't get a peep out of him for a couple of days, which is a shame. I'm hardly in the mood for a discussion about Willy Wordsworth, or Bob the Bastard Bard from Bradford for that matter, but he's the only bloke worth talking to in this hell hole. I should count me blessings. I'll be talking to no one but mesen when I'm shipped off to Willowbeck morgue.

I'm glad I bought some proper fags yesterday from Mrs P. They may taste like shit but at least I don't have to roll. It would have taken me all fuckin' day.

Roy escorts me to the lift. I cough up a nasty and it lands with a splat between me shoes. It's a viscous toffee brown and I nearly follow up with a technicoloured yawn. I am not feeling me best.

"Jesus Alan. Are you alright?"

"I'm fine and dandy Roy," I say, with a long slow wheeze. I take a few long breaths like me doctor told me to and I'm okay. But there's a familiar unpleasant sensation in me chest and I get the feeling I'm coming down with something. I probably caught it off Arthur, although I think his condition isn't quite so transitory. Then again, neither is mine I suppose. I'm not fuckin' daft. The 'bines take their toll on me too but without them, there'd be nowt to look forward to, apart from staring at Beth's arse. I've taken a right shine to that girl and so has me knob. She's got a nice way about her and one or two of the more experienced staff could learn a thing or two from her, that's for sure.

I spark up me fag and plan me day. I haven't seen our Alison since Dr Dofuckall gave me me death sentence. She'll be keeping a low profile. She'll know I've been kicking off. I'm going to spend some of that money she's been sitting on like some fat fuckin' goose protecting her golden eggs. I bet Geoff, that bone-idle husband of hers, will be hatching his little schemes once I'm safely tucked away in a home. Our Alison has been longing to stick the flat up for sale ever since me stay at Murton Croft was starting to look permanent. Me mam left it to both of us but she insisted that it would be a place for me for as long as I needed it. I assumed she'd always figured that I'd snuff it first. She lived through me first suicide attempt and she knew me well enough to know I might give it another crack one day. Alison is wealthy enough and paid her own mortgage off years ago. Still, I always thought that Alison felt a bit aggrieved the flat couldn't be sold and split 50/50. I suppose as me power of attorney she could have sold it anyway but she'd never go against me mam's wishes. She's been dead over ten years now though. I was always her favourite. Alison was me dad's. But unless the flat can be a love nest for me and Cassandra, I don't really need it now. I'm not a total dickhead. There's more chance of Bev cracking a genuine smile than me and Cassandra living happily ever after. Besides, I'd have to fuckin' find her first. Not today though. I don't think I'll be going anywhere today even if I wanted to, not without Big Roy or his shift replacement tugging at me shadow.

Roy doesn't start conversations. To be honest, he'd be

a fuckin' mute if nobody spoke to him first. But he loves being on close obs with me. He smokes like a navvy and he's got a right bark on him and he knows I'll be down here on the hour every hour for me smoke, even if I am coughing up fudge. He's handy to have around. He's lent me a few of those nasty barge poles he smokes in his time. I'd never even heard of them until he offered me one. They cost about as much as ten Bensons for twenty and the baccy inside them smokes like dry pubes.

*

I'm sitting in reception and Arthur's still not up. It's gone eleven. Kevin, a short little bald bloke with a greying moustache, is me new chaperone, whether I'm going for a cig or a posh wank in the disabled bog. Me and Kevin don't get on. Never have. He's another bone-idle support worker. The last time he smiled, Neil Sedaka was number one.

I'm psyching mesen up to call our Alison. It's not that I'm scared of her, I'm just not very talkative today. She'll be giving me twenty questions when I can just about manage one or two. I decide to enlist the help of young Beth. If nothing else, I'll be able to watch her wiggle when she walks back.

"Beth," I croak.

"Yes, Alan?"

"I wonder if I could borrow you for a minute."

"What for?" If I was in the mood for banter, I'd have replied with the mother of all retorts but sadly I'm not.

"I need you to ring me sister."

"Kevin will do that for you, Alan. He's looking after you today."

"Kevin couldn't look after a fairground goldfish. Besides, this needs a woman's touch."

Beth doesn't look sure. She looks at Philippa, the ward manager, who is on hold on the phone. Philippa doesn't miss a thing and she looks over at me, clearly annoyed. She wafts her hand as if she's stopped caring. I don't know what I've done to piss her off but I don't give a toss. Beth nods and comes from behind the reception desk to where I'm sitting.

"What can I do for you?"

"I'd like you to ring me sister for me and ask her to come up. Tell her it's important. And tell her to bring me forty Superkings. I can't roll at the moment wi' me shakes. And can you ask her to bring up £200 in cash?"

"Erm. I'd better check with Philippa when she's off the phone, if that's okay."

"No, it's not okay. I'm running out of time, Beth love. They're all out to get me."

"Sorry, Alan. I'll have to check."

She walks back through the door to the other side of the reception desk. I'm so wound up I forgot to watch her arse.

Philippa is now involved in a heated discussion on the phone. Beth looks down the corridor, ignoring Kevin, who is reading a magazine. She's already figured out that Kevin is about as much use as a chocolate fire guard and she's only been here five minutes.

"Okay, I'll ring Alison," says Beth, "but I'm not asking her for £200. You can ask her for that when you see her."

"Alright, love. You win."

"What's her number?"

I give her me money and she dials from the patient phone. She summons me sister to get her arse up here but Alison can't make it till after three when she finishes work. I decide to go for a little nap. I've got fuck all else to do. If I had me blaster, a bit of Sabbath might have pepped me up but that bastard bitch Bev saw to that. I get up.

"Come along, Kev. I'm off for a nap. You can read me a bedtime story."

I get nothing. He doesn't even change his facial expression. There's no hope for Kevin. I might feel sorry for mesen sometimes but it doesn't take me long to find someone less fortunate. If I was Kevin, I would have chucked mesen off Blackpool Tower long ago.

*

I open me eyes and I'm greeted by Kevin's ugly mush. I order a cup of tea from me bald slave. There's a ham sandwich and a little plate of biscuits on me bedside table. That'll be Jenny's doin'. She always makes sure I don't miss a meal. When I get shipped out of here, I'll have to get her something nice. I'll ask young Beth. She might have some ideas. Our Alison wouldn't have a fuckin' clue.

I have a walk around the ward looking for Arthur, with Quasimodo's brother shuffling behind me. It's a quarter to three and Alison will be here by four. I don't even bother looking in the TV lounge. Arthur abhors daytime TV as much as I do. He'll be either having a fag outside, hanging about in the activity room or reading in one of the quiet rooms.

"Have you seen Arthur today?"

"No," replies Kevin.

I walk up to reception, realising that's all I'm going to get from Kevin. Beth and Jenny are sitting behind the desk. "Good afternoon, ladies. Anyone seen Arthur?"

"He's having a smoke, against better advice. Can you have word with him, love?" says Jenny. "He's not a well man."

"I'll help you do your job if you can get this monkey off me back." Beth and Jenny laugh. Kevin doesn't. Again, his expression doesn't even change. "I've told you before, Jenny. You should never try to get between a man and his tobacco." I cough but I manage to keep down the fudge. There are ladies present.

"You need to cut down as well Alan. That cough sounds nasty," says Jenny.

"Don't you worry about me love. It's just a tickle." Me lungs contradict me and this time I need me hankie to stop the fudge.

Outside, Arthur is sitting on his preferred bench in late winter sunshine, puffing on his pipe like Sherlock fuckin' Holmes.

"Sir Alan! How the dickens are you, old chum?"

"Not ten bad, Arthur. Not ten bad."

"You know, with a bit of a makeover, you'd look a bit like that little shit off *The Apprentice*." It's good to see Arthur is still on form. "I take it that by having that guttersnipe at your shoulder you are on close observation?"

"'Fraid so. I had a run-in with Bev and Roy at two in the morning."

"Oh dear. Young Kevin? Go stand over there, boy," he bellows, like an old school headmaster. "Alan and I have a revolution to plan."

We laugh. We cough. We go purple.

6. Our Alison

Our Alison lives in a perfect three-bedroom semi, with perfect lawns, six perfect garden gnomes, perfect flower beds, a perfect potting shed, a perfect pond with perfect koi carp and a perfect hatchback in her perfect fuckin' driveway that she can't fuckin' drive. If she could drive her husband's car, she'd get her bone-idle arse up here more often.

Our Alison is Mrs fuckin' Average, with an average husband and 2.4 average children. The children are both in their 30s. The .4 is a ginger tom called Percy. He's a fat little fucker who cracks eggs open with his neb and then sups up the bounty if you forget to put them in the fridge.

Our Alison drank from the sane side of our gene pool. She took after me dad. He was as solid as a concrete slab until he keeled over at 66, a year after his fateful retirement. Dad was a grafter all his life and he knew how to keep an eye on the money. If Alison keeps following in his boot prints, she's only got three years left. She's worked in the same lawyer's practice since they laid the foundations. Like Dad before her, she's never had a day off in her life, not even when the old git suddenly pegged it. I can picture her then, fingers lightly clacking on the keyboard at an impressive speed as she listens to one of the senior partners through her little headphones. Then she picks up the phone to her hysterical mother. "Calm down, Mum. Yes I know. It's terrible but I'm a working woman. We can talk about it when I come over at the weekend. You can keep him on ice till then." She's always been a matter-of-fact, cold-hearted bint has our Alison, just like me fuckin' father before her.

Me? I take after me mum. Sensitive, kind (although I do have a nasty streak), workshy, highly strung and totally fuckin' insane to boot. Me mam lasted till 83, on forty Superkings a day and a pork chop eight days a week. She loved her pork chops, me mam. She somehow evaded mental health care and was merely thought of as eccentric. This was despite her bizarre sleeping patterns which meant she'd often be found in the garden hanging up the washing at two in the fuckin' morning, singing at the top of her lungs. She laughed at inappropriate times and could be seen walking to shops, chuntering away to herself, in clothing far too colourful for a wet Wednesday in a Yorkshire winter. She was totally fuckin' barking all her life, but in a nice way. If I follow her all the way to Kansas, I have 15 years in Guantanamo Gardens to look forward to. Not fuckin' likely. I have me belt, me razor and me bucket of pills at the ready. Next time, I'll do all three to make fuckin' sure. Our Alison will be glad to see the back of me.

And speak of the devil – here she is, me dear old sis, waddling down the corridor towards me, her long navy blue skirt hanging over her hips like a quilt over a washing rack. She likes her food, whereas her svelte older brother sees grub as mere shit waiting to happen.

"Hello, Alan," she says, with a half-arsed smile. "How's tricks?"

"Tricks are fuckin' terrible. We'll go in the quiet room. I hope you've brought a pen and paper."

Over the next ten minutes, I give our Alison her instructions, one of which she doesn't take very seriously. I had to remind her I was very serious indeed. I listed the following:

I want a mobile phone in case I get stranded while on one of me jaunts.

I want to get some new CDs and books to distract me from me current turmoils.

I want a new leather jacket and some new T-shirts from the Sabbath and Ozzy fan clubs that she got me into on the internet. I have to think about me appearance.

In future, I will be smokin' real fags as opposed to roll-ups. I've recently lost the ability to roll me own.

I want to talk to Advocacy to see if they can do anything about me impending incarceration.

And last but certainly not least (in fact this fucker should have been at the top of me list), I want to hire a private investigator to track down the whereabouts of a certain

Cassandra Bekker.

Alison immediately changes the subject and starts waffling on about how her twat of a husband needs a hip operation. "No disrespect, love, but Geoff's mobility is not me priority at the moment. Did you listen to a word I said?"

"Of course I did. You said it loud enough. Are you going to give it a try at least?"

"Give what a try?"

"You know perfectly well what I'm talking about."

"Alison, I mean it. The stuff I've asked for – it's important."

"Remind me at the weekend. I'll see what I can do."

"Bollocks ter yer. Just get me a couple of hundred out of me account and I'll ask one of the staff to take me into town. They take Pat shopping every fuckin' week. They can take me an' all. I want to get mesen sorted. I'm going to start enjoying me life."

"Alan, this is serious. A home is inevitable now. There's no point avoiding the issue. Dr Bell said you agreed to a trial period."

"I said I'd go and have a look at it. Are you coming?"

"Yes. It's already arranged. Barry's taking us to see two places in a couple of days. One's in Bingley and one's in Bradford."

"They only told me about Willowbeck Gardens. They've probably lined another one up to make Willowbeck look like a fuckin' palace in comparison. What kind of a numpty do they think they're dealing with?" She didn't answer. She didn't need to. It was a rhetorical question. "Anyway, I'm serious about me list so I'd ask Jenny for some paper and pen so you can get cracking."

"I've told you. Remind me at the weekend. I've got enough on my plate."

"You've got me fuckin' savings on a silver platter, more like it. You might wear the Y-fronts at home, love, but I've had just enough of your fuckin' control-freakin' tendencies to last me a lifetime. I've had a chat with Arthur. I'm arranging a meeting with Advocacy to look at me options with residential care and I'm going to talk about me finances as well. I'm happy with you to stay me power of attorney if yer do as your fuckin' told."

"I haven't worked all day and dragged myself up here to be spoken to like this!"

"Well fuck off home then but write that list first, or as me doppelganger on *The Apprentice* says, you're fired." I laugh when I see her expression of outrage. I'm actually having a lot of fun with this. "Did you bring me fags?"

"Yes I brought your fags. I've been bringing you your bloody fags for as long as I can remember and you never show me an ounce of gratitude. Honestly, Alan, I... I..." Now she's crying like some sad bitch on a soap opera. For fuck's sake. I leave her to it. Before I know it, Kevin's up me arse again. I stifle a scream. When I get to reception, Jenny reads me expression and stops talking to Beth and Philippa.

"Everything alright?" she asks.

"Not really, love. Our Alison is having one of her turns. She's not getting away with it. I don't want her looking after me affairs anymore. She's not got me best interests at heart. All she fuckin' cares about is her dopey fuckin' husband with his fucked-up hip."

"Please, Alan!"

"Sorry, Philippa, but I'm at the end of me tether. It's all getting a bit much today. I've had Bev and Roy on me case and I've got this little prick following me around all fuckin' day. I've had about as much as I can take."

"Can you please stop shouting and calm down? Bev and Roy were on your case because you were cranking out your heavy metal at two in the morning and you are on close observations because you've been a tad lively today." She's smiling now. "Come into the quiet room with me and Jenny and we'll have a chat. Can you make us some tea, Kevin, please? Beth? Can you see how Alan's sister is and ask her if she doesn't mind waiting in reception and I'll have a chat with her afterwards? Sorry, Kevin, can you make Alan a cup as well?"

Philippa doesn't get involved much but when she does

56

she's usually on the ball.

She's risen through the ranks since me High Royds days. I remember her as a student nurse fifteen years ago. I had more lead in me pencil back then and she kept me in wanks for a six month stretch once. If I ran out of fags, she'd always crash me some or get some on her way to work for me and get the money off our Alison later. Both her and Jenny have looked after me for years but as she climbed her career tree she got more distant. I suppose she had to. But I've always felt that she'll do what she can for me when the chips are down.

We go in the quiet room and Philippa shuts the door behind us.

"Right, now what's all this about?"

I don't hold back. I tell her and Jenny about bumping into Cassandra and how I thought we could make a go of it given half a chance. I tell them if I could get a private dick to track her down, I could start the ball rolling, and maybe she's lonely and we just might be able to hit it off and even get married. I tell them that, because of these latest developments, I think it might be a good idea to hold off on the move to Guantanamo Gardens until I have a chance to at least sit down with Cassandra and talk things through. I tell them that I need a mobile phone, some new T-shirts, a new leather and some new fuckin' boots. I tell them I am giving up roll-ups so I don't have to fuck around with Rizlas when it's pissing it down. I tell them I am thinking of sacking our Alison as me power of attorney and I trust either of them over her and her fuckin' hubby with the fucked-up hip any day of the week. I tell them that we all go back a long way and I trust them to do what's right for me and ask them if they understand that I need to see Cassandra and I think that we could be very happy together if Alison kept her fuckin' nose out of me affairs and was out of the fuckin' picture forever. I tell them that Cassandra should have been the love of me life and it's not too late. I just hope it's not too fuckin' late. Because you've got to have hope. Without a bit of fuckin' hope, there's fuck all else to live for.

Then I start coughing. Then I start crying.

They calm me down as best they can and I tell them I need a cig. I manage to stop blubbering before Kevin knocks on the door and brings in the tea.

"Alison has left the building," he says, putting down the tray.

"You make her sound like fuckin' Elvis," I say, and even Kevin smiles.

7. Visiting Day

I seem to have lost a day. I've been sleeping like a toddler on horse tranquilizers. I feel like I've just woken up from a coma. Me mouth's as dry as fuck and me stomach's growling like a fuckin' Rottweiler. It's been an exhausting week, for one reason and a dozen others. I'd be forgiven for suspecting that one of the fuckers in here has slipped me a mallet pill. It wouldn't be the first time. It was a matter of course in the good old days.

It would make sense. It's visiting day. Dr Dofuckall wants me on me best behaviour so the nice people at Willowbeck Gardens or Upshitcreekwithoutafuckinpaddle Lodge get a good impression of me. I'll have to make sure that doesn't fuckin' happen for a start.

I lie awake, dying to begin the day with a bit of Floyd but there's still no sign of me blaster. Bev and Roy have probably procured it so they can hump their night shifts away to *The Dark Side of the Moon* while the guests of this modest hotel dream of better days.

The dawn choruses are getting louder now and me mornings start with that lovely kingfisher-blue sky when I wake around seven. The daffs and snowdrops are on their way and spring will be on us faster than you can say "Please don't send me to a death camp, you sadistic bastards". I love spring. It's the season for new beginnings, not that I'll be having any. Well, not the kind I fuckin' want anyway. For some reason, I think of new-born lambs bounding through fields in that happy, dippy euphoria of their short lives before they end up on the butcher's block for fat fuckers like our Alison to devour. I haven't eaten lamb since the early 70s.

Me day begins like most others; namely: piss, brekkie, smoke and shit. Arthur's having another lie in. It's getting to be a bit of a habit. I'll have to have words. He's acting out of character. Mind you, I must have spent most of yesterday in bed because I can't recall much since me do with me fat sister. I'm pulling the emergency chord on this fuckin' gravy train.

The Siddall Express is temporarily sleeping in a siding.

I sit in reception after me brekkie. Jenny reminds me of me schedule for today before she even takes her coat off.

"Anybody would think you were trying to get rid of me," I say, lethargically. Me mouth's not working as fast as me brain. I don't like it when that happens. If I lose me ability to quip on the day I need it the most, that would be a real fuckin' shame. When I'm a shadow of meself, I prefer to shut the fuck up. I'm feeling far from zesty. In fact, I feel unusually ordinary today.

"Barry's picking us all up at about three-thirty this aft," says Jenny. "We'll let 'em get their dinners before we descend on 'em, eh?"

"I didn't know you were comin', love," I say, surprised.

"I want to check out these two places myself. I like to see where they send my favourite patients."

"I'm a mental health service user if you don't mind."

"I beg your pudding, sir," says Jenny. "Please accept my humble apologies."

She's a good liar. She's always been a good liar. I don't just mean she's good at lying. She tells good lies. She tells lies that are for the good of others. A white lie can be worth its weight in lithium if it's told at the right time. She always makes me feel like an equal. There really is no one like Jenny. She's one in a million. But even she thinks me time is up. I know she does. She's coming in case I kick off. She's the only one that can calm me down without the aid of drugs or a couple of big bastards. She's coming along to help persuade me that this is a good idea. It's a fuckin' betrayal, whichever way you look at it.

It's a quiet morning on the ward. I could do with a pep talk from Arthur but he's either keeping a low profile or he really is in trouble. I heard him cough when I walked past his room earlier on and I was halfway down the corridor. It frightened the shite out of me to tell you the truth. My cough seems to have cleared up a bit. They'll be keeping a close eye on his oxygen levels. I hope to Christ he's alright. I ask Jenny and she says he's fine. But Jenny's telling me what I want to hear today. She can play me like a fuckin' mouth organ. It's a big enough day for me without having to worry about old Arthur turning a nice shade of hypoxic blue.

I miss Arthur all morning. The day continues to drag until Beth picks up the phone at around 11. All the senior staff are in a meeting with Dofuckall. I sit in reception near Beth. We don't chat. I'm in a pensive mood and she's being all keen and keeping herself busy.

Me ears prick up when I hear her stuttering on the phone. She gets interrupted stating her position, saying, "You can't just turn up I'm afraid. You have to... hello? Hello? She's hung up on me," she says, more to herself than me. "Unbelievable."

I feel a bit perkier thanks to this bit of drama.

"You alright, love?"

"Not really." She looks more annoyed than flustered and there's something a bit odd about her reaction, like she's some spoilt kid whose sibling has just got the better of her or something. I can't put me finger on it.

"Tell yer Uncle Alan."

"I'd love to but I can't, I'm afraid."

"Don't say I dint offer. You could learn a lot more from me than half the halfwits in this dump, but it's your call, sweetheart."

Me gob seems to be working a bit more in tandem with me brain, thank Christ. I'll need all me faculties for today's proceedings. Beth looks around and sees no one but Kevin. She comes over to me.

"It was this woman," she whispers. "She told me to get a bed ready for her because she was coming in. I asked her for her name and she told me to do as I was told and that I'd find out her name soon enough."

"Sounds intriguing," I say.

Beth potters around reception for the next few minutes, looking nervy, waiting for the meeting to finish so she can nip out for a smoke. Then, suddenly, there she is. She's standing in front of the reception desk with her suitcase as if she's checking into the fuckin' Hilton. It's only the force of nature known as Janet Chandler. This is more like it.

"There's a taxi down int car park," she says to Beth. "He wants five bar and I ant got a penny to scratch me arse wi'."

"Sorry?" says Beth.

"No need to be sorry, love. Are you new?"

"Yes."

"Be a good girl and go get me someone who knows what they're talkin' about."

Beth gives off this sexy pout. "They're all in a meeting I'm afraid."

"I don't give a monkey's arsehole," snaps Janet. "There's a driver wants five bar and he's a big bugger so I'd put me hand in me purse and get down there if I were you." Beth looks over at me and then looks for Kevin but he's either gone for a dump or a sly wank. Either way, he's out of play at present. "If you've got nowt, tell him it's on contract. That usually gets rid of 'em. It's worked a treat int past for me anyway." Beth looks frozen to the spot. "Go on, love. Chop chop. Meter's running."

I decide to help Beth with this wrinkly whirling dervish.

"Now then Janet," I croak. "Come over here and take the weight off. The poor girl's gettin' run ragged."

"Bloody 'ell fire. Is that you, Alan? The last time I heard owt about you, you'd just tried to top yerself. Get me case, love, and make us a nice cup of tea," says Janet to Beth. "I'll be over there with that hairy bugger. C'mon, look sharp. What's the matter with her?" She walks over towards me.

Janet and I chew the fat while Beth puts the kettle on. I tell Janet about me getting shipped off to a home and she laughs herself into a coughing frenzy.

"That'll put the cat among the bloody pigeons. I can't see you in one of them places, love. I'd try toppin' yerself again if I were you."

"Thanks, Janet. I knew I could count on you for some sound advice."

62

"Well, that's what I'd do. You wunt catch me in one of them places. I'd rather chuck meself off a tower block."

"It would take more than that to finish you off, love. It's good to see you, you evil old cow."

"Likewise, yer sack a shite. Are you comin' for a fag?"

"You can't smoke in here now. You'll have to go outside," I say, but she's already on her way down to what used to be the smoke room.

"Tell that bimbo to bring me tea down, will yer? I'm not freezing me nibs off out there for a fag. What can they do? Arrest me? I'm mad, love. Ant you heard of diminished responsibility?"

Fuckin' marvellous. Just when things are looking like they couldn't get any worse, Janet arrives. Today is going to be fun. I just wish I was around to see it. But I've got other sharks to fry and the clock is ticking.

Beth runs up to Jenny as soon as the door to the meeting room opens. She's in a right flap now. She tries to explain the last ten minutes and she sounds like a schoolgirl recounting a serious playground incident to a headmistress.

Jenny chuckles and tells Beth to take five. She looks over at me and raises her eyebrows.

"This should be fun," she says, and walks down the corridor to the room that used to be the smoke room and is the smoke room once more. I go outside for mine. Jenny's got enough on her plate. But all this has put a smile on me face, and they'll be in short supply for the foreseeable future.

*

We're on our way to one of the prospective residential morgues. The traffic is terrible. It's in Heaton. Yorkshire Ripper country.

Things are a little tense in the car. I insist that Alison sits in the front so I can strangle her from behind if she pisses me off too much. It's why taxi drivers sometimes don't wear seat belts.

Jenny does her best to keep things light but Alison won't shut the fuck up about her hubby's hip, the self-centred cow. This winds me up somewhat and I have a little rant. She just hasn't got a fuckin' clue. Because the decision's been made for her she can pass the buck without an ounce of guilt. She must think I was born yesterday. She could protest. She could look after me interests. But no. She just sits on her fat arse and hopes it plays out to her advantage.

"We're here," Barry almost sings, as if we've just arrived at fuckin' Butlins.

The sun has come out and it feels nice on me face as we get out of the car. It's a big old place, built in Yorkshire stone. I bet you'd get the best part of a million for it in today's market. I can just see Dom, that bald cockney bloke from that property programme, getting all excited about this period property.

There's an old bird framed by a window to the left of the entrance. She's staring out into the middle distance. She's either waiting for a relative or the Grim Reaper.

"What a lovely old house," says our Alison.

"You fuckin' live here then," I say. "There's not much of a garden."

"It's around the back," says Barry. "There's a lovely area to sit out in the summer."

"I don't want to burst yer bubble mate but it fuckin' pissed it down last summer."

"Touché," says Barry, with a hapless grin.

The four of us walk up to the entrance. We used to have a dog when I was a nipper. It was a mongrel. It was crossed between a Dalmatian and a fox terrier. You can imagine the conception. If you ever took it near water, it would pull back on its lead as soon as it clocked it and whine as if it had been badly injured. It didn't matter where you were. You could be walking up to a local pond or in the middle of Roundhay Park. When me mam tried to bath it, she had to get me to help. The poor thing would whine and almost scream with fear. We got him from the RSPCA and figured that his previous owner had tried to drown him as a pup.

Sorry, I digress, but I feel just like good old Marmaduke before we tried to bath him. We approach the main door of Springcroft. If I was attached to a leash, it would have taken all three of them to get me anywhere near it.

Barry presses the intercom, announcing our arrival, and a small dumpy little woman, who looks like Humpty Dumpty in a summer dress, opens the doors.

"Welcome to Springcroft," she announces warmly.

Welcome to Hell, I retort in me noggin'.

As I suspected, Barry has chosen this stinking hovel to make Willowbeck Gardens look more appealing. The smell is the first thing that hits me as we walk into the entrance hall. It's almost ineffable. There are numerous odours fighting for supremacy: cabbage, custard, disinfectant and piss are the only ones I can immediately identify and together they make a formidable fragrance. You could bottle it.

We are greeted by a wrinkled-up troll near the reception hatch. It's gurning and growling, head tilted, hunched over, tottering on the spot, a zimmer frame keeping it just about upright. They should have locked it in a linen cupboard until I'd gone. She, he, or whatever the fuck it is, is hardly helping sell the place to me.

"We'll start you off in the lounge I think," says Humpty.

There's a lovely young woman smiling behind a glass panel. She is the antithesis of the thing groaning and wheezing at the side of us; she has crimson hair shaped in a bob, a ring through her nose and a smile to floor a football crowd. Me dick stirs to let me know I'm still living. It promptly drifts off back to sleep when I nearly knock over Troll Features. She somehow shuffles closer towards me while I am gawping at the pretty girl.

"C'mon, Alan," Jenny says, and links her arm with mine. I can't quite take me eyes off the troll as Jenny ushers me away.

"Christ, Jenny, what the fuck was that?"

"It's called old age, love. It happens to us all."

"That will never happen to me," I say.

"This way," shouts Humpty. We have lagged behind.

We see the lounge. We see the quiet room. We see the

undead. Barry doesn't even glance at me for me approval. He knows this place is a shithole as much as I do. Like I said, he's thought this through.

"We also have a smoke room," says Humpty. "As residential homes are seen as such, *homes*, our residents are allowed to smoke. I'll leave you to it if you don't mind."

We open the door and even I gag. It smells like a thousand tab ends, half of which have been left burning so they smoulder against each other, releasing the noxious fumes from other filters. It's fuckin' horrible.

"I've seen enough," I say abruptly.

"Well, we have other quiet rooms upstairs and of course there's the bedrooms to have a look at. We have a room vacant at the moment should everything work out after your assessment," says Humpty.

"Let me save you the effort, love. I ain't coming here. I'd rather live int sewers with the rats."

She looks at Jenny and Barry, unsure of what will happen next.

I walk away.

"Alan? At least finish the tour," says our Alison.

"The tour?" I laugh. "I'll see you outside. I'll hang mesen by me shoe laces before I come here."

Minutes later, after apologies and half pleasantries, Alison and Barry come out and join me and Jenny by the car. I flick me smoked fag onto a lawn not much bigger than a fuckin' stamp.

"Well Barry. You really excelled yourself with this place," I say.

"It's not that bad," replies Barry. "Willowbeck is definitely the nicer of the two though," he says. "You'll see."

I have no doubt it will be.

We drive through Shipley and Saltaire and then arrive in Bingley and take a right turning past the hideous concrete monstrosity that is the Bradford & Bingley building.

Up towards the moors, we turn into a drive and there it is. Willowbeck Gardens. Me stomach knots, as if it was me first day at school and we've just arrived at the gates. Barry is right. This is definitely nicer. There's quite a view as well. Then I know. I just know. It already feels like home, whether I fuckin' like it or not..

8. Home, Sweet Home

Picture the scene. A large L-shaped lawn, freshly shaved, ready for March's snowdrops and daffodils. Neat borders and beds, promising more roses, chrysanths, hydrangeas and more fuckin' pansies than you could cock yer leg at. You can hear the gurgle and trickle of the stream running off the moors above, snaking its way down to Bingley, past two weeping willows and a gnarled oak tree that still has a rope attached to it from when some kid last swung across to the field opposite, in the mid-70s. It'll be nice out here in the summer, sitting under one of the willows with me cup of tea and me fags, with a nice nursie by me side, giving me todger a tug in the morning sun.

The clouds have just broken and the sun is out. Barry's really thought this one through. Show him the garden first while it's sunny and whip him inside when it fucks off back in. I have to admit, the gardens are stunning, but he knows as well as I do that I'll be behind closed doors for the best part of the rest of me days. And inside will be much the same as any other home up and down the country. No matter how nice the décor or the chandeliers, or the oak fuckin' staircase, there will always be that unmistakable whiff, that heady cocktail of old age and imminent death.

"Shall we have a look inside?" says Barry, as the sun fucks off. Our Alison shivers dramatically.

Barry presses the intercom. We are greeted at the door by a tall, bald bloke with a jolly face of broken capillaries and a thick grey moustache. This man has lived. He looks like a hard bugger as well. His dark grey suit would make him look like the accused was it not for his practised smile that tells you he bats for the goodies.

"Mr Siddall and party?" he says. He's a Glaswegian and sounds like a posh Rab C Nesbit. "Frank Hendrie. We've been expecting you. Welcome to Willowbeck Gardens." He says this with some pride and he sounds genuine. "Check yer shoes for doggy doos. Only jokin', madam," he says to Alison.

"You'll have no grips on them heels." He's done this before. Looks like the lunatics are running this asylum. I'm sure they'll even have the obligatory plaque: *You don't have to be mad to work here, but it helps!*

"Alright mate?" He puts his hand out for me to shake. Well that was a pretty seamless transition from jolly hotelier to me best fuckin' buddy. This bloke is good. I oblige him. It's a decent shake as well. "Right. We'll start you off in reception."

There are no trolls to greet us this time. They've locked the chronics in the broom cupboard. They don't want the place to look untidy. It's all *Ker-Ching! Here comes another £400 a week from the social for our not-a-fuckin'-star-in-sight hotel!* First impressions are everything and this fucker has done his homework.

I look at Barry. He's looking far too pleased with himself. Jenny and Alison both give me that look that means, *Well, what do you make of it so far?* I give fuck all away and follow Frank to another locked door.

He pops in a number: 14768. That might come in handy if I end up here. He opens the door. I brace mesen. We walk along a short hallway. There's a reception room on the right. An attractive young Asian woman flashes us a smile from behind a cluttered desk. She's wearing a dark blue uniform with a white trim. It makes her look more like a cleaner than a care nurse. We turn a corner and all our eyes follow an oak staircase to the next floor. A huge chandelier hangs above it. I briefly fantasise that Dell and Rodney are unfastening the screws on the floor above as we speak, and the big fuckin' thing's about to come crashing down and break me noggin' like a fuckin' egg shell and put me out of me misery once and for all. Chance would be a fine thing.

"We have a lift as well for our less mobile residents," says Frank.

He shows us the lift. It's more like a dumb waiter. It says *Maximum Four Persons* on a sign below the floor display panel.

"I bet you get a bit of a queue for this," I say. I realise

it's the first thing one of our party has said since we walked in.

"Well, most of our residents stick to the day rooms most of the time."

"You should have an escalator," I say, flippantly.

"You know, Alan, that's not a bad idea. I shall suggest it to the board at the next meeting." He's humouring me, the patronising bastard. But in a nice way. This bloke is really fuckin' good.

"I wouldn't bother, mate," I say. "This is a profit-making organisation and you'd be a fool to think otherwise."

"That's a tad cynical, Alan. All I would ask is that you reserve judgement until we've completed our tour." He gives me that practised smile again. It works for me. I look at our Alison. She looks like she wants to straddle him and ride the bastard like a Blackpool donkey. Mind you, I don't suppose Geoff will be much use to her now with his fucked-up hip.

I don't know if it's the sudden smell from the kitchen (a big black woman has just opened the kitchen door, releasing a fusion of nasties from either what they had at lunch or what was to come for dinner) or the image of me sis, bouncing up and down on Bonnie Prince Charlie's pecker, but I nearly toss me Hobnobs over me boots.

"Are you okay, mate?" asks Frank. If his concern isn't genuine, then I'm a pirate from Somalia.

"Aye, I think so. I'd sack the chef if were you. What the fuck is she cooking in there?"

"Alan!" scolds Alison. "There's no need for that."

"Please, madam. Don't worry yourself. I hear a lot worse," says Frank.

The day rooms are what you'd expect, namely ten or so spooks, half of which are watching the box and the other half with their chins on their collar bones dreaming of better times. Only one of them is making a racket, chuntering away to himself, punctuating his soliloquy with little chuckles. We meet some of the nurses, men and women, black and white, fat and thin, all of them busy, busy, busy. There's a large activity room, with cards, board games and bookcases stuffed with thrillers and romances. And there's a paint-splattered table on which many masterpieces have no doubt been conceived. The best of them are on the walls. Any one of them could win the Turner prize but what fuckin' couldn't these days? There are a couple of rows of deformed clay pots from the last pottery class for the infirm and insane. Frank gives us a rundown of the fun one can have at Willowbeck, from arts and crafts, to singalongs with a local crooner. He tells us about the accompanied trips down to Bingley for a spot of shopping. He tells us about trips to the Yorkshire Dales, the Lakes and the seaside. He'll be promising lap dancers dressed as Easter bunnies on Good fuckin' Friday next.

Four of us take the lift. Alison opts out. She gets a tad claustrophobic. Those silly big earrings she wears would take up half the fuckin' lift on their own. The lift creaks up to the next floor. It would be quicker to crawl up the stairs backwards. The door whines open. We step out into a corridor of bedrooms. Various radios and TVs can be heard from the rooms of those who prefer to spend their final days alone.

"Right, Alan. I hear you're a smoker," says Frank, as we reach the end of the first floor. "Follow me." He pops his head into a little room. "Julie? Can you rustle us up five teas love? Throw in a few custard creams and bourbons as well. Let's go mad. After you, mate."

This is more like it. It's twice the size of the TV room at Murton Croft. In one half there's a TV lounge and in the other there's a reading room with a selection of daily papers splayed out across a large coffee table, stained with the rings of countless cuppas. And there are ash trays. They have tall stainless steel ones at the side of some of the chairs and there are glass ones on the coffee tables and window ledges. There's also some kind of machine in the corner that seems to be circulating the air so there's no cancer fog for us to continually choke on. It's all very civilised. What's more, there's a large Georgian window. You can see the sweeping moors above Bingley. I sit in a comfy chair and nod hello to a friendly looking bloke who's reading the *Daily Star*. He smiles. It's the grin of a mad old bastard ogling a pair of tits and remembering what it used to be like to rest his weary head on the baps of former lovers.

"Right, I'll check on those teas. You lot make yourselves at home," says Frank.

That shouldn't be too difficult.

I retrieve me fags from me jacket pocket and spark up. I look at Alison. She doesn't approve of smoking, not since the fat bitch gave up in the mid-80s after a nasty bout of bronchitis. I look at Barry. He smiles like a cat with a fish platter. I look at Jenny. She gives me that "Well, what do you think of it so far?" look again. I smile back.

Then Julie walks in with the tea. Frank's saved her for last. Julie is the finale and I want a fuckin' encore. The woman is sublime. She has legs up to her chin, the body of a film star, long brunette hair and a smile that suggests a whole host of improprieties.

"Tea's up," she says. I actually gulp. Then she turns to the happy-looking perv reading the *Daily Star*. She takes a packet of fags from her blue overall pocket. "You can have yer fag now, Harry."

"Smashing. Time doesn't half go quick when you're looking at the ladies int' paper," says Harry.

"I bet it does," says Julie, comfortable with the banter. She bends over a touch in front of me to hand Harry his four o'clock fag. There's fuck all to see beneath the unflattering uniform, other than the shape of her perfect arse, but it will keep me in wanks for weeks.

Frank appears at the doorway.

"Well, that's all folks!" he says, like Bugs fuckin' Bunny. "I'll be down in reception if you have any questions. Enjoy your tea and biscuits and I'll see you when you're good and ready."

*

Barry turns left at the junction and heads up to the moors.

"I think we're going to miss dinner, Alan. There's a nice place at the top of this road. I might even buy you a pint," he says, cheerfully.

"I should fuckin' think so," I answer.

We find a corner and Barry gets the beers in.

72

"I thought you were a real-ale man," I comment.

"I am," says Barry.

"Then I'm sure you're aware that this pint needs toppin' up. Off yer pop. We'll save your seat." Barry does as he's told. Jenny slaps me knee.

"Behave yourself, you," she says. "So? What did you think?"

"I've never seen her so quiet," I say, looking at our Alison. "What's the matter? Will Geoff be wondering where you've got to? He'll be worried that you'll be running off with the window cleaner now he can't manage it."

Jenny flashes me a mock frown but the corners of her mouth are twitching. I don't think she's ever been keen on her.

"Did you like Willowbeck?" says Alison.

"Not really," I say. "I liked the garden and the smoking room but it was just another death camp at the end of the day."

"Are you going to give it a go?" asks Jenny.

"I'll have to consult me advisers." Barry returns with me topped-up pint. "You took your time." I take a long pull on me beer. "That's a nice drop. Tim Taylor's."

"Yep. Your taste buds are still working," says Barry. "So, what did you make of it?"

"Total shithole," I say. Jenny coughs her mouthful of beer straight into Barry's face. Then I laugh. Then I cough. Then I turn purple.

Alison looks at her watch.

"Are we going to order?" she says.

We order and we're soon tucking in. I ordered a homemade steak pie and chips. The pie is whole, not like those poncey pastry-top pies in a pot. The chips are homemade as well, thick cut, not those anaemic frozen things they usually serve in pubs these days because they can't be arsed to peel a few spuds. This is a nice local. That's another fuckin' tick then.

"Do they have a vacancy, Barry?" asks Jenny after we've finished.

"They're expecting one shortly."

"Nice," I say. "Out with one stiff and in with the next future cadaver."

"Well, unfortunately, that is how rooms become vacant," says Barry, as diplomatically as possible for a total moron.

"And what about those that go for a trial period?" I say. "Those rooms become vacant again if new inmates don't like the conditions of their confinement."

"Of course," says Barry. "Anyone for pudding?"

"I'm off for a smoke," I say. "Are you coming out for a bit of fresh air, Jenny?"

"I haven't got much choice, have I? I can't have you doing a runner over the moors like some bloody werewolf."

We look down into the valley where the lights of Bingley twinkle through the thickening fog. I realise that this is the first place I've been outside Leeds for a good six months. It's also the first boozer I've been in for well over a year. Jenny shivers.

"Do you want me jacket?"

"No thanks love but that's very gentlemanly of you. So, Alan?"

"What?"

"You know bloody well what. Are you gonna give it a go? Can I get a straight answer?"

"All in good time, Jenny. All in good time."

9. Mrs P's Window

I had some alone time last night and I did some serious thinking. Barry and Jenny have played me like a grand piano. By the end of yesterday I was all but packing me bags, ringing a taxi and accepting the inevitable. Then I thought of Cassandra.

There's a ward round tomorrow and knowing Dofuckall he'll want all this resolved so he can move on to discharging me. On the way back from Willowbeck Gardens, Jenny was telling me that the mental health trust managers and bean counters were forging ahead with a programme of sweeping changes. They're trying to ship out the lifers because they're going back to single-sex wards and they just don't have the beds. I'm going to have a real fuckin' battle on me hands to fight this insidious tide of change. The mixed over-65 wards had only been temporary after the flooding of Sycamore House in South Leeds last autumn. The place had been all but gutted and the patients had to be distributed between the five units across the city. Jenny lets me think she trusts me with hospital business. I'm not fuckin' stupid. Like I said before, she tells me what I want to hear, or what Dofuckall and his merry men want me to hear. I don't hold it against her. We go back too long for that.

There's nowhere in Leeds to take someone such as mesen. I fall between the cracks. I don't fit in. I'm a young 68 who's a bit too lively for a bog-standard death camp. There's too much history in me file. Too much volatility. They need a place that can handle someone like meself if I go off on one. I don't make a habit of it these days but I've been known to break the odd plate and crack the odd member of staff in me time. Not the ladies of course but I used to like a tussle with the male nurses if the mood took me. I know what I'm like when I erupt. I've been pretty dormant for a while but the magma is gently bubbling in me boots and I'm likely to pop at some point. Something always has to give. Pressure has to be released. When you shake up a bottle of pop and unscrew the lid, you're gonna get fuckin' wet.

I take the number from the notice board and make a call when the reception's quiet. It always is when they change shifts while they do handovers. I speak to Advocacy Alf. He sounds like a right little do-gooder on the blower and he agrees to come and see me this aft. Jenny will be a bit disappointed but it's tough shit. I can't confide in her now, not at this stage in the proceedings. There's no one looking after me best interests, not really. Even our Alison cares in her own way but they're thinking purely in terms of when I can't so much as undo me fly. I ain't there yet and if I'm to keep trudging around this mortal coil, I want some fuckin' quality of life. I might be fuckin' deluded but I can't get Cassandra out of me mind. I'm as high as Saturn on a string today and I feel like being pro-active for a change. They've let me off close obs now so they'll let me go for a wander. When I had me morning fag I could almost smell spring, and it's a gorgeous day. It's time to get me shit together for the final battle. Me chest feels a bit better. I haven't coughed too much for a couple of days. I'm sure I can make it to Mrs P's without keeling over. If not, then I might as well chuck mesen in front of a bus.

*

At first I thought I might write a letter and ask Mrs P to give it to Cassandra next time she comes into her shop. But I have no idea if Cassandra goes in regularly or if it was just a one-off. She said she works around here but that doesn't necessarily mean she'll be frequenting Mrs P's on a daily basis. There are three corner shops around the immediate vicinity. If I hit them all, I might just strike it lucky. Then it comes to me. If you are looking for something, or have something that someone else might be looking for, you advertise.

I stand outside Mrs P's and look in the window. Okay, so there's no other mad bastard seeking long-lost loves but I see enough in the window to make me think this might not be a bad idea after all.

I must admit, I've never once looked in Mrs P's window before and now I do, it's quite fun. Me favourite ad is about pets. It reads as follows:

GOING ON HOLIDAY?
OWN A RODENT?
WANT IT LOOKING AFTER?

From just £5 per day you can go away
and relax while your beloved rodents
have a holiday of their own!

CALL FRED AND ALICE ON **** ********
LEAVE YOUR RODENTS IN SAFE HANDS!

Another advert catches me eye and I realise that a splash of colour might not be a bad idea. It's another belter, advertising a children's entertainer:

HAVE FUN WITH NAUGHTY NORMAN
Magic Tricks   Balloon bending
And other party games
NAUGHTY NORMAN LOVES KIDS
AND KIDS LOVE NAUGHTY NORMAN!
Call Now on **** ********

There's a picture of Naughty Norman surrounded by a group of kids and Naughty Norman looks very happy indeed.
I look at me right hand. It's hardly as steady as a rock but I think I can manage to write a few lines.
I walk into the shop. Mrs P clocks me nervously.
"Morning love. I need some paper and a pen so I can put an ad in your window."
She didn't expect this and it takes her a beat or two to compute me request.
"I have postcards."
"I don't think I'm on holiday love and if I did, I wouldn't wish any other bugger was here with me."
I've lost her already. I don't think she's forgiven me for the Milk Tray incident. She'll always give me an uneasy

moment or two but as usual, she's given me that feeling that she'd like to teleport the fuck away from me if it's humanly possible. And then a thought strikes me. I've only seen one Pakistani bloke in the nuthouse in all these years. His name was Dilip. I used to call him Dill for short. He didn't like that. Anyway, me point is, Asian people are either in some way immune to the genetic anomalies that the likes of yours truly fall victim to, or there are loads of mad old Asians locked in the attics of their children, frothing at the mouth and howling at the moon like the rest of us nutters out here in Never Never Land. And the latter wouldn't surprise me at all. Asian people look after their old. The English send them to their deaths at dives like Willowbeck fuckin' Gardens.

Mrs P drags me off me train of thought.

"I have blank postcards. You can use one for your advert." She puts one in front of me and hands me a pen. "25p a week. How come you always wear sunglasses?" It's the first time she's ever asked me a question in all the times I've frequented her establishment. Now it's my time to be thrown.

"If I could answer that, love, the blokes with the white coats would be out of a job."

I thought this light-hearted remark might put her at ease but it has the opposite effect and she backs away and turns to the cigarette counter to refill the Regal King Size shelf that doesn't need refilling.

Another customer comes in.

"You can write it on the freezer," she says, and flicks her hand to her left. It's a gesture that can only be read as *Now fuck off out of the way, you mad bastard. You're making the place look untidy.*

I walk to the little freezer that contains the ice creams and lollies. I put the card down on the cold surface. I check me right hand. It's fluttering like a swallow-tailed butterfly. I take a deep breath in an effort to compose mesen and write me headline.

Where art Thou Cassandra?
Alan Siddall would like to hear from his old Friend

Cassandra Bekker.
Please call **** ******* and make an old man very happy.
His address is:
Murton Croft, Leeds, LS3 1TL

It feels right in the third person. For half of me miserable fuckin' life, I feel like I've been narrating me own story rather than living it.

I practically peel the postcard off the little freezer and I gently curse. It wasn't Mrs P's best idea but it will have to do. I walk back to the counter.

"It's a bit wet, Mrs P. You should have let me write it here, to be honest." I pat the counter below me. She doesn't know how to respond so she doesn't. As usual, she wants any transaction between us to be over almost as soon as it's begun but she'll have to bear with me for the moment. "I'm trying to track down a lady," I say. "You might remember her from a few days ago? I was talking to her over by the sausages. She's about the same height as me, but a big lass – you know, she's got a bit of girth – and she speaks with a slight accent. She's from South Africa originally." It may be me overactive imagination, but I swear she's going red. I'm getting nowhere so I decide it's time to put her out of her misery. "Are you putting this in the window, love, or do I get to pick the spot meself?"

"How long?"

"How much is it?"

"I told you, 25p per week."

She's getting impatient now, which is a first. She's got brave all of a sudden.

"No need to be like that, love. Even the mad have feelings."

I get nothing.

"Eight weeks," I say and put two quid on the counter. "How much for the card?"

"It's okay," she says, flicking her hand dismissively.

"You better give us forty Mayfair as well. I'm off the roll-ups so you'll make even more dosh out of me if you play your cards right," I say, a little too belligerently.

I don't get a "Good day" or jack shit. She's just lost me custom. I have some fuckin' pride. After I've found Cassandra, me and Mrs P are history. You should not treat your regulars like that, even if they do wear shades when the sun hasn't got his hat on.

*

I walk back up to Murton Croft, stopping every hundred yards or so to catch me breath. I spark up a 'bine before I enter the grounds. I spot Janet ranting about something or other to Kevin. I walk over to say hello.

"Now then, Janet. You don't look happy."

"I'm not bleedin' happy. I'm sick of freezin' me nibs off in a bloody car park whenever I want a bloody fag. It's an infringement of me rights, that's what it is. I'm going to me MP's surgery."

"It's the law, love. I don't think they'll pass another to bring it back. There's more chance of 'em bringing back hangin'."

"It's them buggers in Westminster that want hangin'. For Christ sake. Look at this silly cow." She points towards a fellow service user who was admitted last night. She's standing at the top of the stairs leading down to the car park. "I'd watch her, love," she says to Kevin. "You need to get her back to the ward. She's bloody gormless. She'll break her neck on those stairs. Anyone can see she's not steady on her feet."

"I'm here to watch you," Kevin says, in that tuneless voice of his.

"You might as well talk to a traffic cone. You'd get more sense out of one," I say. "Kev's strictly a one-task-at-a-time bloke, aren't yer mate?"

Kevin doesn't reply.

"The blood'll be on your hands if she goes arse over tit," she shouts at Kevin. "You'll be bloody sorry. No bugger cares for no one these days, apart from their bloody selves."

"I'll catch yer later, love." When Janet goes off on one, it's best to keep your distance or you might get caught in the crossfire. She's never been a fan of close obs. It brings out the worst in her. It's great to have the vinegary old hag back though. I don't know what she did to get herself on close obs but I wish I'd been there.

When I eventually get upstairs, Arthur's sitting in reception, and in my seat. I won't go all three bears on him; he'd make a poor Goldilocks in this nuthouse panto. He must have just reeled off a one-liner because Philippa is laughing her tits off and he's coughing himself a few shades south of crimson. I wait for his face to return to a relatively normal shade of pink.

"I'd ask if you're feelin' better but you've already answered the question."

"The old wheeze-box is playing up, squire. Any suggestions?" says Arthur, with another bout of hacking.

"You could try laying off the pipe and cancer sticks for a start."

"Don't be absurd," says Arthur. "My chest complaint is viral in nature," he says, with a cheeky grin before coughing again. "Are you coming down for one?"

"Not likely. It took me ten minutes to get up two flights of stairs. The lift's out. I'd wait till the cleaners have stopped fuckin' about with it. It'd take you till fuckin' May to get back up here."

Arthur starts laughing again and I instantly regret the joke.

"There's been a call for you, Alan. It was a bloke called Alf from Advocacy. Everything okay?" asks Philippa.

"As well as can be expected." I wink at Arthur.

Then Arthur sings, "There may be trouble ahead," and I do a little dance around him. Do they really expect me to go quietly into that good night? Not fuckin' likely.

10. The Ward Round

I stare at the circle. The circle stares back. Jenny breaks the silence.

"How's your chest, Alan?"

"Not ten bad, love. Not ten bad."

The occupational therapist smiles. We're still not on first name terms after all this time. Mind you, I've never had much call for her. I've never wanted to go home and I've always been quite happy to be looked after until now so she's never had to assess me ability to make mesen some chips without burning me flat down, or supervise me getting the skid marks off me jockeys. It's a bit late to want me independence but that's just how it is.

"Can we get started, Alan?" says Dofuckall. "We can always recap when your guest arrives."

"Are you trying to be funny, Doctor?"

"Sorry?"

"You will be. He's not me guest. He's the one person someone should have told me about. You should tell service users that they have people like Alf to talk to, especially when you're sending them to their deaths."

"I think that's a bit over-dramatic, Alan," says Dofuckall, with a cocky little snort. "Besides, we don't hide the service. It's all over the notice board."

"You might not hide it, doctor, but I've expressed me considerable reservations about leaving this place to almost everyone in this room, and that includes you, Jenny, and not one of you has mentioned Advocacy. Forgive me for being cynical, but anyone would think you weren't that keen on me talking to them."

I feel as big as a grizzly bear on two paws today. I'm on form. I'm in pole position and no fucker in this room is getting the better of Mr Siddall today.

"Alan," starts Dofuckall, but Beth opens the door and saves him, allowing him time to get his thoughts together.

"Sorry to interrupt," says Beth, "but I've had a call

from Advocacy. Alf Coulter's mother has been taken ill so he won't be able to make today's ward round."

"Well that's very fuckin' convenient. Who got to him?" I shout. "This is a fuckin' conspiracy. Did you warn him off, Philippa?"

"Of course not," she says, looking surprised at me outburst.

"Well it doesn't make a soddin' difference. I'm not agreeing to anything till I've spoken to me brief again." I sound like Phil fuckin' Mitchell. "He's as close to a legal representative as I'm gonna get and I'd like to postpone this meeting until Mr Coulter is fit for fuckin' purpose."

I'm in a right rage now. As usual, all eyes turn to Jenny when the going gets tough.

"Alf can come to the next ward round, Alan, if you want him to be here," says Jenny.

I try to calm down but I'm not doing too well.

"I expected more from you an' all. You've betrayed me, Jenny, and I won't forget it, no fear."

No one says anything for a minute or two, while I quietly seethe, like a punctured can of pop.

"I mean, our Alison couldn't even be arsed to show up. There's no one on me side in this whole room, not even you, Jenny, or you, Philippa. I've known you both for years."

And that's it. I'm crying. I'm crying like a fuckin' baby and I can't quite believe it. Suddenly, I want Arthur and Janet in here, in me corner, mopping me brow between rounds, warning me to stay off the ropes. I'll try to stop blubbering.

"I'll organise another meeting with Advocacy for you, Alan. Okay? If Alf Coulter can't make it, we'll get someone else here to see you. Okay?" says Philippa.

"Can we talk about the other day, Alan?" says Dofuckall. "Can we discuss Willowbeck Gardens?"

"I should have been told I had options," I shout. "If it wasn't for Arthur, I wouldn't have even considered talking to Advocacy." I stand up. "You're all full of shit, you lot."

"Alan," says Philippa, rising from her chair. "You've

always liked it here. You still do. There's never been a reason for you to talk to Advocacy before. It's never come up until now."

She's got a point but I pretend she hasn't.

"You can all go fuck yourselves," I shout, and walk out of the room.

I storm to the reception desk. Beth is looking at a card in her hand and she's smiling.

"What are you looking so happy about?"

"Nothing. Are you okay?"

"I'm dandy, love. Go on, share it with the group. What you grinning at?"

"It's Arthur. He sent me a lovely birthday card. He's written me a poem."

I feel a stab of jealousy.

"I do me talking under the sheets, love. Always have done, always will. What will your boyfriend say to that randy old sod writing you sonnets?"

"I don't have a boyfriend," she says, with mock sadness. She's being friendly, not flirtatious. She's being herself. She's lovely.

"Well, if you're looking for an old man, Arthur's had his day. Poor bastard's running on empty. I'm available though. You better be quick. I'm getting me made-to-measure incontinence pads from Savile Row delivered in time for me move to Willowbeck Gardens." I get nothing but an uncomfortable smile. "Can I have a tenner from me money, please?" She gets the key for the nutters' piggy bank from Kevin, who is trying to look busy in the back room.

"Are you sure everything's okay?" says Beth with genuine concern as she hands me the tenner.

I sigh. She can go fuck herself as well. I'd just like to be there when she does.

*

It's a lovely day for mid-March and I head for the park. I haven't been here since last summer.

I see me first snowdrops of the year in a shy little cluster by a big oak tree. I follow the path that leads down

84

towards the benches in the middle of the park where I usually
go in the summer to sit and watch the world go by. I pass a
lanky teenager who nods at me as he passes. He's smoking a
spliff disguised as a roll-up but that distinctive aroma gives
him away.

I used to smoke shitloads of the stuff with Babs. I had
a mate who grew his own in the attic of his terrace house. He
used to give me a good discount an' all and me and Babs
would go round and score and smoke half of our stash before
we managed to leave his fuckin' house.

Babs was insatiable when we got home on those
nights. I'd be so out of it that me prick and me tongue were
the only things that could function, but I could never come
during penetration when I was stoned so she'd just ride me
until we were both sore and then she'd blow me. I'd have to
return the favour of course and she always insisted that she
parked herself on me face because it was the only time I could
find her clitoris. It was also the only time I could make her
scream like an angry fox. It was more her doing than mine.
Me face was just in the wrong place at the right time. Then
we'd raid the fridge and cook some meat, no matter what time
it was. They were good times they were.

I could just smoke a spliff. We did LSD once as well
but I saw something I really didn't like. I never talk about that.
We did mushies every so often but they didn't really do it for
either of us. Babs was terrible on them. They just made her
talk incessantly and I'd have to shove me cock in her trap just
to shut her up. When I think of what we used to do and I think
of her and Derek, I still get a horrible feeling in me guts, even
after all these years. I've never managed to exorcise the filthy
whore from me life. She's like an ulcer that just can't be
removed. That's why Cassandra is so important to me now.
I'm not fuckin' stupid enough to think that we will live
happily ever after and all that shite, even if me advert does
work, but I'd rather think about her than that evil bitch. I
mean, I still get hard every time I think of Babs. That can't be
right. There must be something I can take for that. There must
be something I can take that can stop me remembering her

riding me as if I was a Cheltenham Gold Cup winner, or her smothering me with her sopping cunt.

I'm so hard now and I'm frothing with anger. I head back to the oak tree where I saw the snowdrops. I get there and take a moment or two to catch me breath. Then I take out me cock. It feels good for it to be out in the cold air. It hasn't been this hard since I was last inside a woman fifteen years ago. That was with Lillian, a randy old bitch from St Ives, who I once fucked in the bushes behind the tennis courts at High Royds.

Me eyes dart in the only two directions where I can be spotted but it's a bit late to be worrying about being seen. I close me eyes. I imagine Beth, her eyes wide and crazed, staring up at me as she takes me deep into her hot mouth. And then I'm coming. It shoots out like a wax dart. I open me eyes. There's an old man with a Highland terrier on a lead about twenty foot in front of me. The dog is dressed in one of those little tartan coats. I get me hanky from me pocket and give mesen a good wipe. The dog starts yapping. The old bloke is still staring at me, his mouth wide open in shock. I put me hand up, like tennis players do when they've just fluked a winner. I pop mesen back in. Then I take a fag from me packet to enjoy a post-wank fag, leaning against the tree so I don't fall over. That's quite enough adventure for one day.

*

Beth calls me back as I try and pass reception without being spotted. "Alan?" I stop and turn but I can't look at her.

"Dr Bell said he'll pop back and see you tomorrow."

"Okay," I say and turn to head to me room.

"Oh, and there was a call for you while you were out. It was a woman. She didn't leave her name."

I can't believe it.

"Did she sound a bit foreign?"

"Yeah, a bit actually, yeah."

"Did she leave her number?"

"No. She said she'd call in later this afternoon."

I get hard again. I haven't recovered so quickly after coming since I fucked Babs above the Cow and Calf in the summer of '71. I fucked her at the Twelve Apostles twenty minutes later. This could be me lucky day after all. Cassandra's coming to see me.

11. Butterflies

It's lovely outside and if it's warm enough for an al fresco wank, I'm sure it's warm enough to wait for me special guest. After I've made a mug of tea, I head for the lift. I lose half of it and give mesen third degree burns on the way down the corridor but I've got enough left to keep me hydrated while I wait for Miss South Africa.

I haven't felt this excited since England came out of the Wembley tunnel on that fateful summer day in 1966. It was the only bloody time that set of sorry buggers delivered.

I spark up and prepare for me date. I've got butterflies the size of fuckin' eagles flapping away inside me gut.

As much as I enjoy their company, I've got some serious thinking to do so I hope I don't get distracted by Janet or Arthur if they turn up for a fag. This meeting with Cassandra is potentially life-changing. Mind you, I don't suppose I'll be seeing much of old Arthur for much longer unless I'm very much mistaken. It'll take more than a shot glass of Benylyn to shift that fucker off his chest. I heard him wheezing when I passed his room earlier.

In all the excitement, I realise I haven't even changed me undies since I bashed me bishop in the park and it feels a bit moist and sticky down below. I take a whiff under me right arm and it's not too fresh under there either so I decide to go powder me bollocks and talc me pits so I'm nice and clean for the old girl. You never know, she might feel like a bit of al fresco fun herself. I let out a Sidney James cackle as I head for the lift.

Again, I don't look Beth in the eye when I pass her. I head for me room and strip off to freshen up. I wish I could lock me door. It's one of the many indignities us mental health service users have to put up with, just because the staff are shit scared we will all top ourselves at will the minute we get the chance. I hope one of the nurses doesn't decide to look in on me. It's times like these you wish you had a Do Not Disturb sign to hang on your door knob. I could hang it off me own knob. It's still as stiff as a starched shirt collar. Not bad for a bloke of 68.

I give mesen a good wash and spray me pits. I decide to put on a fresh T-shirt as this is a special occasion. I opt for me Black Sabbath *Masters of Reality* T-shirt and the irony is not lost on me. Alison got me it off one of those website things. She may be a hapless old cow at times but she has her uses. After me little Shakespearean drama plays out this aft, I'll give her a bell. I'll remind her of me list and ask her why she hasn't got off her considerable behind and granted me wishes. I don't expect a lot from her but it's about time she started pulling her weight, as difficult as that may be for that fat old boiler.

"Hello Alan. Bye Alan," says Beth with a chuckle as I pass her again. I give her a quick glance out of the corner of me right eye to see if I still can without burning up with embarrassment. I feel like I've committed a crime. I don't feel the urge to confess as yet but I just might feel the need to when I'm not thinking clearly. I just hope I manage to keep me little lapse of decency to mesen. I don't want to be thought of as a sad old pervert, even if that's exactly what I am. You'd think I was fuckin' Catholic. I spent too long with Babs. Her sordid Catholicism must have left its mark on me along the way. I insisted that she converted to the Church of England before we married but her father would have rather been burnt at the stake and have had his charred body sodomised by an angry vicar than have his daughter turn her back on her faith. The fact was that his precious daughter was the epitome of evil who would have had St Peter impaling himself on the pearly gates rather than let that evil bitch into heaven. If Babs had been at the last supper she'd have turned it into a fuckin' gang bang.

The mere thought of Babs can ruin me day. Me good mood has already dissipated a bit but if today goes to plan, all will be well in the kingdom of Alan Siddall. I will be king and Cassandra Bekker shall be me queen. Dilly fuckin' dilly dilly. There's fuck all to worry about regarding Babs. It's really about time I let all that stuff go. Easier said.

Half an hour passes and I'm ready for another cuppa. I look at me watch. It's nearly 3.30. If I had a mobile, I could ring in an order and get Beth to bring me a drink. I'll have to get on to our Alison. She hasn't got off her bone-idle arse and got me even one of the things off the list I gave her. She's keeping a low profile of late. When the shit hits the fan, you can only rely on yourself. That's the sad fuckin' truth of it. Maybe if me and Babs had had kids I might have been supported better in me years of madness and infirmity. Mind you, if I ponder again on what me and Babs could have produced, it sends a shiver down me spine. The world is probably a better place without the appalling offspring of Mr and Mrs Siddall (nee Kelly).

I just can't get that bitch out of me mind. Luckily, Janet has appeared. She walks over to me with Kevin skulking behind like a puny secret service agent. She'll have some complaint or other about our little heartbreak hotel to take me mind off Babs.

"Who you waiting for? You look all excited. You on a promise?" she snaps.

"I am as a matter of fact. Give me a sip of yer tea. I'm spitting sparrows."

"Sod off. I don't want your filthy mouth anywhere near my cup. I don't know where it's been. You might give me some 'orrible disease." I give her me best puppy look and she hands me her cup. "Kevin, go get Mr Siddall a pot of tea. Make yersen bloody useful for a change. Go on. Off yer pop. Look at him. What a sorry excuse of a man."

Janet and I have a good laugh at Kevin. But he doesn't move. He turns his head to let us know he's ignoring us. Someone like Kevin will walk in here with a gun one day and start shooting. He looks the type. He's good to have around the place. No matter how fucked-up us lot in here are, we look at the likes of Kevin and thank the good Lord for our blessings.

"I take it you're still on close obs?"

"Aye. I went a bit doolally last night. It's me sleeping patterns. They've been shot to shit since I came back in here."

She puts a fag in her mouth and I light it for her with me shaking right hand. Kevin will have hers. Janet's not exactly a pyromaniac but I wouldn't trust her with a lighter when she's in this kind of mood any more than they do. "I had a run in with that Bev last night, the effing heifer, her and that big ugly sidekick of hers. They think they're bloody *Sapphire and Steel*, them two."

"What?"

"Never mind. Anyway, they came running into the TV lounge at three in the morning. I'd only put the radio on for a bit of music. I was doing me Dusty Springfield with me hairbrush when they came barging in. She can move fast for a fat bugger, that Bev. Anyway, we had a bit of a row and I was sent to me room like a bloody teenager. I still couldn't get to sleep. To be honest... No, I shouldn't be telling you this..." She had me attention. The time was passing quite nicely now I had a bit of entertainment.

"What?"

"Well, I got a bit... aroused."

"I'm pleased for yer, love, but there's some things a lady like yourself should keep private. Besides, you'll put me right off me tea."

"You wouldn't say no, you big hairy brute. You've got a short memory."

"As a matter of fact I happen to be spoken for."

"The last time someone spoke for you, you were in court for indecent exposure." She laughs at her own little joke and then takes a big slurp of tea, before realising she has a bit more laughter in her belly. A jet of warm liquid shoots out of her mouth and lands on me left thigh.

"For fuck's sake, Janet. You've spat all over me jeans."

"Temper, temper. What are you so edgy about, anyway?"

"I'm waiting for Cassandra."

"Who the bloody 'ell's Cassandra?"

"It's a long story but this could be the best day of me life if I play me cards right." She laughs again, a right old mocking cackle, and for a second I feel like lamping her.

"I don't want to burst yer bubble but you're hardly the catch of the day, love. You do smell better than usual though, I'll give yer that. Anyway, if it doesn't work out, you can always pop and see me in the wee small hours." She winks at me and laughs again. "C'mon Kevin. Let's leave Casanova here to wait for his Cassandra. They'd ride off into the sunset if he could manage to get on his horse." Even Kevin laughs.

I feel all agitated again. Suddenly, I have a flashback to a long lonely night in mid-winter long ago. I took solace in the arms of Janet in High Royds back in the 80s. It's a night I'll never forget. It was pretty gruesome. We were found by a nurse on the night shift in one of the linen rooms, a certain Philippa Green, but the damage had already been done. I'll have to live with those images for the rest of me life. Janet's face in the throes of passion is not a pretty sight, God love her. She looked like something from a fuckin' horror film. Still, I obviously made an impression on the old hag to get an invite back into her bed. If it doesn't work out with Cassandra, I might just take her up on her offer. It's been too fuckin' long since I got me end away and I need to again before I shuffle off this mortal coil, even if it is with Janet.

I need to stop thinking about sex. I've got another stiffy to contend with and I'd go get rid of it in the gents if I wasn't scared I might miss Cassandra's arrival. Besides, one wank a day is more than enough for a man of my years. But when I see who's waddling up the drive, me little soldier soon falls back to sleep. Talk about bad fuckin' timing. But at least she's got a bag with her so she might just have something from me list. She better had or she's in deep shit. I'll make this quick. I need to get shot of her as quickly as possible.

"Now then, sis. You took yer fuckin' time." Her eye twitches from the short, sharp ferocity of me greeting.

She sits down.

"You smell nice for a change," says Alison, with a weak smile.

"Toufuckinché" is me terse reply.

She opens up the bag and I look inside. It's full of

92

goodies. She must feel guilty.

She puts the bag down and puts her hand in her right jacket pocket. The next thing I know, I've got a new fully charged mobile phone in me hand. The only problem is, I have no fucker's number other than the woman sitting next to me. I'll have to remedy that pretty sharpish. I feel a rush of excitement as I look into me palm at me new toy. But then I focus on me present situation.

"Thanks for the stuff, love, but I haven't got long today. I've got someone coming to see me."

"Who? Someone from Willowbeck?"

"No, and we have to talk about that as well but not today. Can you come by tomorrow?"

"I can't, Alan. I'm at work tomorrow. I've got all afternoon though. What time is your appointment?"

I can't help but smile and I see her expression change to one of concern rather than curiosity.

"It's not an appointment exactly," I say. "It's more of a social visit."

"Who with?"

"An old friend."

"Alan, you don't have any old friends, apart from ex-patients."

"Fuckin'ell, love. Tell it like it is, why don't yer? Well that's just where you're wrong. In fact, she might just be more than a friend."

"Don't be ridiculous," she snaps. "I don't have time for games. If you're in one of your silly moods it's perhaps best we talk later in the week."

By "silly mood", me dear old sis means the all too frequent manifestations of me lifelong bi-polar disorder, bless her cotton socks.

"I'm not in a silly mood," I reply calmly. "I'm waiting for a lady who just might make me fuckin' miserable life worth living so either be happy for me or go back home to that prick of a husband and stay away until you can have the decency to consider what I want for a change."

"Why are you so mean to me, Alan? After all I've

done for you. Why do you treat me so badly?"

I stand up.

"Just fuck off home, Alison. Thanks for the goody-bag, I mean it, I'm grateful, but just fuck off home and leave me alone. I'll call yer when I need yer."

Then come the waterworks, and when me sister turns on the tap, she could flood the fuckin' Aire Valley within minutes. I really can't be arsed so I take the bag.

"Get yourself home, Alison. This is no place for histrionics," I say.

"Is that right, Alan?" she snaps bitterly. "You've been a bloody drama queen since we were kids so please don't lecture me on histrionics. You should be ashamed of yourself. You treat me like a skivvy and I've had enough of it."

"Understood. Now pop off home and calm yourself down. I really don't want a scene. Me guest could turn up at any minute." Ironically, or maybe it's not that ironic when you think about it, she looks at me like I'm stark raving mad.

"You really are a nasty bastard," she spits, and retrieves a hanky from up her right sleeve and honks into it. I almost feel guilty.

"Fuck yer then. I'm off back to the ward. Look at the state of yer. You're a disgrace. Just go home, woman."

I leave her sobbing. Bev turns up at the entrance and she goes to sit with her. Bev looks up at me as I take a look down the path, pretending this whole drama is nothing to do with me. She shakes her head, tuts and puts her arm around me babbling sibling.

"I'm a nutter, Bev. I'm allowed to upset people," I shout. Zahid gives me a fierce look from behind the check-in desk and I give him the finger before heading for the lift. What a fuckin' farce. All I wanted to do was wait for Cassandra in peace and it's all gone to shit. I don't know why I fuckin' bother. This is going to be a disaster. I start to hope that she doesn't turn up, not when I'm like this. I'll try and snap out of it but me mood is darkening fast. Why can't people just leave me the fuck alone?

*

94

Beth gives me a big smile when she sees me.

"What's in the bag? Anything exciting?"

I look at her lovely face, the very face I imagined earlier, the very eyes I imagined crazed with lust as she sucked on me. I feel mesen stiffen again and then I feel the tears coming and I can't stop them. I drop me bag and start blubbering and before I know it, Beth is beside me rubbing me shoulder, and I cry harder because I feel even more guilty but me cock doesn't care and it's harder than ever as she rubs me shoulder and I just want to yell and I do, then I double over and cry and howl like I've never done before, and instinctively, that sweet young woman grabs hold of me, and, without thinking, puts me arm around her shoulder and walks me over to the chairs where Arthur is sitting and staring at me, his eyes red with exhaustion and wide with shock. By this time, Philippa and Jenny have appeared from nowhere.

"You sit here with Arthur. I'll make us all a nice cup of tea. How's that sound?" says Beth.

"Sounds fuckin' great," I say, meaning it. She smiles at me and that smile has such warmth, such genuine warmth that I feel a fresh wave of shame. "I'm sorry, Beth," I say. "I'm so sorry." She puts her hand on me shoulder and tells me not to be silly. But I feel silly. I feel so fuckin' silly I could open me wrists with a rusty razorblade.

I don't get a peep out of Arthur as we drink our tea. He just pats me knee once and that one little gesture says more than a thousand words can say. In short it says, *I don't know what the fuck you're going through but whatever it is, I hope you manage to cope with it before it finishes you off.* And just like Beth helped me a minute or so earlier, that little pat helps me too and I realise, no matter how bad things get, I am amongst friends here. And I realise I really don't want to leave here even though I know, I just know, that's exactly what I'll be doing.

Bev enters the ward and starts talking to Jenny and Philippa behind the ward station. Beth brings her tea over and sits with us. She doesn't say a word. She's only been here a few weeks and she's learnt more about mental health treatment in that short time than Bev and Roy in the forty years of experience between them. Well, she hasn't learnt it exactly, she just knows. She just fuckin' gets it.

After me tea, Jenny and Philippa come over and walk me down to me room. There's a chair outside me room ready for close obs. I hope it's not Beth. I really hope it's not Beth. I'm in the mood to confess. I'm in the mood to expose mesen and confess.

I walk in me room, take me leather off and collapse on me bed. Jenny gets the job and takes a seat outside. I lie down and for once, I take me shades off. Jenny looks into me eyes and then I watch a tear, just one tear, roll down her left cheek and then we smile at each other. She looks away and she opens her book. She's always got her nose in a book that one. I don't know how many books I've watched her read while she's kept a vigil on me but it's a lot. I close my eyes. A minute or so later, I feel a sheet being pulled over me and then I feel her taking off me boots. I'll just have a little nap. I open me eyes.

"Jenny?"

"Get some sleep, Alan."

"I need you to promise me something."

"Okay."

"If Cassandra turns up you have to wake me up, no matter what."

"Who's Cassandra?"

"It's a long story."

"Okay. I promise."

"Thanks."

I close me eyes.

*

There's a ham salad, a piece of chocolate cake and a beaker of juice on me bedside table when I wake up. I put me shades on. I have no idea what time it is and then I realise I can look at me phone rather than carting mesen down to reception to look at the clock. It's 6.25 pm. There's a box on me phone that tells me I've got a text message but when I try and open it, it tells me the phone is locked. I have no idea how to go about

96

unlocking it so I open the door. Roy has replaced Jenny in the chair.

"Can you unlock this for me, Roy? I've got a text message."

Roy hands me back the phone. It's from our Alison.

ALL THIS IS HARD FOR ME TOO YOU KNOW. I'M DOING MY BEST. WE HAVE PROBLEMS OF OUR OWN. PLEASE CUT ME SOME SLACK AND TAKE MY FEELINGS INTO CONSIDERATION ONCE IN A WHILE. I WILL ALWAYS DO THE BEST I CAN FOR YOU. LOVE ALISON.

Because her message is in capitals it feels like she's screaming at me.

"Are you any good at this stuff, Roy?"

"Yeah. Do you want to text someone?"

"I want to reply to that one."

"Okay. I'll show you."

"Can you do it, mate? It's a short message."

He sighs.

"What do you want me to put?"

"Go fuck yourself. Only joking. Put I'm sorry and a couple of kisses. That ought to do it. What do yer think?"

"It might take a bit more than that, mate, but it's a start." He smiles and sends the text. "There you go." He hands the phone back to me. "Someone came to see you earlier on."

"What?"

He is startled by me sudden change in mood.

"Some woman came to see you."

"Who?"

"She didn't leave her name. But she said she'd pop back in the morning, first thing."

"Okay," I say.

I go back in me room and sit on me bed. The eagles are back, flapping their giant fuckin' wings, trying to churn up me stomach but there's fuck all in there to churn up. I down me juice and decide I should really eat something. Cassandra is coming tomorrow. That's good enough for now. I look at me mobile. The morning is a long fuckin' way away and I'm wide awake. I hope a patient or two will join me on the night shift otherwise I'll be stuck with Roy and Bev. I'd rather be stuck with a bad case of Legionnaire's disease.

12. Porn

I try to sleep again but it's no use. I get out of bed and shuffle to the TV room. Roy has probably decided I'm not on close obs anymore because he can't be arsed to observe a sleeping man. It's like that *Big Brother* programme. I went into the TV room one night and Pat was watching them all sleep. I've never known owt like it. It's amazing what passes for entertainment these days. They should put some cameras in here on a night. We'd certainly be worth watching, especially at bedtime. That's when we face our demons.

I'm not really a TV person but I've got to pass the time somehow and there's no one interesting to talk to.

"Good evening," I say, as if I'm walking into a hotel bar. There are five people in the TV lounge: two old geezers are asleep and three old birds are watching *The One Show*. I'd rather watch tarmac set so I decide to go for a smoke. I cough and have to catch me breath as I struggle to breathe for a few moments near the nurses' station. I won't be far behind Arthur I suppose if I carry on like this. I might stop if Cassandra doesn't like it. I'd do anything for her. Anything. I feel mesen getting a bit weepy again and it doesn't go unnoticed.

"You alright?" says Bev, sounding like she doesn't give a shit either way.

"What do you care?"

"Only asking," she says, without looking up from her paperwork. Roy reads me mind when he sees me and gets me cigs and lighter from the safe.

"You gonna be alright?"

"Think so."

"Okay. I'll let you go on your own then."

"Thanks, Roy."

He's softened up a bit. He's alright really. It's Bev that's the problem. It's amazing what a bloke will put up with to get his dick gobbled.

Colin has replaced Zahid on the check-in desk downstairs. He looks brown. He must have been somewhere nice.

"Now then, fella," he says, as I saunter up to the desk.

"Good holiday?"

"Aye. We went to Egypt. Lovely. Mid-nineties every day. Great food. We even had a go at that scuba diving. Our lass went into a bit of a panic. She saw some drift wood and she thought it were a bloody shark. She started screaming like a loony. Sorry. No offence."

"None taken, Colin."

"How are you?"

"I'm hunky fuckin' dory."

"Going to a home, aren't ya?"

"Haven't you heard of service user confidentiality?"

"I hear everything behind this desk, mate."

"If you must know, plans are afoot to ship me out of here but I just might be saved by a special lady."

Colin nods as if he believes me. He's been here a long time. But his eyes tell me he's just humouring me.

"Who is she then? It's not that woman who came to see you earlier, is it?"

"You saw her?" Me gut tightens. I cough. I probably turn purple.

"Yeah. She popped in at five when I was doing the changeover with Zahid. Nice lady. Very smart."

"What did she say?"

"She just said she was here to see you, asked for you by name."

"Did she sign in?"

"Yeah."

Colin hands me the signing in sheet for the day. I quickly scan it and nearly throw up me heart.

"She's a bit young for you, mate. She didn't stay long with you, did she? She was back down here after about five minutes. Said she'd be back tomorrow morning."

I look at her name. Sidra Begum. Advocacy. Unfuckinbelievable. After all this. I should've fuckin' known. Why do I do this? Why do I always live in some fuckin' fantasy land?

I walk outside for a fag feeling like I've been punched in the stomach. I can hear Colin asking if I'm okay but me mouth just won't work. It's not dark yet. We'll be putting the clocks forward soon and then it will be Easter before we know it. I usually go to Alison's on Easter Sunday. Whoopeefuckindoo.

I sit down on the bench, spark up a fag and I'm crying again. It's about time I snapped out of this nonsense. It's about time I packed me bags and went gently into that good night. Willowbeck Gardens is me future. I've got no fight left in me. I need to talk to someone. Where's Jenny when I need her?

I finish me fag and decide me next move. Colin is on the phone. I just might make it down the stairs to the staff car park and then I can go out of the back and head down to the university without anyone seeing me. I look in me leather pocket. I've got eight fags, a lighter and £3.50. That'll do nicely.

I won't have long to get anywhere before they notice I've gone so I plan me route quickly. Roy will shit a brick when he sees I've fucked off. I'm still supposed to be on close obs. He might get a disciplinary. Tough shit. I have to think about numero uno for a change.

I opt for the university way down to town. It's pedestrianised for a good while and those lazy plods are hardly likely to get out of their cars and hunt me by foot through the campus once they hear about me escape. I'm hardly a danger to the public.

When I get to the main road I can head through the Merrion Centre, down to Vicar Lane, then down to the market to the Duck 'n' Drake. There's more chance of bumping into Greta fuckin' Garbo than Cassandra but I'm in the mood to reminisce.

To be honest, I'm making this up as I go along. It reminds me of a time I decided to go to Babs's and Derek's love nest. It was a similar evening to this only then I was in High Royds and had to catch two buses to get there. I'd found out their address from the phone book. It was that easy. Babs had never been scared of me enough to hide her whereabouts.

It's not as if I was a wife beater. It was the other way around. She hardly feared me turning up at the doorstep to beg her to come back to me. After all, it was me who got stabbed in the leg. I should've pressed charges on the crazy bitch.

Anyway, I turned up at their house on a damp spring night. I'd already started wearing me shades at inappropriate times so when Derek opened the door to what must have looked like a Hells Angel wearing a pair of shades at 8pm on a darkening March evening, he looked like he'd just met the Grim Reaper. Derek wasn't much of a man, to tell you the truth. I'm hardly Clint Eastwood but Derek was puny as fuck. He looked a bit like that bloke from the *Carry On* films, the one who was a bit camp – not Kenneth Williams – the one with the round glasses, only Derek didn't wear glasses.

I had always imagined Babs with some huge hairy-arsed fucker with a cock the size of a rolling pin and dirty fingernails; a mechanic maybe, or a fuckin' panel beater. Even I could take that little wisp. She obviously picked a little 'un so she could dominate him.

"Step aside, pal. I'm here to take me wife home."

He tried to shut the door but I was already half in and I pushed him out of the way and stormed through into the lounge.

"What the..."

"Hello, Babs. I've been thinking about it and I think you should come home."

Babs was in a white dressing gown and her long brown hair was still wet from the bath. Christ, she looked better than ever and I remember thinking if I just went up to her, disrobed her there and then, I could shag her right in front of that skinny little bus conductor and there would be fuck all he could do about it. But Babs was in shock. Her brain was trying to deal with who was in front of her eyes. I hadn't seen her for five years. She had moved on. I was still trying to catch up. She finally composed herself and picked up the nearest object, which happened to be a rather cheap and nasty looking candelabra, a dangerous weapon in the hands of a woman like Babs.

"Get the fuck out of my house, you mad bastard, or I'll crack yer fuckin' skull open." It was nice to see that Babs hadn't lost any of her sophistication. I backed away realising I hadn't thought this through. "Don't worry, love," she said to Mr No Muscles. "My ex-husband's not staying for supper."

He gave me a wide berth as I backed away from me irate ex-wife.

"You fuckin' whore," I screamed and she came at me and I turned and ran. I got as far as the bus stop terminus about a half a mile from their house when a police car showed up. She'd obviously rung the fuzz. We still had mutual friends so I guess she must have heard I'd gone mad. That was the last time I saw Barbara Siddall (nee Kelly). I have replayed that scene a thousand times, and on every occasion Babs has opened her robe, let it drop to the floor and I'd fucked her senseless under the quivering form of a whimpering helpless bus conductor called Derek. And I made her scream with pleasure. I don't care if Derek's got a prick the length of a garden hose, there's no way he's ever made Babs come like I could have that night. But I didn't. I wasn't man enough. I couldn't show her who was boss because we both knew who the boss actually was.

I'm ready for another battle with me little python but a ham shank in the park like I had earlier is a long fuckin' way from whipping me pecker out in the middle of the city centre. I might be mad but I'm not fucking stupid. I've already been glared at by a quartet of knuckle-draggers on their way to some pub or other.

I nip down through the Merrion Centre and then down towards the Wrens pub. The Grand Theatre is to me right as I'm about to head down to Vicar Lane. There's a line of people entering the building for some show or other. It reminds me of the time I once screamed obscenities at Eliza Doolittle from the upper circle of York Opera House, but I wasn't a well man at the time. Mental health service users have as much right as the next person to enjoy a good musical but you have to question the judgement of an activities committee that decided to take the likes of me to any public performance, particularly when I'm riding on the crazy train. Pat Jenkins was off her fuckin' head that night as well. She called Professor Higgins a cunt. I swear that's the one and only time I've heard her say the C word. He brought out the worst in old Pat when he started singing "By George I Think She's Got It". There were more laughs for me and Pat than any of the cast and chorus that night. No wonder they were so pissed off.

I cut down a side street and me nostrils fill with the tantalising smells from a couple of curry houses. Me stomach howls as I pass the second, willing me to fill it. A bloke who looks in his early twenties stares out from his window seat and I give him a wave. He says something to his girlfriend and they both look at me and laugh. If I wasn't on one of me ill-conceived missions, they'd be fuckin' wearing what was left on their plates.

The smell of curry automatically makes me think of Babs again. I consider banging me head against a wall to shift the bitch.

She used to cook us both curries now and again but cooking was never her strong point. Come to think of it, nothing much was apart from – don't go there Alan. You always walk into another fuckin' sex flashback. I could chop it off right now after the grief the little bastard has given me today.

Suddenly, I want to sit down but there's nowhere handy unless I want to slouch in a shop doorway like some dirty tramp. But I'm no bloody tramp. You might disagree if you saw me at this particular moment but I still smell pretty good, even if I do say so meself, after sprucing mesen up for Cassandra earlier. Well, we all know what a fuckin' glorious waste of time that was.

I pass the Templar Arms and nearly walk in but I haven't got too far to go and it seems a shame to turn back now. I just need to take a little break before I puke out me left lung. I cough hard and I see stars.

The Templar Arms was a popular haunt for me and Babs when we started courting, until a fellow market trader pinched her arse one Friday night. She didn't seem to mind that much. In fact, if I hadn't been there she'd have probably sucked him off in the gents for a packet of pork scratchings and a pickled egg. She was pissed as a rat, mind. I offered him outside. The bastard just decked me where I stood. It was the last time I defended the honour of me lovely wife. She could take care of herself and it saved me getting me face re-arranged on a weekly basis. Besides, you should never mess with a fruit and veg man. Lugging sacks of spuds around the place gives them muscles like Johnny Weissmuller.

I take out a fag and spark up. A chap who looks a Woodbine away from lung cancer joins me outside the pub.

"Evening," he mumbles suspiciously.

"Hello."

"Not a bad night," he says, when he decides I'm no threat.

"That depends on your perspective," I say, and by the look on his face he's already decided to raise the threat level to critical, like the MI5 do when they suspect a terrorist attack is imminent. "Sorry mate. It's been a bad day. I was expecting me lover but me fat sister showed up instead." He nodded and let out a little grunt to acknowledge me remark and decided to try and ignore me, but that wasn't going to work. "I've been waiting for this woman all me life, to tell you the truth. She's broken me heart," I say, and feel the tears coming. He flicks his half-smoked fag in the pavement gutter and fucks off back inside. I suppose he cut an unlikely figure to provide me with a shoulder to cry on. I compose mesen and finish me fag.

I start walking again and I'm just about to cut across the big car park where the bus station used to be when I'm drawn to a neon sign like an Irishman to a pork butcher's.

I open the door, activating a little bell. A chubby woman with jet black hair, ghost white skin and a pierced nostril pops up from behind the counter and flashes me a big warm smile. I look around where I stand and see enough sexy underwear, rubber dresses and skimpy outfits to give the pontiff himself a stiffy.

"I think you want to be downstairs," she says. "Can

you manage?"

Me shades have thrown her. "I'm not blind, love. If I was, there'd be little point in coming through these doors. I have a rare condition."

"Oh. Are your eyes sensitive to light?" It's obviously been a quiet day for the lass and she'll be well trained in making the customers feel as comfortable as if entering a sex shop is as normal as nipping into the post office.

"No, love. I'm as mad as a box of frogs."

She actually laughs.

"Me too," she says. "But don't tell anybody. I like your T-shirt," she says.

"You a Sabbath fan?"

"Not really but I like the odd song. Me older brother used to love 'em. I like Marilyn Manson."

"Who?" She opens her jacket and to reveal a fantastic pair of tits and a T-shirt with what must be the face of Marilyn Manson. "What the fuck is that?"

She laughs again. "He's a god."

"Is he now? He looks like a fuckin' freak to me."

"Of course he's a freak. That's why I love him."

I'm perfectly happy talking to this plump and pleasant young woman but I'll probably get the wrong end of the stick and ruin the memory of the pleasantries that have just passed between us. It's not every day that I am treated with any kind of respect and I don't want to push it too far. She knows I'm a mad bastard and she doesn't give a fuck. If more people were like that, us nutters wouldn't have to be cooped up like fuckin' pigeons for most of our miserable fuckin' lives. Besides, I can always stick the scene in me wank bank for withdrawal at a later date.

"Right, love. Think I'll take a look around if that's okay."

"Knock yourself out," she says, as if I was about to check out a new line of sofas.

I walk downstairs and by the time I've reached halfway down, I can already hear someone getting fucked. Me eyes rest on the projector screen that fills the far wall. On it, a big-titted blonde is getting fucked from behind by one black man while another has his cock in her mouth. I haven't seen anything as remotely filthy as this since me one and only visit to the Plaza cinema back in the early 70s. The Plaza showed nothing but adult films and was full of dirty old men like mesen, pulling their pork and shooting their muck all over the seat in front.

I watch the screen, transfixed, not quite believing what I'm seeing. It's just too much. It's fuckin' horrible really.

I notice a bloke with a shaved head and muscles like Popeye after his spinach. He's putting out new stock, not even registering the screams of ecstasy of the woman as she reaches climax. I suppose this filth is normal to him. I had no idea that these types of places existed these days. There's always been a couple of places hidden away on the backstreets of Leeds but this shop's in the middle of Vicar Lane for fuck's sake, like it's the most normal establishment in the world.

The black man inside the woman's mouth pulls himself out and covers her face with the product of his labour. This stuff leaves nothing to the imagination. I feel a bit sick.

"You okay mate?"

"Not really, no. Do people actually buy this rubbish?"

"Oh yes. Bit much for you, is it?"

"I'm sixty-eight, lad. I've seen and done all sorts in me time but this filth, it's... it's..."

"Mate? You okay? Julie? Julie? Get down here, will ya? I need a hand with this bloke."

I'm on me knees now and I just can't stop the tears. I'm roaring like a toddler who's grazed his knees. I just can't stop and then I feel it coming and before I can even attempt to stop it, I throw up all over the floor in front of me.

"Jesus Christ!" shouts the bloke. "I don't believe this. Fucking hell."

"Dean! He can't help it, can he?" I look to me left and see the feet and chubby ankles of the woman from upstairs. "Put the closed sign on the door and put the kettle on. Make him a cup of tea, will yer?"

"I'm sorry," I croak.

"Don't be silly." She rushes behind the counter and brings the chair out and after helping me away from the splat of puke, brings the chair to me and helps me into it.

"Have you thought about a career in mental health, love? You could do a lot better for yourself than working in a place like this."

"You need qualifications for that stuff," she says, glancing at the mess I've made a few feet to our left. "I was too busy bunking off to learn owt at school."

I try and sit up straight, trying not to look at the giant screen in front of me, trying to block out the grunts and moans from another scene that's just begun.

"It's never too late, love. Me sister used to work in a butcher's. Now she's a legal secretary." I feel more puke coming and I don't have time to warn her so I put me hand out to push her away a bit and throw up all over the floor again. She sighs heavily. Now she's finally losing patience and I realise I've outstayed me warm welcome. I fumble for me mobile in me jacket pocket and I hand it to Julie. "Can you ring Murton Croft for me? You'll find the number under M."

"No shit," she says, smiling. I try to smile back but don't quite manage it.

"Tell them you have Alan Siddall with you and he needs picking up."

I look back up at the screen and there's two Oriental women going to lunch on each other, top and tail. I look away but can't keep me eyes off the screen for long. Julie notices me and raises her eyes and tuts. "You're obviously feeling a bit better." I put me hand on me crotch and squeeze at mesen and that's where I cross the line.

"Right, I better get this mess cleaned up. Don't... yer know, start... We can't allow... well... yer know."

I take me hand off me crotch.

"Sorry, love. I haven't had sex since 1994."

"Jesus," she says, with a short fast laugh. "I thought I was going through a lean spell! I'll get this lot cleaned up and see about that tea. I'm going to turn the film off now. Okay?"

"Aye, that's probably for the best, love. What's yer

name?"

"Julie." She doesn't give me her hand to shake.

Dean turns up with the tea while Julie mops up me puke.

"That's lovely, Dean. Thank you, young man. You're an angel." He looks at me like I'm some hideous freak of nature. I catch Julie's eye while she squeezes out the head of the mop in the bucket. She raises her eyes again and gives me a big smile. She was born to be a support worker at the very least. She should job-swap with Bev. I can just see that fat bone-idle bitch watching porn and fucking herself in full view of the public with one of the big dildos that are hanging on the wall behind me. I feel me stomach churn and retch again. Julie looks up, waiting for another eruption.

"Don't worry, love. It's a false alarm."

"Well, thank fuck for that," she says, with a smile.

I really ought to stop thinking about sex so much. It's really not good for me.

I finish me tea and wait for me ride. I should have done a Janet, ordered a taxi and got them to pay it once I got back. But when you're knee-deep in your own puke, surrounded by giant dildos, butt-plugs and fuck knows what else, you'd be forgiven for not thinking straight. It's enough to put you right off sex, this lot.

The night shift staff are going to love this. It'll be one of them stories that circulate on their debauched nights out. *Do you remember the time we got the call from that porn place, when Alan Siddall was found wanking and puking in the middle of the shop?* Chinese whispers stretch a lot further in a nuthouse. You can exaggerate as much as you like about someone like me. You'll always be believed.

I'm left alone with the sex toys, DVDs and magazines and briefly consider sticking a niff mag up me T-shirt for a souvenir of me little adventure, but then I hear voices and decide against it.

I just hope it's not Bev. Anyone but Bev. I hear Julie bringing whoever it is down the stairs. Then I recognise the voices. It's Roy and Philippa and suddenly I don't feel so bad.

"Hello, Alan," she says, with a gentle smile, as if I was sitting on a chair in a doctor's waiting room.

"This isn't what it looks like," I say, and I see her and Roy both trying not to laugh.

I thank Julie and Dean for their hospitality. Julie says "Anytime" and I'm not stupid enough to believe her. Dean looks like he's still trying to cope with what's just happened and he just wants to get back to his little porn bunker, stick on some atrocious sex-fest and pretend our paths never crossed.

I get in the back of Philippa's car with Roy. I wasn't expecting the gaffer to come down and rescue me from this den of iniquity. I feel almost privileged.

"You're lucky I was around. I only popped back in after dinner in town. I'd forgotten my house keys," says Philippa.

Me mind's racing. When me mum was a little on the high side she used to rant at will. She used to say, "Eh, boys! I've got me talkin' back," after one of her relentless bouts of wittering.

"I was on a trip down Memory Lane. I was trying to track down an old friend in a boozer down by the market but I got a bit distracted by the neon sign. It's like somewhere in Las Vegas. Anyway, I just popped in and then it all went tits up. Nice girl, that Julie. You should pop down with an application form for her. She'd make a great addition to the team. She treated me like bloody royalty. I didn't get a chance to thank her properly. Do you think she'd mind if I got her some flowers or something? No, that's probably not me best idea. I just nipped out for a pint, Philippa, to get over the shock of what happened earlier. They've fucked everything up, those Advocacy bastards, getting me all worked up for fuck all. I've a good mind to take legal action. I mean, that woman, creeping around like a fuckin' CIA agent. If she'd left her name for me I would've known it wasn't Cassandra, instead of cleaning me bollocks and getting mesen in a right state for fuck all. I have to find her, Philippa. I have to find Cassandra. I can't just give up on life when there's a possibility that I could spend the rest of me days with the woman of me dreams."

"Who's Cassandra again? I thought your ex-wife was called Babs?"

"Haven't you listened to a fuckin' word I've said? Cassandra is the one. Me one true love. Don't you get it? She's what me life should've been. It's fate that fucked it all up. It's so clear to me now. If I could only get the chance to explain, we could still be as happy as pigs in shit, me and Cassandra. It's just fate that fucked it up. That's all it is. Fuckin'ell. I've been dealt one lousy hand after another. What have you stopped the car for?"

"I want you to try and calm down a bit, please. I know you're going through hell, love, I really do, but I don't want you getting yourself too worked up, okay?"

"Okay, drive on. I need to go see Mrs P though. Make sure me mobile number's still in her window. I could put an ad in the paper an' all. It's not as if I haven't got the money. I'll talk to our Alison. There's the internet as well. I could ask Beth to show me how to use the internet. She might be on that somewhere. Are you any good with computers, Roy?"

"Not really."

"No. I didn't think so. I thought you might prove useful for a change." I hear Philippa giggle in the front. "I'm glad you're all having a good time at my expense. It's a right fuckin' laugh, innit? Let's all have a good fuckin' laugh at Alan's love life. I'm serious about all this. I'm going to need everyone's help tracking down Cassandra. As Bill Shankly once said, 'It's not a question of life and death – it's more important than that.'"

Philippa parks up the car. "We're home," she says.

"It's not me home anymore, love. You've all seen to that."

"C'mon. Let's get you back to the ward. I'll see if we can rustle up a sandwich."

"I've just tossed me chips in the middle of a porn market. What makes you think I want a fuckin' sandwich?"

"A cuppa then. A cup of tea cures all."

"There's no cure for what I've got, love. Apart from a

bullet to me brain."

We walk into the light of the reception. It's like walking out of the cinema into a summer's day in reverse. Colin is behind the desk. He looks up and says hello. He looks sheepish, like he knows something he shouldn't. It's time for some damage control.

"If you're thinking of spreading any nasty rumours, Colin, I'd think again. We've all got skeletons in our closets, mate."

"Sorry?"

"You fuckin' will be."

He's been warned. Now for the rest of them. Little tales like the events of this evening spread like forest fire in here. It's time to piss all over that fire.

13. Three's Company

I wake up and feel like I've slept for a week. I know how late it is because instead of a bowl of Weetabix that would be there if I'd missed breakfast, there's a ham sandwich, a slice of chocolate cake and a beaker of squash. Same shit, different fuckin' day. I should really stop skipping meals at my age. I need all the nutrition I can get. I need to get mesen back in shape.

The events of yesterday come flooding back. I wouldn't mind but I only went for a pint. I should've gone to a boozer closer to home rather than trekking down to the Duck 'n' Drake in the vain hope that Cassandra might be in there. I would guess that snowy night was the only time Cassandra ever frequented the Duck. It's a man's pub, always has been, always will be. Beth and Jenny will know by now. There's no such thing as confidentiality in here. If it was just Philippa, she'd keep her mouth shut. But there's Roy and whoever took the call in the first place. I'm 90% sure of who that would be. It would be just my fuckin' luck. Bev. I bet she loved that. I bet she just fuckin' loved it. I'll be able to tell if she knows with one look at her fuckin' ugly face.

I wonder what time it is and remember I've got a mobile phone. It's 3pm. Fuck me. No wonder I feel refreshed.

I get dressed and go for a smoke. Beth and Jenny are behind the nurses' station. They say hello, almost in harmony.

"Fags, please," I say.

Before I know it, Kevin's attached to me arse like a giant boil and we make our merry way to the lift. At least Kevin won't try to make conversation. I'm not in the mood for pleasantries right now.

It's a lovely spring day and I fancy a walk in the park again but we all know how such innocent little jaunts turned out yesterday. No. I'm grounding meself. I'm not fit to wander amongst the population at this moment in time. I'm better off behind closed doors with all me fellow misfits, and that includes half the fuckin' staff.

I start coughing and once I start I find it hard to stop. When I do, I have to deal with a painful wheeze that almost burns. I sit down from the shock of it and spark up. I just don't care anymore.

"Can I borrow a quid, Kevin? I'm dying for a coffee. I've got money upstairs. I'll give it back to you when we get back up to the ward."

"Sugar?"

"Yes, sweetheart?"

"Do you want sugar?" he replies, with not even a hint of a smirk.

"I was trying to cheer mesen up with a bit of friendly banter, Kevin, but I obviously picked the wrong person. Let's try again. Latte. Two sugars. And make it fuckin' snappy."

He trudges off to the machine.

I take me time with me coffee. The sun is pretty hot for this time of the year and I really do feel like a walk but I know that will be out of the question. They don't have to tell me that I'm confined to the grounds for the foreseeable future after me porn adventure. Any attempt to abscond and I'll have the fuzz on me tail. Not that I've got anywhere to go.

I wonder what Cassandra is doing right now. I'd like to think she's in some studio in front of a big canvas. I imagine a long airy room full of natural light; cream walls that suit the sun that floods in on days like these.

I remember her eyes, that concentrated expression of hers when she did me portrait by the fire in the Duck 'n' Drake, how her eyes darted from me to her pad, her pad to me, and back again and I imagine those eyes on me now.

Of course, the Cassandra I picture now, with me eyes closed, is the one I knew all those years ago, not the woman that I saw in Mrs P's. That woman had lived another thirty-odd years. The Cassandra I'm looking at now is frozen in time. She's immortal, like some goddess. She will never grow old and she'll paint and draw in this lovely room for the rest of her...

"Now then, face-ache."

"Janet."

114

"You sound disappointed, love. Are you still waiting for your fancy woman? I hate to break it to you, love, but I think you're flogging a dead cat there," she cackles. "I notice you've got Kev on your arse today. I'm behaving meself for a change," she says. "I see. You're in one of your moods. Don't worry, love. I'm not stopping. I'm watching TV with all the corpses this aft for a change. I need something to pass the time. That Pat never takes her eyes off that bloody box. She..." I get up and walk back inside with Kevin close behind. "Sorry I spoke, you ignorant get! Don't be coming to me..." Her rasping voice fades as I head for the lift. Zahid smiles. I don't smile back.

Back on the ward, I sit in reception and don't move a muscle for the next hour. Beth and Jenny are about to leave for the day. They both look worried about me. They try and get something out of me but I say nothing. I wish Arthur was up. He's the only one who could get me out of this mood. They say goodbye. I give them a little nod. I don't want to be rude.

I decide to go to me room when Bev and Roy arrive. Bev smiles at me but it's a loaded smile. It says, *I've heard all about your antics in the porn shop, you dirty old bastard. Fancy, puking up all over the place, you filthy little man. Don't worry. There'll be no more porn where you're going. There'll be no more city jaunts when you're wearing incontinence pants and pissing into a catheter, you sad old bastard, you...*

In me room, I take off me boots and lie down.

*

It's dark when I wake up again. I put me bedside lamp on. There's another sandwich, another slice of cake and another beaker of juice. If there's one thing I'm looking forward to at Willowbeck Gardens it's a bit of variety in the grub department. I'm ravenous. I practically swallow the sandwich whole even though the bread has already curled up. I scoff me cake and drain me juice. I'm still hungry. I check me mobile. It's 9.30. I'm certainly getting me beauty sleep. They'll be round with tea and biscuits soon so I can fill up on Hobnobs.

I put me light on. I feel like a bit of company so I have a wash, change me clothes and go to see who's knocking about. I poke me head around the TV room but there's no conversation to be had in there. It's just Pat and the rest of her cronies watching something with that bloke who used to be in *The Professionals*.

Bev and Roy aren't around when I get to reception. I'm pleased about that. Roy is okay in small doses but me and Bev are heading for a big fall-out. Can't stand the bitch. I don't know Phil and Gavin that well but they're young and enthusiastic and seem to like it here. It makes a huge difference. They both greet me with a cheery "Hi Alan" when I approach the counter for me fags.

"I'll have one with you, actually," says Phil, pretending to be joining me out of choice rather than duty. Phil's in for a fun night. I feel like a good rant. He gets me fags and we head downstairs.

"So, lad, how old are you?" I ask, as we spark up.

"Twenty-three, mate."

"Twenty-three, eh? Woman? Bloke? One of each?"

"Girlfriend." He gets out his flash mobile and shows me a picture. "Anne."

"Not bad," I say, ogling a beautiful brunette. "Funny name for a young woman. Family royalists, are they?"

"No. Named after her gran, I think. It's not her name that matters though, mate."

"She's a keeper, that one. Does she blow?" I say, hoping to embarrass the arrogant little southern bastard.

"Oh yes. Like you wouldn't believe," he says with a giggle.

"Well, make sure you return the favour. If you need any tips you know where I am."

It seems to be the new style of the younger nurses and support workers. They treat you as if you were one of them. Beth's the same. It beats apathetic twats like Bev and Kevin who look like they'd rather be cleaning out the sewers than working at Murton Croft.

"So what about you, Alan? Any special lady?"

"Is that supposed to be fuckin' funny?"

"No I was just…"

"Yeah, well. Change the subject. I've just had me heart broken."

"Sorry, I didn't mean to…"

"That's the trouble with your generation. Always fuckin' sorry but yer never know what for."

We finish our cigs in silence.

"Sorry I snapped at you, kid," I say in the lift back up to the ward. "It's been a bad couple of days. I don't know if you know but they're carting me off to a death camp soon. I'm not dealing with it all too well. I bumped into an old flame last week and I haven't been right since. The thing is, I know we could make a go of it. I've been in this place too long. I thought this was it for me but when you start getting all hopeful when the truth of it is that you haven't got a hope in fuckin' Hades, it can turn you inside out." The lift doors open. "I mean, I've been mad as the mayor of Never Never Land for as long as I can remember but I've really blown a gasket over the last week. A part of me wishes I'd never bumped into her again but at least she's put a bit of fuckin' fire in me belly. You know what I mean?"

"Yeah." says Phil. No you don't, you little arsewipe, but thanks for doing me the courtesy of pretending you do.

"Anyway, I might need your help a bit later. I need you to help me track her down. I bet you're good with computers. I'll come and see you in a couple of hours and we'll have a chat. You could be me last chance, mate. I'm relying on you."

Phil's gone a funny colour. He's glad to be scuttling back to his little bum chum. I leave him gassing about nothing to Gavin and I go see if anyone's in the quiet room. I open the door and see Janet nattering away and I'm just about to fuck off back where I came from when I hear good old Arthur talking in hushed tones.

"Is this a private party or can any old tosser join in?"

"Siddall! Take a seat, old boy. It's good to see you. I've been hoping you'd show up. Janet and I just might be pulling an all-nighter. We're both higher than Sherlock Holmes after an opium binge and taking a stroll into our respective pasts."

He coughs again. He turns purple again, only this time he remains purple for a tad longer than usual and it takes him a while to recover.

"Jesus, Arthur. No wonder you've been laid up. I'd seriously think about quitting, old China. Me own lungs aren't in the best of shape but, bugger me, you're a wheeze away from an oxygen tent." He starts laughing again but thinks better of it.

"Yes. Best not get the funny bone tickled too much. Dear old Janet here wasn't far away from inducing a coma when she was retelling a tale or two from our days at High Royds." He takes a deep breath again. "She tells me it's a new housing estate these days. We should take a trip up there. We could get ourselves a nice two-bedroom place and have our bottoms wiped by the rapid response unit at the touch of a button." He changes a darker shade of crimson this time as he laughs. "I'm serious, Siddall," he rasps. "We can live like kings! We'll get a couple of floozies in once a week to give us the once-over and clean up our filth." He manages to stop himself laughing again.

"I'd stop it with the jokes, you silly old sod," says Janet. "You can't even bloody breathe. Anyway, have you forgotten about your wife? You know, that silly cow who's put up with you all these years? You don't know how lucky you are. She'd have left you years ago if she had any sense."

"My word. Don't hold back, dear. You spit it out," says Arthur with one of his big smiles. He knows what a nightmare he's been for that woman and he doesn't really give a fuck any more than I do about our Alison. It's a sad indictment on us both.

"You've had it easy," continues Janet. "No one's ever helped me, not since Alf died." Janet starts crying. Fucking hell. What have I walked into here? It's like that *Jeremy Kyle Show* but for old nutters. It's easy to forget that Janet was happily married once. That was a long time ago now, but, like

me, she's never managed to move on. She's right about
Arthur. He's never so much as ironed a shirt. He left home,
married young and he's been looked after by his long-
suffering wife ever since. People rarely spare a thought for the
ones that have to look after us. Like our Alison. I should show
her some appreciation now and again. She's been good to me I
suppose. But she doesn't half get on me tits.

"C'mon, Janet, cheer up. He's only winding you up," I
say. "It's you who's fuckin' lucky. You'll be back in your flat
in a couple of weeks, with your nice neighbours and friends.
I'll be at Willowbeck Gardens surrounded by the undead and
filling me shorts cos I haven't got the strength to get to the
little boys' room. Stop feeling sorry for yourself."

It's really not nice seeing Janet cry. I've known her for
donkeys' years and I think this is the first time I've seen her
shed one tear, to tell you the truth. It makes her seem more
human.

"You know what, folks? I don't think I'll see out the
year," says Arthur, a little too morosely.

"Tell us something we don't know," spits Janet, and
then we're all laughing again. Me and Arthur start coughing
and wheezing and we all decide it's time for a smoke, even if
it's the last smoke we ever have.

We walk to reception slowly. Phil and Gavin suggest
we put Arthur in a wheelchair after realising they can't talk us
out of taking Arthur for a smoke. When Phil realises me and
Janet aren't in much better shape, he offers to push him for us
as well.

The moon is almost full and the four of us sit there
smoking in silence. Then Arthur farts. We all laugh like
school kids and I'm sad again because I know I'll be leaving
all this behind. But maybe it's the end of an era for all of us.
Arthur will be lucky to see the month out, let alone the year. I
look at Phil. He's texting. I watch his right thumb. It's like
he's on fast forward. Better than living on rewind like yours
truly. I've been living on rewind for as long as I can
remember.

"Are you texting your bird?" I ask him.

"Yep," says Phil.

"You keep hold of her, lad," I say, in a serious tone. Then Arthur farts again. We laugh again. Two of us turn purple again. Which lying bastard said that laughter was the best medicine? Not for fuckin' Arthur it isn't.

We get Arthur back to the quiet room. Phil makes some tea and brings us some biscuits. We're all quiet for a while. At first I think it's because they're both knackered but they're awake enough. There's something on both of their minds and by the looks on their faces, it's nothing good. It's all very depressing so I decide to raise the mood.

"You'll never guess what I got up to yesterday," I say, and begin my tale.

14. It's Good Night from Me... And it's Good Night from Him

I miss breakfast again. There's a bowl of slop resembling cereal next to me but I'm not hungry. Me and me two amigos didn't finish setting the world to rights till well after three. We had another fag at about two in the morning. Arthur only managed a couple of drags. For a few seconds we thought we'd lost him. He went a colour that I don't want to see again in a hurry.

I'm just getting dressed when there's a knock on me door.

"Hang on. I'm not decent," I shout, not wanting to be seen with me orchestras in full view. I put on me trousers and go and open the door. It's one of the bank nurses covering for someone on holiday. I'm not being a racialist but she's one of the blackest women I've ever seen. She has amazing hair that looks more like an exotic shrubbery.

"Morning, love. What can I do for you?"

"There is a lady to see you in reception."

"Who is she?"

"I am not sure."

"Is she a big lady with brown hair to here?" I put me hands on me shoulders. Okay, it's a long shot but when you're heading for the knacker's yard, a smidgeon of optimism is all that stands between your dainty wrists and a rusty razorblade. It could be Cassandra.

"No. She is a small lady. Asian, I would say."

"Okay. Tell her I'm on me way."

I don't rush. For some reason I decide to grease me hair back with some of that posh wax that Alison brought me. It's not often I examine me forehead but there's not even a suggestion of a receding hairline. I might be grey but I still look a young 68. I could get some of that Just for Men and knock another ten years off mesen just in case me path does cross with Cassandra's before I leave Murton Croft.

"Morning," says Beth, when I reach the ward

121

reception. "You look different. It suits you."

"I'm thinking of dyeing it blonde. What do you reckon?"

She laughs and it's like soothing music.

"I'm not sure I'd go that way, Alan. I think it's fine as it is."

"That's very kind of you, sweetheart, but I need a change. Got to look me best for the ladies."

She smiles uncomfortably.

"There's a lady here to see you, now you mention it. She's in the quiet room. Fancy a tea?"

"No thanks, sweetheart, but I'd kill for a pint of bitter."

"Sorry, we're all out. The pumps are dry." She laughs again. Me days are going to be a lot less sunnier without Beth.

I walk into the quiet room. A tiny, young Asian woman, who looks about eighteen, stands up to shake me hand. Jenny appears behind me. It's not for moral support. She knows as well as I do that this little meeting is bound to get me all riled up.

"Ah, Mr Siddall. We keep missing each other. My name is Sidra Begum. I'm looking after the case load of your Advocacy contact while he's off. Hi again, Jenny. Shall we sit?"

"I'd rather stand, sweetheart, if it's all the same. Nice to meet you, love. I've been otherwise detained. I haven't got long, to be honest, so if we can make this brief I'd appreciate it."

She's on the back foot already and I've hardly started. It's a considerable gift of mine.

"That's fine. Well I suppose what we have to find out first is how you think we can help?"

"You tell me, love. You're the one with the adverts on the patients' board."

"Okay. Well, we can help in many ways, really. Erm, I understand that it has been recommended by your psychiatrist that you should be thinking about residential care. How do you feel about that?"

"To be honest, love, I've had it up to here with talking about me feelings. I've been talking about me feelings for the last thirty years of me life. There's only one thing I want to know so we don't waste any more of each other's time."

"Okay. Fair enough. Fire away."

"Can you put a stop to it?"

"Sorry?"

"I don't want to go to Willowbeck Gardens. I want to stay here. Can you make that happen? Do you have the power?"

"Well that depends on a number of..."

"Give me a straight answer, love. I don't want a debate. I just want to stay here. Can you make that happen?"

"On what grounds?"

"I don't want to go. Simple as that. There's no grounds. I just don't want to go. I want to stay here."

"If we can just..."

"No offence, love, but I'm all talked out. I'm hanging up me gloves and going quietly into that bad night. I haven't got the energy for a scrap. There's a special lady in me life and she's the only one that can help me now. Jenny here thinks I should go. Beth thinks I should go. Even me own fuckin' sister thinks I should go. Pardon me French. Thanks for your time, love, but there's nothing left to say."

"You're obviously upset. Maybe we..."

"It's me destiny, Sidra. I can call you Sidra, can't I?"

"Of course."

"It's written in the stars, love. It's in the bloody tea leaves. I've shot it. I appreciate your concern but I'm sick of having me hopes raised time and time again for nothing. It's time to accept what's coming and make the best of it. I've been told I can go for a trial period. If I suffer any abuse or they try and bump me off, you'll be the first to know. Do you have a card?" She gives me one, resigned to the fact that this is the end of our meeting, whether she likes it or not. "I'll stick it in me mobile. I might even put you on speed dial, whatever that is. Cheerio, love. Thanks for nothing."

I leave the room. Jenny stays, to apologise for me

abrupt behaviour no doubt. I shut the door behind me and look back at them through the little door window and give them me soldier's salute. Sidra's mouth is wide open in disbelief. It's nice to know I can still control proceedings when I see fit.

I go for a smoke. The nurse with the plant on her head is me new shadow. I don't know what the fuck she's supposed to do if I decide to do another runner or whip me little soldier out. I might just put her to the test.

*

Neither Arthur nor Janet made it to lunch. Fuckin' lightweights. I don't know what to do with mesen so I retire to me room. I slap some Ozzy on. Randy's solo in "Flying High Again" perks me up a bit, and after a bit of air guitar practice I pick up me phone and try to work out how to send one of them texts. I think of something shocking I could say to Sidra now I've got her number in me phone but decide against it. I've got three numbers in it now: Alison's, Sidra's and the ward number. I wonder if Beth and Jenny will give me their mobile numbers? I doubt it very fuckin' much.

I try and sleep while Ozzy sings his little heart out but it's just not happening so I change the CD and go for a bit of Dylan. It starts raining outside and it starts thrashing against the window. I feel like reading a good book for the first time in years. I might text our Alison to get me a couple of thrillers from Oxfam.

I'm just about to nod off when I hear a scream. It sounds like Beth. I bolt upright and head for me door at a speed that surprises even me.

Arthur is on the floor, his head resting on Beth's knees as she bawls for assistance. Arthur's not looking too good. He's mumbling and coughing up blood. I notice that there are little spatters of blood on the right wall of the corridor which he no doubt deposited seconds earlier before he collapsed. This is not good. This is not fuckin' good at all.

Jenny, Kevin and Philippa come running down the corridor with the oxygen tank and I back into me room and close the door behind me. I can't watch this.

I turn up Dylan. I lie back down. The rain is really

going for it now.

Part 2

You Make Me Feel So Young

15. The New Boy

It's a lovely spring day and I'm sitting underneath a weeping willow tree. I've got a mug of tea in one hand and a cig in me other. The spacious L-shaped lawn in front of me has just been mowed. The smell of freshly cut grass never fails to lighten me mood, and boy do I need me mood lightening today.

I had me second meeting with me new shrink this morning. Why Dofuckall couldn't keep me on his books I'll never know. It's all about catchment areas these days. Nobody gives a fuck about the continuity of care. Instead I've got this cold, battered old hag called Dr Beiger. A fuckin' German, no less. I tried cracking a few jokes to break the ice the first time we met but she scared the hair off me ball bag, to be frank. It takes a lot to scare me. Power does not belong in the hands of people like this nasty old bitch. She's not much younger than me. There's nothing more dangerous than a jaded shrink. This woman is old school. I bet she's caused her share of misery and pain throughout her working life. She knew how to deal with me straight away. I'll have to get up with the fuckin' milkman to get the best of Dr Beiger.

I've been a bit lively in me first week at Willowbeck Gardens. It's to be expected. It's a big step for me. I've caused a few scenes, smashed a few cups, scared a few stiffs and insulted the odd member of staff. Dr Beiger soon put a stop to me shenanigans. She gave me some nice anti-psychotic smarties which brought me crashing back to earth from Cloud 999. Speaking of 999, I thought I was having a heart attack on me second night. It turned out to be fuckin' heartburn. It was almost death by cheese-and-bacon flan. The next day, I called the cook a fat Nigerian coon. I'm not proud of meself. I'm no racialist as you know and Esme's a smashing lady. She'll be gobbin' in me food till the day I die and it's nothing less than I deserve.

Anyway, I made a complaint to Murton Croft about Beiger. I told Philippa over the phone that me and Dr Beiger would never sing from the same lyric sheet. But I heard fuck all from Dofuckall. I never thought I'd miss that lazy bastard but his heart was always in the right place. That's one organ that is not functioning too well in that dried-up hag. Does it count as being racialist if you call someone a kraut? Fuck knows. If it does then I'm guilty as charged. I don't mind the Germans, to be honest, though. I never had any trouble with them while I did me national service. In fact I have some very fond memories of German ladies, even if I did pay for the company of all but one of them.

Arthur's death has hit me hard. A bi-polar bear like yours truly could just shut himself down and retreat into the land of the loony. I could laugh me way through the grieving process like when I was a younger man. That particular defence mechanism hasn't kicked in this time. It certainly did when I lost me mum and dad. The day of me mum's funeral I caught a bus to Scarborough and walked up and down Marine Drive with a bottle of Bell's for company, laughing like the laughing policeman they used to have at the Pleasure Beach in Blackpool. There was fuck all to laugh about. I spent the next six months in High Royds.

Me dad's death didn't hit me quite so hard but he'd had a long illness. I made it to the old bastard's funeral but I had to be held back during the sermon. I wanted to say a few words but it wasn't my turn. The vicar was still talking.

I've known Arthur a long time. I've known his wife for just as long. She's always given me the fish eye but she knows me and Arthur go way back so she shouldn't be too surprised when I turn up on Tuesday morning, with our Alison, if she can be bothered. She's booked the day off work to take me, bless her. She took me measurements to get me a suit from Asda. They knock them out for twenty quid these days and when you get to my age you get a lot of use out of funeral suits.

There'll be a good turn out from Murton Croft so it will give me a chance to catch up with them all. It's only been a week but it feels like a lot longer. I also want to check that young Phil managed to get me mobile added to me advert in Mrs P's shop window. If I could get hold of her number I could check mesen actually. I could ring that directory of enquiries or whatever the fuck they call it these days. No. It'll wait. Fuckin' pipe dream anyway. Phil even tried tracking her down on something called Facebook, whatever the fuck that is.

I do like it out here. The views are fabulous either way. I can look down into the valley and see Bingley stretched out below or I can look up onto the moors. There's no one else seems bothered about the views from Willowbeck Gardens. They're either waiting to die or they have their eyes glued to the box. Most of them only wake up for their three squares a day. They can take care of other business while they're asleep. The day I start filling me boxers because I can't get out of me chair to pop for a turnout is the day I'll be smashing a glass and choosing an artery. No fear.

I am trying. I just can't get used to the place. I feel like I don't belong here. Simple as that. I told Dr Beiger but I might as well have said on Sundays I like to dress up as a little girl and spank me monkey on Ilkley Moor. It would have induced the same reaction: abject indifference.

I fancy another cuppa so I ring reception.

"Hello? Willowbeck Gardens? Josie speaking?"

"Now then, Josie. It's Alan Siddall here, the new boy. I'm under the weeping willow tree and I wondered if you'd be so kind as to make us a brew. I'm spitting sparrows, love. Nice and strong. Two sugars."

"It's not a hotel, Alan. They'll be round with the drinks in a half hour or so. Come inside and help yourself."

"I would, love, but I'm a bit unsteady on me pins since Dr Beiger drugged me up to me eyeballs. Go on, love. Save an old man from traipsing about."

"You'll have to wait a few minutes. I'll see what I can do."

"You're a treasure. What are ya?"

I could get used to this to be honest. A hotel is exactly what it is. The only trouble is that its guests are made up of forgotten souls, the undead. It's the kind of hotel with a minus zero rating that should be fuckin' paying me to stay.

It's hard to believe that people have to pay for accommodation like this. If I hadn't been admitted on a Section 117 our Alison would have to find £400 a week for this shithole. You could live in a fuckin' villa in Spain for half the price. It's all about the money with these places. It's a business and the business they're in is fuckin' death. Simple as that.

There's no sign of me tea yet. I'm just about to put in another call to Josie when it rings. I nearly shit mesen. I'll have to keep me ring tone turned down. Phil downloaded it for me before I left Murton Croft. The song seemed nice and appropriate that day because I was telling Phil that the entire mental health trust was out to get me. If "Paranoid" by Sabbath starts cranking out while I'm with the stiffs in the day room I'll be responsible for multiple coronaries. Still, it would put the wrinkly old fuckers out of their misery.

"Hello. Alan Siddall speaking."

"Hello?"

"Hello. Is that you, Cassandra?"

"Who is this?"

"This is me, love. Who's thee?"

"Sorry, I'm looking for Terry Bateson. He's my mortgage broker. I've obviously got the wrong number."

"Don't be sorry, love. You've done nothing wrong up to press." She laughs. Sounds like a nice young woman. "To be honest, I'm glad you called. I was feeling a bit lonely."

"I see," she chuckles. "I've obviously got a digit wrong somewhere. I do apologise."

"I can give you some mortgage advice for nothing, love. Don't bother buying. Rent. Nobody's buying at the moment, love. Don't you watch the news?"

She laughs again. "You're probably right but hey ho. It's been nice talking to you... whoever you are."

"To be honest, love, I could do with a minute of your time. I've just lost a good friend of mine."

There's a pause. "Oh, I'm sorry to hear that. But I really must be..."

"I'm not a well man mesen. They've put me in a

home. I'm in the garden now. It's a cracking day, init?"

"Yes it's lovely. Listen, sorry, I have to dash. Bye."

"Bye, love, bye. Thanks for your time anyway."

Where's that fuckin' tea? Well if you want something doing, do it thesen.

Josie is on the phone when I get back in. I shake me head at her and tut as I pass to let her know I'm far from happy with the service.

I stick me head through the kitchen hatch to ask for a cuppa. Frank Hendrie is doing his best to look busy with a couple of the kitchen staff.

"Frank? Make us a pot of tea, mate, there's a good lad." He flashes me that shit-eating grin.

"No can do, Alan. We are in the middle of a kitchen drill. Ask one of the staff in the day room. They'll be more than happy to oblige."

"I see. Get him settled and then show him how we really deal with the old bastards, is that it?"

"Alan, I know you've had a few tough days but... I'll tell you what. Seeing as it's you I'll make you a brew. You look like a strong and two to me. Am I right?"

"That's quite impressive, Frank. Bang on. Chop chop. I'm spitting sparrows. Throw in a couple of digestives as well. You know I'm good for it."

He smiles. I'll crack the bastard eventually. He's far too good to be true. I'll test his patience to the limit and then we'll see who the real Frank Hendrie is. I bet he ties his dog up and fucks it with a tyre iron when he gets home. There's something not quite right about that big Scottish fucker and I'm going to find out what it is.

He brings me me tea. I don't thank him but he doesn't seem to mind. I drink half of it and then get the dumb waiter up to the top floor with the rest to have with me next fag.

Harry is reading his *Daily Star* when I walk into the smoke room. He takes an anxious look at the clock. He gets a fag on the hour and he's got ten minutes to go. The delicious Julie will be in to spark him up at 11am.

"Morning, Harry," I say.

132

"Hello, Alan," says Harry, with his usual smile. Like Frank Hendrie, Harry has a sunny disposition, although Harry is totally genuine, which is more than I can say for that shifty pillock from the Gorbals. I don't know what pills old Harry's on but I fuckin' want some. I dread to think of what he escaped from to be so happy here at Guantanamo Gardens.

"What's happening out there in the big wide world?" I ask.

Harry looks at me over his paper. "I couldn't tell you, Alan. I've been too busy looking at the ladies. There's more tits in here than in Esholt Woods." He chuckles, revealing his sharp gums, his eyes smiling more than his lips. "I like to start the day with a pair of boobs or two. It's good for the circulation."

Harry must be the only old smoker I know who doesn't nearly shit himself coughing when he laughs. Inevitably, Arthur pops into me thoughts, until Julie turns up, that is. As much as I enjoyed Beth's company, I don't suffer from any guilt when I imagine Julie with her lips around me shaft. Julie's been around the dog track a few times. I bet she's really dirty in the sack.

"Morning, lads," she says. She takes a packet of Silk Cut from her unflattering royal-blue uniform pocket and sparks Harry up. "Tea?"

"Thought you'd never ask," replies Harry.

"Alan?"

"Yes, please."

We don't need to ask for biscuits. Julie always brings biscuits.

She brings us our tea and bourbons and then Harry does his little routine.

"My little friend's been asking about you, Julie. He's very lonely. I've given him a stroke this morning but he's still not happy. He wondered if you'd give him a little tickle under his chin." He laughs again. Julie ignores him and clears away the cups from earlier. "I'm sorry, old friend," he says to his crotch. "You're stuck with me for now. Don't worry though. Julie might give you a Christmas kiss in December."

Julie sniggers and raises her eyes at me. "Frisky old sod." Me mouth fills with saliva like one of Pavlov's puppies. I try to speak, to sound normal, to look normal, but by the look on her face I suspect I've achieved neither. When Julie's around, I'm reduced to a fuckin' caveman. I could start a fire, hunt a wild boar, cook some meat, eat and then give her a good seeing to. Conversation? No fuckin' chance. She takes the words right out of me mush and renders me dumb. When Julie's around, I'm like that Indian bloke in *One Flew Over the Cuckoo's Nest* until he says "Juicy Fruit".

I leave Harry talking about his cock and head back outside. It's getting harder to fill the time. Now that Dr Beiger has slowed me down a bit, the days are starting to drag. Frank promised to take me into town next Wednesday but what the fuck do I want to go to Bingley town centre with him for? I've got everything I need. The woman who does the painting and the Reminiscence Club comes on Wednesdays. Maybe I could start painting. I'd better find something to occupy me time with. I didn't seem to have this problem at Murton Croft. There were real people to speak to. Okay, there's Harry and there's the staff, for what they're worth, but as for the rest of them, they just bring out the worst in me. It's just not healthy for a bloke like me to be mixing with these corpses. I'm just not there. I'm just not ready. But there's no place for the likes of me. I've fallen through the net. That's why they should've kept me at Murton Croft. I've gone along with this little charade but as soon as I see Barry I'll be asking him about me options when the trial period is over. I don't know. That's how I feel today anyway.

*

Later, I'm woken from me siesta. I was dreaming about Cassandra. It was a weird one. She was working in a big butcher's shop but she wasn't serving customers. She was in the back spattering pig's blood onto a big canvas, like Jackson Pollock. She was naked and she was totally lathered in blood. I walk in, ready for action, when me fat fuckin' sister turns up like some battered old chamber maid, fuckin' up me sexy dream.

She's brought me a black suit, a black tie and a white shirt. I ask her to turn her head and I try it all on. It takes me a while so she's stood in the corner of me room like some naughty schoolgirl with her back to the class.

It's a struggle but I finally manage it. Alison helps me straighten me tie. "The legs are about an inch too long. Can you turn them up for us?"

"They look fine to me. Remember, you'll have your shoes on."

"Really? And here's me thinking I could turn up barefoot with me toenails painted pink. Listen, if it's too much trouble I can always ring a bespoke tailor, get some spiv to come down here and cup me balls and get one made-to-measure. I've certainly got the money. How is me money, by the way? I don't want that scrounging husband getting his thieving hands on me hard-earnt dough."

She lets out a bitter laugh and it stings. "You haven't lifted a finger since the mid-80s."

"Maybe not but I worked hard up to then. Anyway, it's beside the point. I want to start enjoying me money. I don't see why I should be scrimping on a suit just so I can leave you a pot of gold at the end of your fuckin' rainbow."

"Alan, you asked me to get you a cheap suit. I got you a cheap suit. If you want an expensive suit, that can be arranged but Arthur is getting buried in three days. You might find it tricky to get a made-to-measure suit in that time frame."

"What the fuck's up with you?"

"Oh, nothing. Shall we go outside? It's a lovely day."

"I'm off back to bed. You can please yourself."

"Alan, take your suit off at least. You'll crease it all. If you think I'm pressing it before the funeral you are sadly mistaken."

I ignore her and get in bed with me new suit on and smile at the wall. I hear her sniffling and when I sense she's about to cut her losses and leave, I say, "I hope you've brought me some fags and some money. Frank's taking me into Bingley next week. I'm going to treat meself. It's about time I started thinking about mesen for a change." I just push the buttons.

"Have you listened to yourself, Alan? Do you know how long it takes me to get to this place? I have to catch a bus into Leeds, the train to Bingley and then I have to catch a bloody taxi from the station, which you are paying for by the way."

"You should walk up from the station. It's only a mile or so uphill. It would do you the world of good. You could do with losing a couple of stone."

"Why are you so nasty to me? I really don't deserve it, Alan, and it's getting to the point where I just can't do this anymore."

She sits in me easy chair and starts blubbering. I do some fake snoring to avoid any more unpleasantness. She stops whimpering after a couple of minutes and shuts the door behind her. I'll send her a little text later to finish what I started. If she doesn't want to visit anymore, she can fuck off and rot in hell with that good-for-nothing twat of a husband. I really couldn't give a toss. I can ring Sidra Begum and get her to sort out another power of attorney. Maybe Jenny or Beth would do it. They wouldn't make such a big fuckin' deal of it either. Or I could ask Julie. I could be her sugar daddy with all me brass. She can't get paid much for cleaning out fuckin' bedpans. Or I could ask the other Julie, from the sex shop. I could set her up for life. I close me eyes and imagine the possibilities.

*

After the latest leg of me beauty sleep I head down for dinner. Food in here tastes a lot better than it fuckin' smells but that's not saying much. The odours of cabbage, custard, mince and spuds seem to permeate every inch of carpet and wall in this shithole around 3pm every day when they start cooking. It doesn't get the stomach growling so much as crying in protest. I'd take that re-heated shit that was delivered to Murton Croft any day. The puddings are pretty good though. Esme does a mean jam roly poly with custard.

Apart from Julie, Frank and Josie, the rest of the staff at Willowbeck Gardens are foreign. It doesn't bother me. It makes for an interesting life. Half of them have about as much command of the English language as Manuel from *Flowery Twats*. There's a couple of Polish women who aren't the prettiest women I've ever seen, there's three Asian women who are friendly enough and there's a tiddlywink with a nice pert pair and an arse to match. Slim pickings really.

I even get a reaction from those closest to the grave when I walk into the dining room in me funeral suit. I'm like a chef walking into a fuckin' chicken coop. Elsie, a shrunken troll with a face like a creased shirt, lets out this hideous noise that's half shriek and half grunt. It's not as if I'm sporting a black cape and a scythe but I suppose I'm the next best thing to the Grim Reaper. I take a look in the mirror again. I look pretty cool even if I do say so meself. The suit and shades go together rather nicely. I look like one of them *Reservoir Dogs*. I think I've just discovered me new look. I've been wearing a leather, T-shirt and jeans since I was 30, well, when I wasn't wearing me whites and butcher's pin-striped pinafore. Maybe it's about time I changed me image. I wonder what Cassandra would make of me dressed up to the nines. If it wasn't for me shades I'd just be another regular old fucker who goes to that many funerals he's decided to keep the suit on permanently to save him the trouble of changing.

I spot Harry. He's smiling as usual.

"Now then, squire. What's on the menu for this fine evening?"

"You brush up well for an old hippie," he says, with a chuckle. "Who's died?"

"An old friend of mine. I don't just wear black for funerals. I like to dress this way for the entire mourning period. In fact, I could be dressed like this for quite some time." Harry chuckles again. Me own expression tells him that I don't find this particular conversation particularly amusing. But that won't stop Harry. His sunny disposition knows no bounds. I might make it me mission to wipe off that fuckin' cheerful smile once and for all. And that's one challenge that I would cherish in me current mood.

"Well, it's tomato soup for starters so that white shirt

of yours has had it," he says, with another chuckle, undeterred by me hostility.

I take me jacket off and hang it over the back of the chair as dinner starts being dished up.

Harry's right of course. Me third spoonful of soup explodes all over me right tit and it looks like I've been shot. Harry starts laughing his head off. Suddenly, he's not laughing anymore. He's wearing the unmistakeable expression of a man who has just followed through. It puts me right off me dinner.

After a tasteless stew with tasteless mash and gravy like weak tea, Esme finally comes up with the goods with a treacle sponge and custard. It's been a while since I smoked any weed but Esme's puds are as close as you can get to a mellow high without skinning up.

After dinner, Frank walks in and chats up some of the old ladies, the smarmy bastard. Then he clocks me.

"Can I have a word, Alan?"

"I'm listening."

"Perhaps we could go somewhere a little more private."

"Are you sure a word's all you want? You're getting me worried now. I've heard about what goes on in these morgues." Harry chuckles again. He's obviously recovered from his little accident. Frank's smile weakens.

"Come on, big man. It will only take a moment."

I follow him out of the dining room and into his little office.

I take a seat before I'm asked. "Will this take long? I fancy a bit more of that pudding if there's any left."

"Ah yes. Esme's a dab hand in the kitchen alright."

"I wouldn't go that far. Most of what she cooks is not worth feeding to a dog, to be frank, Frank, but she can make a decent pudding. I'll give her that."

He glares at me and tries to smile without quite managing it. I have no trouble smiling at all right now.

"Alan, it's about your sister, Alison. She was in a bit of a state earlier and I wondered if we could have a chat about it."

"You wondered wrong, mate. It's got nothing to do with you. If you're wanting to fuck her, mind, I could put a good word in for you. Her husband's hip is fucked so she's not getting much." I smile again but I sense I might be pushing me luck. He's from the soddin' Gorbals after all and every man has his breaking point. He might not do the damage himself. One word to Dr Beiger and I could be visited by a Nazi dentist in the middle of the night like the one Lawrence Olivier played in that film with Dustin Hoffman.

"This is obviously a waste of time. I just don't see why you can't try to be a bit more civil, that's all, not just to her, but to all of us. Is that too much to ask?"

"You worked in High Royds for years, right?"

"Yes."

"And did you ask the chronics on Ricton to be civil when they were trying to chew their right hand off, just to have something to throw at you?"

"Not exactly, no."

"Diminished responsibility, me old China. Haven't you heard? Us bi-polar bears can get away with murder."

"Oh, stop being so bloody facetious, for fuck's sake," he snaps. And me work is done.

"Now, now, Mr Hendrie. Temper, temper. Is that all? If we're finished, I think I'll see if there's any pudding left. I could eat another helping. You need to calm down a bit and reflect on your behaviour."

I walk back into the dining room grinning from ear to ear.

16. The Funeral

Of all the days Alison decided to let me down it's today. She's forgotten to bring me a clean shirt.

"Didn't you get me text?"

"No. I've already told you. You can't have sent it."

"I sent it alright. You're fuckin' useless. What am I gonna do now? These trousers need turning up an' all. I can't go. You've fuckin' ruined it."

"Why the hell did you wear it, you bloody idiot!" she screams. That's no way to talk to an old man.

"Haven't you noticed? I'm not right in me fuckin' head, sis."

"What's all this shouting, Alan?" Frank has appeared at me door like a knight in shining polyester in his cheap grey suit. Mind you, I can't talk, in me Asda special. Mine's better though. "Are you okay, Alison?" Fuck me, they're already on first name terms. When the fuck did that happen and where the fuck was I?

"She's forgotten me shirt. I texted her. It's a fuckin' disaster."

"There's no need to swear, Alan. Your sister does her best..."

"If I want your fuckin' opinion on me gormless sister I'll ask for it. Oh, that's right. Turn on the taps, Alison. They'll be ringing Dr Beiger next and they'll stop me from going to me old mate's funeral. I can't believe this is happening. I just can't believe it."

"I didn't get your bloody text," she screams. I almost jump.

"I'm going for a cig. Forget the whole thing."

Harry's in the smoke room as usual, gurning like Les Dawson on cocaine, and he's a very lucky man. If Julie hadn't been bending over by the big metal ash tray I'd have lamped that jolly old bastard right there and then just for being happy. Julie's arse saved him from a broken nose and me from a six-month stretch at Her Majesty's pleasure.

Harry tries to engage me. Even Doug, a bald and bearded corpse from the other side of the room, asks me a question but I can't hear anything but me own internal screams.

I finish me fag and Frank appears with a light-blue shirt draped over his arm.

"This should fit. I borrowed it from Alfred. He's about your size. Interested? It's up to you."

I do me best to ignore him but he's done something useful so I stand up, mumble thanks and walk back to me room.

*

Frank comes along for the ride. I think he actually wants me sister. He's certainly going beyond the call of duty today. She was in no fit state to drive though. Fancy. Making such a scene on a day like this. Arthur would be turning in his grave if he was already there. Actually, he'd probably be pissing himself. And that's exactly what I do. I start laughing and once I start, I can't stop. I beg Frank to stop the car before I piss mesen. He does. I nip out and take a slash behind a bush near the garden centre on the way to Bramhope.

Oh, yes. He's even taken us in his car. That means Alison will have to come back to Willowbeck so they can spend even more time together.

"Are you married, Frank?" I ask, as we enter Cookridge.

"No."

"Didn't think so," I say, and start laughing again.

"Let's have a bit of music, eh?" says Frank. Classic FM. The sad old bastard. He wants to fuck her. He wants to fuck me fat useless sister.

*

I decide to try and behave meself. It's been a long time since I attended a funeral. I never get invited, for some reason. Arthur will have insisted on having a few nutters at his send-off. He liked putting the cat amongst the pigeons. And I feel like a fuckin' tiger today.

"Are you going to take your sunglasses off?" says

Frank, when he turns off the engine.

"I've been wearing shades for twenty-five years. I never take them off. Didn't you read me notes?"

"I thought today... well... as a mark of respect."

"What the fuck do you know about respect?" I say, squeezing the words together in me lips so me rage is more or less a silent one. "If it was up to Arthur, we'd all be in fancy dress. What the hell do you know about anything?"

"Okay, okay. Don't make a scene. Let's try and get through this without any trouble."

Alison gives me that look. I take a deep breath. The Scottish bastard is beating me at me own game. I just can't let that happen.

After all the shirt drama, we're actually early. There are a few people already outside the church but I don't recognise anyone. And then I see Jenny pull up in her silver Fiesta. She's got Philippa in the front and Beth in the back. Then some other familiar faces show up in a Volkswagen Polo, namely Bev, Roy and Kevin. I don't know what they're doing here. Arthur wouldn't have pissed on them if they'd been stung by jellyfish. There's no sign of Janet but she's never been a fan of funerals.

The funeral car arrives. There's no flowers. Just a simple coffin. The pall bearers and three others carry Arthur in. I step towards them when they pass me to give them a hand. Frank reads me and holds me back with a firm hand on me arm. He's strong alright. Too strong for me. Yvonne's eyes meet mine. I nod. She smiles weakly. Arthur's wife has never liked me.

It's a nice service but nice just doesn't do it for me. The vicar does his best to dress up Arthur's passing but it doesn't stop his wife blubbering unashamedly. Good on her. This is no place for stiff upper lips. I feel like blubbering mesen. I'll bet a bit of her is relieved though. I imagine our Alison will be relieved as fuck when me own wooden box is set on fire. I imagine I will be, come to think of it. There'll be no burial for me. There'll be no stray dogs cocking their legs on me final resting place.

A couple of Arthur's old colleagues from the university say a few words after the vicar has dispensed with the God stuff. Arthur was a man of letters, not faith. This God stuff is all for his wife's benefit. That's fair enough I suppose. Funerals are for the living more than they are for the dead. That's my take on it. I don't give a flying fuck what happens at mine.

One of his old colleagues tells a funny story about when some obscure Conservative politician was invited to the university to open a new block and Arthur refused to shake his hand. Arthur also had a word with this particular gentleman in private about the government's disastrous policy for higher education.

There's nobody here to represent the Arthur I knew though, the mad Arthur. But the mad are rarely celebrated. And we have better stories to tell than most. That's what's missing from this farce. I could certainly tell a few tales.

There was the time when his wife returned from shopping and Arthur had decided it's about time they got a new kitchen. He thought it best to destroy the old one first. Yvonne thought a bomb had gone off. There was the time when Arthur walked around the ward wearing nothing but his old panama hat, singing "That'll be the Day". He was a big boy, old Arthur. He'd even put a twinkle or two in the eyes of the female cadavers in the TV room back at Willowbeck.

The service ends with an extract from his favourite piece of music. I'm fucked if I know what it is. It's some pretentious opera bollocks. Arthur liked his opera. He once made me sit through *Madame Butterfly* on Channel 4. It was a couple of years ago now. We were both as high as pylons that night. It was the only time I saw him cry. I cracked a few quips but Arthur made it clear with one flash of his eyes that if I didn't just shut the fuck up, surgeons would be surgically removing me shades from me arsehole at some point that evening. That was old Arthur. He was as meek as mutton until you got his blood up.

I made him sit through an Iron Maiden concert one night to get him back. He cried then as well but for very different reasons.

I give Yvonne an inappropriate hug on me way out. It's not reciprocated. I think she's playing dead. Frank didn't stop me, for some reason. I wish he had. I feel like a right cunt now. It's the look on her face. Maybe me hands were a bit low. I didn't have a hard on or anything. Honest, officer.

It's pissing it down as we leave the church. I haven't had a chance to speak to the girls from the ward yet. They haven't even looked at me. I want to loiter around to say hello but Frank ushers me and me sis back to the car.

"What are you doing? I want to have a chat with some of the staff from Murton Croft."

"This day isn't about you," whispers Frank. "People are here to grieve, not chat."

I let this one go. Frank is playing hardball. This will take some thinking through. He's a lot smarter than he looks.

The rain is incessant at the graveside. The priest does his little ritual while Yvonne cries some more. Nobody has thought to bring a brolly. Come to think of it, do people ever bring brollies to funerals? At least Yvonne is wearing a hat.

I fire a sideways glance at me Murton Croft girls. Beth's hair is soaking and dripping like she's just got out of the shower but this is no place for such thoughts. I look away quickly. I look at Bev instead. That's the finest antidote for inappropriate erections right there.

Arthur is lowered, dirt is thrown on the coffin by Yvonne and a few others and we slowly disperse. Again, I want to try and get to the girls but I figure I'll have ample opportunities at the reception.

We drive off in a different direction to everyone else. It doesn't take me long to realise that I won't be going to the ball after all. It's probably for the best. At least I got to see the show.

I don't make a fuss. Like I said, I need to think this through. Frank is getting the better of me. He chats our Alison up all the way back towards Bingley. She even laughs a few times, the filthy heifer. They have taken a real shine to each other. I suddenly imagine him going at her from behind and a guffaw escapes me.

"What are you laughing at?" she says. I don't reply.

"Does anybody fancy some fish and chips?" says Frank. He wants to make a day of it. I'm about to tell him to fuck off and to show some respect for the dead but I am a bit peckish and I'm not ready to return to Willowbeck Morgue just yet.

"You know, that's not a bad idea, Frank. But don't be touching me sister up with those greasy hands. Don't force me to defend her honour."

"Oh yeah," sniggers Frank. "You and who's army?"

Alison laughs. It's a strange laugh I've never heard before. It's her "You're making me wet so come and fuck me, you big Scottish brute" laugh. This just might become a problem.

Me stomach churns. Suddenly I'm not so hungry anymore.

17. The Reminiscence Club

It's Wednesday and the rain is coming down in torrents. It seems pretty fitting for what lies ahead. It's Reminiscence Club time and I can barely contain me excitement. Rain and reminiscence go together like tortured souls and lithium. Frank has put little reminders up everywhere so it gives me and all the other stiffs something to look forward to.

He's used one of those plastic stencils which always leave gaps between bits of the letters. I'm no expert but with the advances in technology, you'd think they could come up with one that could do whole letters. He usually does his little notices on the computer but the printer's fucked. I know this because I heard him tell Josie that the printer was fucked. It's not often you hear Frank swear. I've only managed it the once but I'm sure I'll manage it again. I'm surprised Josie lets him get away with it. She's quick to let me know when I've crossed the boundaries of decency. Needless to say, that's pretty much half the time I open me mush. Frank shows his true colours now and again. I'll get the better of him one of these days.

Frank meets us at the entrance to the activity room. He has a sheet of stickers with everyone's name on which he applies to each one of us as we go in. He hasn't bothered with the stencil this time. He's just scrawled the names on in pen, the lazy good-for-nothing fucker.

The usual woman has chucked a sickie so her husband's turned up. He's got all the tell-tale signs of a former mental health patient, giving something back to the loonies and all that. He's a nervy little sod with more twitches and quirky mannerisms than Frank Spencer. He's brought slides. He's brought videos. He's brought a box full of old food items. He's also armed with a selection of CDs that will have our merry little troopers rolling back the years. But it does strike me as a tad ironic that at least half of his current audience probably can't remember what they had for breakfast, let alone the vital roles they played in the war effort.

It suddenly strikes me that not only am I the youngest resident of Purgatory Towers, I'm the youngest by a country fuckin' mile. Still, I have a tale or two to tell from me time in Germany and the song that's playing now brings one memory in particular rushing out at me faster than Esme's Nigerian stew.

It's "In the Mood" by Glenn Miller and his Orchestra, and, man, was I in the mood that night.

There was me, Alfie Turner, Stan Briggs and Danny Boy. We got a pass to go to a local dance so we got ourselves spruced up and went to try our luck. It was a beer hall and they had a band playing the hits of the day. German accents don't do justice to much, especially songs from the great American songbook, but we had a remedy for that. After they'd finished their first set, Alfie went to have a word with the singer. Alfie could charm the panties off Vera Lynn and he was no different when it came to asking a favour of our new German friends.

Danny wasn't Irish but he had a good set of pipes on him. He was the singer in the barrack's band. He wasn't blessed with looks. He had a long thin face, crooked teeth and a chin you could hang your hat on, but when Danny sang, fuck me, he had the girls eating out of his hands like hawks at a falconry. And if we were lucky enough to be with him, we got the ones left behind. Danny could dance an' all. And he taught the rest of us a few steps to aid our woeful attempts at pulling a fraulein or two. Anyway, he got up and sang "Someone to Watch Over Me", and then another and then another. Not only did we not have to buy a drink or so much as a bratwurst for the rest of the night, but before long we were surrounded by women. With Danny's voice and Alfie's charm, we knew we were on to a winner. The only trouble was, as friendly as our new-found German friends were, the men didn't take kindly to risking the future of the master race by letting us impregnate their women. Times had changed but not that fuckin' much. We had to be discreet. If Alfie Turner was anything, he was discreet and he managed to set up a rendezvous with three gorgeous girls and one not so good looking, a mile down the road by the river.

We were just about to turn around and head back to the barracks when we heard a chorus of giggles accompanied by a sack full of clinking bottles. Danny sang another couple of tunes and then we started a fire. It was a gorgeous night. There was a full moon. We soon paired off. I got the ugly one. She wouldn't let me fuck her but the blow job I got from dear Aneka has been at the top of me wank bank for half a century. The best bit was, it didn't cost me one single deutschmark, not like all the other sex I had in that fine country.

This Reminiscence Club lark is a lot more fun than I expected. And I've got me first boner since I arrived at this hell hole. I let out a cackle of excitement when I imagine the reaction I'd get if I whipped it out here and now and shot me load over the back of Evil Elsie in front of me. It could turn into an orgy of the undead. I'm suddenly laughing. It feels good. I haven't laughed much recently and it feels good. Then everyone's eyes are on me and I realise I've just been asked a question by Jim, our very own reminiscence guru.

"Sorry, mate. What was that? I was miles away," I say, struggling to keep me laughter where it belongs. In me fuckin' head.

"That's the whole idea... Alan," he says, reading me name tag. "Are you reminiscing?"

"Oh yes," I manage, and I know, I just know what's coming next.

"Would you like to share it with us all?"

I want to say no, I really do, and I know I should but Frank has just walked in to see what's going on and, I...

"I was remembering the time I was sucked off on a riverbank in Germany."

Those unlucky enough to be taking a sip of their tea either half choked or spat all over their laps. The majority of the others were lost in their own memories or as catatonic as usual. Only Harry laughs, and boy does Harry laugh. It takes a while for his laughter to subside but when it does, the silence is as deafening as the flash bombs that went off at the end of "Paranoid", Ozzy's final encore at the Queen's Hall, Leeds, in

1982.

"Excuse me," I say, standing. "I have to pop to the little boys' room. Please continue."

Eyes burn into the back of me as I leave. I look at Frank. He already knows me well enough to know that I'm a bit of a loose cannon, but despite all the things he's witnessed throughout his illustrious career in mental health, this reminiscence session will rank pretty highly when he finds himself reminiscing in his dotage. His face tells me that and it tells me something else. Frank really doesn't like me very much.

*

When I walk into the dining room later that afternoon, it's like nothing has happened. It's the only advantage to being cooped up in a death camp that I can think of. When you're sharing your final days with old second-hand Siddall the lack of a short-term memory is a blessing in disguise. Of course, Harry is grinning from ear to ear and looks at me as if I've just found a cure for cancer. He even claps. I bow.

I join him at his table with Evil Elsie, who grunts at me (she had a lucky escape today), and another catatonic of the not too distant future named Elizabeth. We haven't had the pleasure of being formally introduced but she's still got her name tag stuck above her left tit.

The food comes and before we eat Harry raises his green beaker.

"To Alan Siddall and the best bloody Reminiscence Club I've ever been to."

Elsie grunts and Elizabeth raises her beaker with her shaking right hand. She's not sure why I'm getting a toast but she's happy enough to go along with it.

I spot Frank helping dish up shepherd's pie at a table opposite and I raise me beaker to him. Harry does as well. He just might turn out to be me partner in crime. Frank nods with a smile that seems genuine enough. Maybe he's resigned to the fact that he's finally met his match.

*

It's a lovely evening now the rain has buggered off. I watch the sunset over Bingley under the willow tree. I think I might take up painting if they let me back into the activities room next week. Then me and Cassandra might actually have something in common if the fate fairies get their arses in gear. I could paint that little riverbank scene with Aneka snacking on me pork sword. It will make a change from all of the crap that's up on the wall already. Too many still lifes for my liking, and I'm not just talking about the paintings.

I'm still in the mood for reminiscing but when you've had a life like I've had, the past is a country you'd rather not visit too often.

It was fun today, I actually had a good time.

18. Bad News Comes in Twos

It's Monday. Me and Harry are in the garden. It's a lovely spring day and I've introduced me new best friend to me shady spot under me weeping willow tree. Harry took some persuading. It's the first time he's been out of the home since his daughter came to see him in February. She lives in Staffordshire. He tells me I don't know how lucky I am having our Alison at me beck and call. Chance would be a fine thing. I haven't seen the lazy bitch in over a week. She reckons she's ill. She's never fuckin' ill. I left her a little message on her mobile telling her what I thought about her. That probably wasn't a good move. I might have overstepped the mark a bit. Fuck it. If she's not here by tomorrow, well, I'll... I'll shout and insult her a few more times. That's all I can fuckin' do.

"Shall we go back in?" says Harry.

I've been a bit quiet for him, I think. Harry's a talker and I'm in one of me more pensive moods.

"We've just got here. Are you missing yer girlfriend?" If he doesn't get to see Julie on the hour, he's a broken man.

"Aye, I am. Her arse is a lot nicer than yours, for a bloody start." He lets out his gummy laugh.

Since the Reminiscence Club me and Harry have been inseparable. We've played cards, watched the box and wound up Frank Hendrie at every conceivable opportunity. We've had a pretty good laugh swapping stories about our upbringing. Harry doesn't talk about the war though. He doesn't talk about his wife either. Those two subjects are off limits. He made that quite clear the other day. He didn't say anything. He didn't have to. He just disappeared into himself when I asked about his wife. He did the same when I asked him where he fought in the war. He just disappeared for a few minutes. That's the only way to describe it. He just left his body behind and left his eyes staring at the wall. The trouble with me is that if someone makes it clear that they don't want to talk about something, it's usually worth talking about and so I want to talk about it. I just have to. It's like I've been set a challenge. I've always pushed buttons. I'll be pushing Harry's before too long. It's inevitable. He might even thank me for it one day. If we just wisecrack, moan or have the odd natter about our childhoods, or about the shape of Julie's arse, as nice as it is, we're going to run out of things to talk about pretty fast. And seeing as he's the only person worth talking to in this shit tip then I would like our friendship to be based on a little more than talking about what it would be like to fuck Julie Curtis.

He's the only thing I like about this place. He's getting excited, is the lad. There's the annual trip to the seaside coming up and he won't shut the fuck up about it. Blackpool, of all fuckin' places. Me and Babs used to go nearly every year and the mere mention of the place triggers a fresh batch of painful memories that I'd rather not revisit.

I can tell he wants me to come. He looks up to me, you see. I think I represent some part of himself that he's lost somewhere along the line. He's like a kid on me shoulder, a sidekick, egging me on to wind up Frank or some of the other staff; lighting me fuse, stepping back and watching me go. The truth is I think we both make each other feel a bit younger.

He starts going on about Julie and I just switch off. Me thoughts return to Cassandra. I wonder if she ever spotted me card in Mrs P's window. I'll have to give me laddo at Murton Croft a ring. I've already forgotten his fuckin' name. The young lad on the night shift. What's his fuckin' name?

Harry's still talking. "She's not married, yer know, Julie. I can't believe she hasn't been snapped up. I'd have had her in a shot in me younger days. I bet you wouldn't have said no thirty years back either, would you, Alan?"

"I like a woman with a bit more upstairs, Harry."

"Yer what? Julie's got a lovely pair!"

"Fuckin'ell. You're not even joking, are yer? Brains, Harry. Brains. There's only one woman for me."

"Is she still alive?"

"Course she's fuckin' alive."

"Were you together long?"

"No, mate. We had one date back in the fifties. She's the one that got away, Harry. The woman I married was a psychotic bitch."

"You can bloody talk. When did she get rid of yer?" He's trying to keep things light but he's in dangerous territory now. He's crossed enemy lines. He better watch his fuckin' mouth. "Tell me about the one that got away," he says, grinning.

"Her name was Cassandra. She was beautiful Harry, stunning. And she was an artist."

"What, a piss artist?" I don't even bother with a reply. "And you say she's alive?"

"Yes, for the tenth fuckin' time. She's alive."

"Alright. Keep your sunglasses on. I just thought... well, yer keep saying 'she was' instead of 'she is'." I fire him a warning look but he can't see the intensity in me eyes because of me shades.

"It's the biggest regret of me fuckin' life, Harry." Harry's uncomfortable now. The minute you say anything real, he starts losing interest. I don't think our Harry's as content and jolly as he appears to be. I think our Harry is kept awake at night by memories and big fuckin' demons just like me. "She wanted to see me again but I didn't turn up. I'd already asked Babs to marry me, yer see. I was betrothed, Harry. I had principles." I get nothing, but I continue. "I bumped into her a few weeks ago. I hadn't seen her in all these years. It was like being struck by lightning, Harry. I love her, Harry. Are you still with me?"

"I think we should go back in."

"What the fuck's up with you? Are you not capable of having a normal fuckin' conversation that doesn't involve Julie's arse?"

"I'm going back in," he says, dismissively.

I smoke a fag in the time it takes him to get more than halfway to the reception doors. He looks a bit unsteady on his feet. He's had his arse parked in that fuckin' smoke room armchair for too long, that's his problem. Fuck him.

He stops in the driveway, out of breath. I know that

feeling, gasping for your life, when your chest lets you know that there's fuck all chance of you catching so much as a molecule of air. I stub out me fag, cough, probably turn purple and go and help Harry back into the home.

We eventually get back to the smoke room. I could have walked to fuckin' Skipton by now. I guess that's why Harry doesn't get outside much.

Julie comes in with a cup of tea for us both. "You missed your eleven o'clock fag. That's not like you, Harry."

"I went for a wander with Alan."

"He didn't give you a cig, did he?"

"No, love." He winks at me when she's not looking. She pops one in his mouth and lights it. She turns to look at me.

"You're as thick thieves, you two, aren't yer? I'm glad he's got someone else to talk to," she says quietly. "Harry never gets much conversation up here."

I look around at four fellow smokers and realise I haven't said a word to any of them. Come to think of it, I don't think I've heard them talk to each other either. There's Doug, with his perpetual frown and half-mast trousers; there's Ralph, who is the oldest resident at 94; there's Rose, who talks to herself but no other bugger; and there's a woman with the look of constant surprise, who always looks like she's just bumped into a friend she hasn't seen for thirty years.

"Aye," I finally say to Julie. I still can't talk to her. I still go into a fuckin' trance every time she walks into a room. I still imagine her naked every time she walks within ten feet of me. I still imagine her on all fours... that's enough. I'll only give mesen a stiffy and I'd rather not bother, thank you very much. I'm getting too old for that malarkey. Unless Cassandra suddenly turns up. I'm saving mesen for her now.

"Are you gonna come to Blackpool, then?" Harry asks me, breaking me out of me trance.

"I've got fuck all else to do, I suppose."

"It'll be a laugh."

I look around at our fellow smokers again. "Oh, yes. I'm sure it will be a fuckin' scream."

*

After lunch, we go back up to the smoke room. Frank comes in and asks for a word with Harry.

"You can speak to me here, Frank. *Murder, She Wrote*'s on soon."

"I would prefer to speak to you in private," says Frank.

"Whatever you've got to say, you can say in front of Alan," says Harry.

Frank looks at me. I grin. Me blossoming friendship with Harry is really starting to bother him. Harry's suddenly got all rebellious and I can tell by Frank's expression that he blames me for upsetting the apple cart.

"Very well. We've had a call from your daughter, Harry. She's on her way from Staffordshire. It's your brother, mate. He's taken a turn for the worst. She wants to know if you'd like to go see him at the LGI when she gets here."

"He's been ill for ages. He'll be okay," says Harry.

"I think you should go and see him, mate."

"Harry can make his own decisions," I interject.

"This is not the time, Alan," he almost hisses.

"Not the time for what?" I say.

He turns back to Harry, pretending I'm no longer there. That's a really silly move on Frank's part.

"I think you should go, mate," he says to Harry.

Harry's disappearing. He's got that vacant look again, like he's just floated up into the ether, leaving his limp body behind, leaving his eyes staring into space.

"Not the time for what?" I repeat to Frank.

"Can I have a word in the corridor, Alan?" says Frank, trying his best to keep calm.

"*Murder, She Wrote*'s on in a minute, Frank. Come back in about an hour. We can have a natter then."

I smile again. Frank doesn't smile. Frank's not happy at all. He sighs, turns and leaves.

*

Harry doesn't go to see his brother. He tells his daughter he's not feeling too good. His daughter leaves the room and tells him she's staying over in a hotel and will come back to see him tomorrow to see if he wants to go then. Harry says he's busy tomorrow. The only time Harry's busy is when he's on the pot or stroking his little friend.

Harry goes to the toilet. His daughter comes back into the room. She is very upset. She is still in pretty good nick. I'd give her one. She's not much younger than me but she hasn't got a grey hair on her head. She has long brown hair, tied back with a flower thing and she's still got a good figure. She's got plenty of meat on her but I like something to grab onto when I'm backscuttling. But I'm not going there. I don't want to say anything that might upset her, not when she's going through the mill with her uncle.

"You've got lovely hair," I say.

She smiles. "So have you! I haven't seen you in here before."

"That's because you don't visit your dad often enough, love." I didn't expect me to say that any more than she did.

"I live in Staffordshire. It's difficult."

"How long does it take in a car? A couple of hours? It takes me sister that long to get to see me on public transport. She comes three times a week. Where there's a will, there's a way." I think I've blown me chances of getting me dick sucked now.

"It's not that simple," she snaps. "I have other responsibilities."

"I see."

"Why are you grinning?"

"No reason, love. No reason."

She tuts and leaves the room. I'm just trying to help.

*

We're back in the smoke room after tea. Harry has cheered up now after the unpleasantness earlier. He does his little friend routine with Julie. "I'll tell yer, love, he's still waiting. Why won't you stroke me little pet? Go on. You know you want to." Harry's intensified his gentle sexual harassment of Julie and she's noticed it.

"Stop showing off in front of your new best mate," she says, playfully putting him in his place.

"Frank tells me your brother's taken a turn for the worst," she says.

"Aye," says Harry, losing his smile.

"You should go and see him, love. Don't you think so, Alan?"

"I don't know. I don't like to interfere," I say, feeling me face go all beetroot on me.

"That's not what I've heard," says Julie, meaning it. I look up. She looks down at me, her eyes wide and accusing. She flicks her head in Harry's direction.

"Maybe you should go, mate," I say to Harry. "You might not get another chance. You'll only feel worse if you don't say goodbye."

Julie pats me right knee and a surge of electricity shoots up me thighs. She mouths a silent *Thank you*. I think I'm in love again.

"I'll go tomorrow. What time's she coming?" he asks Julie.

"I'm not sure," says Julie. "I'll ask Frank."

"Righty-o," says Harry and he shuts his eyes to have one of his naps. Julie gives me a big smile and leaves the room. I bet she's like fuckin' dynamite under the sheets.

*

The next morning, Harry comes into the smoke room all spruced up. His hair is greased back and he's got a shirt and tie on and a blue blazer with an insignia on it. It's obviously something to do with some geriatric old boys' club from the war. He looks quite dashing for a wrinkly old bastard.

"Are you on the pull or what?" I say to him, when he marches over to the window. I get nothing. I'm being inappropriate for a change.

He sits down and I can tell by his eyes that he's not dealing with his brother's impending death too well. Even an old cunt like me has the odd platitude tucked up me sleeve and now's as good a time as any to pull one out.

"He's going to a better place, Harry," I say, as sincerely as I know how. I can do better than that though and I feel almost ashamed of me lame attempt. "He's been ill for a

157

while, hasn't he? It's better to go sooner rather than later. When you're hanging on, there's no point. I wouldn't want me loved ones to see me wasting away to nothing. It's hard enough to lose someone as it is. Is it cancer? Cancer's a horrible disease, Harry. I've seen some sorry sights in me time with cancer sufferers. There was a bloke on me ward at Murton Croft who had lung cancer..."

Harry looks at me finally. I can't quite read his expression. Me words have obviously made an impact but I'm not sure if they've had the required effect. I wasn't trying to cheer him up exactly but I was going for a philosophical approach. I've clearly made the old git feel worse.

"The thing is, Harry," I say, "when you're..."

"Why don't you just bugger off downstairs and leave the lad alone?" says Doug. "You're always trying to get a rise out of people. You should think before you speak. You should learn when to keep your trap shut."

I'm genuinely lost for words. Not only is it the first time I've heard Doug say more than a thank you to Julie for bringing him a cuppa or a fag but I'm just not used to being put in me place and I really don't know how to react. I could go over and chin the old fucker but I'd be up for assault. I stand up. I do something I haven't done for years when faced with a confrontation. I walk away. Fuck me! That's a first.

I bump into Harry's daughter near reception. "Lovely morning, love," I say. She's fallen out with me as well. I chuckle, get one of me fags off an incredulous Josie, and fuck off outside to sit under me willow tree to reflect on me behaviour and have a right good fuckin' laugh about it.

I'm still laughing when I see Frank walking towards me a couple of minutes later.

"Now then, Bonnie Prince Charlie. What can I do for you this fine morning?"

"I've got some sad news for you, mate."

"What's that then?" I say, in the aftermath of me inappropriate mirth.

"It's your brother-in-law. He's passed away."

Now, give me some credit. I've got the giggles already

and Frank is giving me that look which says *I've just said something very serious and this is really not the time to be laughing, so please, act in a socially acceptable way for once in your miserable fucked-up life and at least try to look like you give a flying fuck, you nasty old twat.*

But it's not going to happen. The first splutter escapes and I'm struggling to hold onto a second infinitely more powerful one that just might turn into a violent, unstoppable guffaw. I feel me cheeks expand as I struggle to keep the fucker in but then it's out and once it's out I'm off and I'm heading for the first fence. I double over. I'm in total hysterics. It's like I'm floating above meself, watching this performance, and the floating part of me is laughing his tits off as well.

"I'll leave you to it," says Frank, in a tone of total disgust. He leaves me here, under me willow tree, laughing like a total fuckin' lunatic. Well, if the cap fits I'll gladly wear it.

I am not an evil man. I'm just a victim of circumstance. This little drama began with me trying to do the right thing. I won't be doing that again in a fuckin' hurry.

19. Inheritance

Last night's smarties from the supper sweet-trolley have made me miss breakfast. It's all a part of that Scottish fucker's plan. I'll be five stone by Christmas, like some fuckin' AIDS sufferer. I should demand to see a full list of what they're giving me, if I can fuckin' remember. This is not on. They never let me miss a meal at Murton Croft. If I slept through meal times, I'd wake up next to a sandwich, some juice and a slice of cake or some fuckin' thing. In this shithole you don't get so much as a cream cracker.

I've been well high for a couple of days but I feel low today, as low as I've been since I got here. I often wonder what I'd be like if they just took me off everything they've been slowly poisoning me with for the best part of thirty years. Something's not right. Something is very wrong. I felt on top of the world last night. Okay, it's been an interesting week. I'd got Frank all riled up over me Reminiscence Club shenanigans and me reactions to me brother-in-law's death and it looks like I'm paying the price. The world of mental health is often just like fuckin' school: if you misbehave, you get punished. Simple as that. Instead of the cane or the slipper, you get a few more drugs so you don't know where the fuck you are or how the fuck you feel. They might as well cover us in fuckin' leeches as far as I'm concerned or just let nature take its course. Let the mad be mad. Live and let live. Maybe the world would be a better place.

I stagger out of me room. The door opposite is half open. It's been closed since I arrived at Willowbeck Gardens and I've never set eyes on its occupant until now. Unfortunately me first impression will last. He must be over twenty stone. He's sitting on what looks like a commode, his face wearing the strained expression of a man attempting to pass a stool the size of brick. I get the sound effects too. He glances to his left but he doesn't register me presence. He's got a towel over his legs. There's a horrendous smell coming from the room but it's not the smell I expect, given his current

160

situation. It smells of death.

The only time I've ever smelt anything remotely this bad was on a beach in Harris on the Hebrides. We went there on a rare family holiday when I finished me national service. Me dad knew a bloke with a house up there that he rented out. This bloke was from the island himself and had settled down in Leeds. It was in the middle of nowhere but only ten minutes' walk to a lovely secluded beach. Anyway, we could smell something peculiar in the air around the cottage and the closer we got to the beach, the closer we got to the source of the smell. But the allure of the turquoise Atlantic proved too strong despite the four of us almost retching with each step. When we got to the beach we came across bits of pink flesh sporadically situated at various points along the shore. It was quite a spectacle, like something from a horror film, a beach strewn with gore, the blood, guts and innards of some huge sea monster. I was a fan of Jules Verne in me younger years and me imagination went wild when I thought of the sea beasties breaking the surface in *20,000 Leagues Under the Sea.*

Me and Dad went for a pint in Stornaway a couple of days later and it turned out that a huge whale had beached the week before. The whale was too big to shift so they packed it with dynamite and blew the fat fucker to smithereens, hence the hunks of pink flesh, scattered over a square mile of beautiful coastline.

Anyway, that's what this bloke's room smells like now. The Chinese chick with the nice arse shows up.

"Pwease don't look. Mr Collins no well."

"Sorry, love. What's that bloody smell?"

"It's his weg. Very, very bad. Disease."

"Jesus. Well have fun. And get him to wipe his own arse. Some of these in here just take the piss."

I go get some tea and a sandwich and then go back to bed. I don't feel meself at all. I don't even go for a smoke.

*

I've just had a fuckin' horrible nightmare that I'd rather not go into. I'm parched dry and a bit dizzy on me pins. I ring the emergency bell. I want tea and some biscuits.

It seems an age before this Scouse giant turns up and he's not happy.

"What you playing at?"

"Get us a cup of tea and a couple of biscuits, mate. I haven't had a drink or a bite to eat since yesterday morning. I put me head down for a kip and I lost a day. It's the new tablets. They're trying to kill me off."

"It's not bloody room service. That bell's for emergencies. You can't ring it for a cup a tea. I thought you were in trouble."

"Well, seeing as you're here you might as well sort me out. If you let me have me own kettle there wouldn't be a problem. I could make me own."

"Oh yeah, that's a great idea. You'd be in the burns unit before you could say Jack Robinson. You'll have to come down yourself if you want a drink. We've had an incident and we need to sort things out."

"Somebody snuffed it?"

"I'm not at liberty to say, Mr...?"

"Siddall. Alan Siddall."

"Well, I'm Kenny." *Hi Kenny, you sanctimonious Scouse prick.* "You look fit enough to me, Alan. Get yourself up and come down. There won't be anyone about so you'll have the place to yourself. I'm sure you know where everything is by now. I don't know what it was like where you came from but we don't encourage all-nighters. We just don't have the staff, to be honest."

"I didn't say you could call me Alan. I could just as easy burn mesen down there as I could up here. As usual, you lot talk shite."

"I can see you're going to give me trouble, Mr Siddall."

"You ain't seen nothing yet."

"I've got to go. We're expecting someone."

"You sound like a bloody prison warden. You're supposed to be looking after me, not fobbing me off."

He opens his mouth and then thinks better of it. He

162

wafts a hand at me and disappears.

I meet another new face when I finally make it downstairs. He makes me a cup of tea reluctantly. I ask him if I can nip out for a smoke. I need some fresh air. I promise him I won't make a run for it and he says he'll join me. He's a black fella called David, another big bastard. He's a man of few words and I'm not in the mood for small talk meself so we smoke in silence.

An ambulance shows up. You can imagine how the silent flashing light permeates the dreams of me fellow residents. It won't be long for any of them. I bet they get a pretty high turnover of *incidents* in here.

David makes me a cuppa while they go to retrieve the corpse I and watch them cart the body out in a posh-looking bin liner. I play a little game with meself to guess who the lucky fucker is. I suppose I ought to get used to it. This is purgatory after all.

In all the excitement, I don't feel too good so I go back to bed. The Scouse giant passes me in the corridor when I get up to me floor.

"Did you get your cuppa?"

"Yes I did, no thanks to you."

"Sorry about that. You caught me at a bad time. Can we start again?"

"Fuck off," I say and stagger back to me room.

There's been way too much fuckin' death recently for my liking. It makes a man feel a little too mortal.

*

I go down for a late breakfast or an early lunch. Alison hasn't been for days and I'm going to put a call in. She'll have to surface at some point. I need to stock up on supplies, seeing as me sleeping patterns have gone to shit. I don't like prowling the corridors of this dump at three in the morning, not with all the stiffs dropping like fuckin' flies. It's not like Murton Croft, where there's always someone to talk to no matter what time it is. They promised they'd look after me here. It's total fuckin' bullshit. They don't even feed and water you properly. There's fewer staff per person and people keep fuckin' dying. What the fuck am I doing here?

After a poor breakfast, I'm sitting in reception. Various members of the staff try talking to me but I'm in one of me quiet moods and I might say something I'll live to cherish. The body bag from last night put the willies up me. Maybe he was a bit of a wisecrackin' maverick like meself. Maybe he made one wisecrack too many. There's something not right about this place and I need to plan out a strategy. Frank and the giant Scouse bastard are old school, just like that fuckin' kraut shrink. I am genuinely concerned for me own wellbeing. I get the feeling that they don't tolerate bad apples for long. We are the forgotten children of the earth. We are the undead. Nobody will miss us, not even our families. We are here to die and no matter how we die, no one will ask questions.

After lunch, it's brightened up so I take the rest of me tea to sit under me favourite tree. I'm feeling pretty fuckin' sorry for mesen and I'm scared. I haven't been scared since Babs pulled that knife on me and I saw that murderous look in her eyes.

Like magic, they appear in front of me, two familiar faces; as if they'd teleported here as soon as they had sensed that all was not well in the land of Siddall. I can't help but grin. Me poker face has abandoned me. I'm still not happy about being snubbed at Arthur's funeral but I can't help but fuckin' grin. Jenny and Beth have come all this way to see me.

"Now then," I say. "You two took your bloody time. I thought you'd forgotten about me."

"You're not easily forgotten, love," says Jenny with a big warm smile. "In fact you've been sadly missed."

"I'm not dead. I'm just on a sabbatical. I intend to return to Murton Croft at me earliest convenience. Hello, Beth. It's nice to see you."

"You too, Alan."

Jenny gives me a little hug. I suppose she can now. She's not breaking any rules, showing me affection. I'm an old friend now rather than an old patient, service user or whatever the fuck they call us these days. It's a nice thought.

Beth keeps her distance till I let Jenny go. She gives me a big smile. That's enough. That'll do. Any physical contact with young Beth will just put me back on the slippery slope of involuntary drooling and al fresco masturbation.

"I was sorry to hear about your brother-in-law," Beth says.

"Don't waste your tears on him, love. He never wasted any on me."

"Are you going to the funeral?" says Jenny.

"Alison won't even speak to me so I'm fucked if I know. I don't give a toss either way, to be honest."

I try and stay laid back but after we've finished with the pleasantries, all me ugly fears and frustrations come spewing out.

"You've got to get me out of here, Jenny. There's something not right about this place. They're killing us all off. A bloke died last night. He was as fit as a fiddle yesterday." That's a total lie. I still haven't found out who the lucky corpse once belonged to. "It's all about profit, this place. It wouldn't surprise me if they've got some rich bloke's son lined up for his room. That's how they play the game, Jenny. It's all about profit margins. They've put me on these new drugs and I don't know where the fuck I am. They want to turn me into a vegetable like all the other stiffs so I won't give them any trouble. Get Barry, Philippa and Dr Bell up here. I want a meeting. I need to put a stop to all this before they finish me off. Our Alison's nowhere to be seen. She's probably in on it."

"She's just lost her husband, love. She might need a bit of time."

"And who's gonna take care of me affairs? She'll have to belt up and get on with it like we all have to do. That's life. You lose people along the way. You've got to take it on the chin and move on. It's no good her moping around. She needs to get up here and focus on her brother's care before I end up in a bloody body bag meself. I hate this place, Jenny. I really fuckin' loathe it."

"Calm down, love. You have to give it time. It was

bound to be a bit of a shock to you, coming here. Give it a few weeks. We wouldn't have put you here if we didn't think they could look after you," says Jenny.

"Look after me? They don't even feed me. I can't even get a cup of tea in the middle of the night. I need someone to have a word with them. They have no rules up here, Jenny. There's no rules of engagement in this fuckin' war."

"Come on, Alan. We haven't seen you for ages. Try and calm down a bit, love," she says, stroking me arm like I'm some fuckin' docile Labrador.

"What happened at the funeral?" I say.

"What do you mean?"

"You didn't even say hello."

"We were grieving, Alan, just like you. We thought we'd catch up with you at the reception."

"Yeah, well. That Scottish prick put a stop to that, carting me off from me mate's funeral. I wanted a word with his wife."

"Listen, just calm down a bit, okay?"

Beth is staring into space, clearly uncomfortable. She looks gorgeous. Her lovely brown hair is hanging over her shoulders. She looks like a film star. I want to touch her face but I don't think she'd like that.

"Sorry, but I want a meeting. I won't say another word but I'll be talking to Advocacy again, not that those useless sods... We're the forgotten ones, Jenny. We've been sent here to die. Don't you get it? This is where me journey ends."

"I think that's a bit dramatic, Alan, to be honest. Frank is well respected. You should see the other places. This is like a hotel compared to..."

"I want out of here, Jenny. If you don't make it happen, I will."

There's a silence and it feels longer than any other silence I've ever been responsible for causing, and believe me, I've caused a few in me time. Beth won't look me in the eye. This is not how I wanted this to go. I need to calm down or they won't come and visit me again.

"Don't cry, love, please. I was really looking forward

166

to seeing you. We haven't got long. Please? For me?" says Jenny.

"It's the new tablets, Jenny," I whine, trying to compose mesen. "They're turning me into God knows what. I can't bear it. I can't."

The sky has clouded over as if it's trying to mimic me mood. There's a huge black cloud forming and it looks like a nasty shower is heading our way.

"Shall we pop inside for a cup of tea?" says Jenny.

I get up and walk a few paces in front, looking down at me boots like a condemned man. What a fuckin' disaster.

We find a quiet spot in one of the lounges. Frank comes in, acting like the lord of the manor.

"Now then, ladies. Can I get you a drink?"

"A tea for me, please. Milk no sugar," says Jenny.

"And you, darling?"

"No, thanks," says Beth.

"You do right, love. Frank can't make a brew to save his life. You don't know what you'll catch in here, anyway."

Frank doesn't react.

"I'll leave you to it," he says and heads to the kitchen. There's a silence again. This time, Beth breaks it.

"Have you made any new friends?"

If it had been anyone else, including Jenny, I'd have told them to go fuck themselves for being so patronising but I really don't think that Beth has a patronising bone in her body.

"Half of these people don't even recognise their own flesh and blood when they can be arsed to show up so what chance have I got of them remembering me?"

"Alan!" snaps Jenny.

"Sorry, love. There's Harry. He's okay. He's a mucky old bugger though. He's always saying inappropriate things to the female staff."

I catch their eyes as they look down into their laps. Their eyes tell me exactly what they're thinking, namely *pot*, *kettle* and fuckin' *black*.

"I'm not getting the care I need in here. I'm not right for this place. Anyone can see that. I was better off at Murton

Croft. I rang down for a cuppa in the middle of the night and I got a right bollocking from this big Scouse bruiser."

"It's not for room service, Alan. They probably had other things to attend to," says Jenny.

"What's the point in having a bell if you can't fuckin' ring it?" I shout.

Frank appears with the tea.

"Everything okay, ladies?"

"Leave the tea and sod off. This is a private conversation," I shout.

"Ladies?"

Jenny gives him a sharp nod that lets him know his presence is not required.

There's another silence. Beth breaks it again.

"The bell is there for if you're in distress, Alan. If you use it too much they might not come if you really need them. You know what I mean?"

"I see what you're saying, love, but I was in distress. I had a terrible nightmare. It was Frank. He was raping our Alison. He slit me throat and raped our Alison, right in front of me. No man should have to put up with that." I haven't got a fuckin' clue where that came from but it sounds plausible enough!

"It was just a nightmare, love," says Jenny, tenderly.

"It was so real, Jenny. It could have been a sign. There's something not right about that bloke. I'm telling yer."

"Calm down, love, please."

I look out of the window. The sun is out again. The shower never came.

"Can you take me out somewhere? I haven't left the grounds since I got here. It's like a prison. I used to be able to nip to Mrs P's at Murton but there's fuck all around here. Please?"

"We can't, love. We have to get back to work. Let's go for a walk around the grounds while the sun's out."

We walk around the gardens and sit on a bench overlooking the beck.

"We've got something for you," says Beth. "It's from

Arthur. His wife brought it in, a couple of days after the funeral."

Beth hands me a white carrier bag. I pull out a present. It's wrapped in plain red paper with a sticker on the front that says: For Alan.

I tear at the paper.

I look at me inheritance. I'm not a sentimental man but I have to fight back me tears.

It's a CD. It's *Madame Butterfly.*

20. Frank Pulls Out the Stops

If there's one thing I'm good at, it's winding up psychiatrists. I've worked with a good few in me time and I've got the better of most of them at some point or other. However, Dr Beiger is 2-0 up and she's not even broken into a sweat. I think she plays on her nationality. Psychiatrists can be scary at the best of times but a psychiatrist with a German accent can give you nightmares for the rest of your fuckin' life.

Personally, I don't have a problem with Germans. When I served in Germany, the people I met were nice enough. They were on their fuckin' knees with apologies after wiping out half of Europe but the Germans I got to know were decent, hard-working people. Or whores. They work hard as well. But I am relatively young compared to me fellow residents. These lot lived through the real horrors of the Second World War. I might be a war baby but as a kid the war was exciting and, to be honest, I was glad when me dad fucked off for a few years. It stopped me getting the shit kicked out of me for no fuckin' reason at all. Okay, there were times when I filled me pants with fear when the sirens went off but a few bombing raids aside, it was the rations that I remember more than anything. But we ate a lot of fish and chips; we might have suffered with powdered bloody eggs that made me ma's baking taste like shite, but we always had fish and chips.

When I got to 15 he stopped hitting me and our Alison, and me mam. I made it quite clear if he ever laid one finger on any of us again I'd take a meat hook to his face.

Harry just won't talk about the war. It's somewhere he just doesn't go. Harry's not the type to forgive and forget either. In fact, the only time he's not wearing that ridiculous gummy grin is when he's due to see Dr Beiger. He goes all pale and it takes him a while to recover after he's had his meeting. I watch him come back to the smoke room and he doesn't say a word for a while. He's been quiet for ten minutes now while I wait for Julie to let me know when it's my turn.

I'm just about to nod off when Julie comes to get me. I walk into the meeting room. Frank is there, cocksure and strong-chinned once again. He's recovered from our recent proverbial bouts and he's ready for another round.

And then I get a lovely surprise. It's Philippa. I try me best to look indifferent but me face cracks into a smile as soon as she gives me her own familiar warm smile.

"Hello, Philippa."

"Hi, Alan. How's it going?"

"Don't ask," I say, taking me seat. There's no Alison but that's fair enough. She's got enough on her plate. Always has had, the fat cow.

"Mr Siddall? Nice to see you. How are things?" says Dr Beiger. I don't say anything. "Frank tells me you're having some problems settling in."

"Where's Barry?" I ask Philippa, as if we're the only two people in the room.

"He's off sick," says Philippa and widens her eyes. It's a not so subtle expression to tell me to behave mesen and to stop ignoring the German shrink and Bonnie Prince Charlie.

"I hope he feels terrible," I say, with a chuckle.

"Mr Siddall," says Dr Beiger, raising her voice (she's not used to being ignored), "how are you feeling?"

"I've lost that loving feeling, Doctor. Me head's all over the shop and this dump has made me realise that maybe it's best if I just walk in front of a bus and put an end to this joke of a life of mine."

"I see. And why do you think you are having troubles?"

"Is she for real?" I say to Philippa.

"I think what Dr Beiger is trying to say..."

"You don't have to talk for her, Philippa. You're one of the good guys." I turn to Frank and Beiger. "This woman knows how to look after people like me. You two haven't got a clue. You're old school. You're still stuck in the Dark Ages. You'd both just as rather give me a lobotomy than try and figure out how to treat me. If you knew the first thing about me, you'd know how many times I've been diagnosed, how many drugs they've tried. The only vaguely settled time I've had in the last ten years has been at Murton Croft. As far as I'm concerned, this is just a huge step backwards. Haven't you heard that song, Doctor? 'The Drugs Don't Work'?"

"Have you finished, Mr Siddall?" I don't answer. "Okay, the thing is you are still getting used to us and we are getting used to you also. It takes time to settle anywhere. I would guess that you didn't like this Murton Croft when you first left High Royds. Correct? It is like the new boy at school. He doesn't know many people, everything is different..." I start laughing. "Is something funny?"

"You are, Doctor. You should have been a comedian. You'd have made a fortune. Mind you, a little bird told me you lot get about a hundred K a year anyway. That's not bad for asking mad people a few silly questions a few times a week and writing out a few prescriptions to keep us all under control."

There's a silence.

"I understand you have suffered a few bereavements recently," says Dr Beiger. I look into me lap. "Your friend Arthur, your brother-in-law..."

"I won't be shedding any tears for that waste of space," I say. "Me brother-in-law never gave a toss about me and vice versa. To be brutally honest, I'm more interested in how it affects our Alison."

"Well that is good. You are thinking about your sister."

"That's one way of looking at it. She hasn't been near me in more than a week. I wasn't even invited to the funeral. I've left her alone up until now but if she's doesn't get her arse in gear and pay me a visit, I'll be cutting her off."

"Sorry, I don't understand."

"She's me power of attorney, Doctor. She only comes to visit me so she can keep her eyes on me cash."

"That's a bit harsh, Alan. I don't think..."

"If I want your opinion, Frank, I'll ask for it. I know your game, an' all. You'll be trying to get your leg over with the merry widow faster than I can toss a caber."

I glance at Philippa who looks like she's trying her best to keep her lips fixed in a serious expression but her smiley muscles are twitching and I can tell she's struggling not to laugh. She disguises it well with a sympathetic smile. Philippa never takes anyone or herself very seriously. Bizarrely, it's made her very good at her job. Nothing fazes the woman. And she loves a scrapper, even a nasty old twat like meself.

"Okay, well, we think you should try and get a little more involved with the activities on offer, and maybe you are going on the trip to Blackpool?" says Dr Beiger.

"I might go for Harry's sake. He's just lost his brother and he could do with the company. I'm running out of brass though. You'd better ring our Alison. She's not returning me calls." What I don't tell them is that I left her a pretty firm message letting her know if she didn't snap out of her mourning period pretty sharpish, I might as well slit me wrists and join her cunt of a husband in hell. I might not have phrased it quite like that but the sentiment was the same. I did tell her life was for the living and I was still alive the last time I checked.

"Alison sent up some cash, Alan. No worries there," says Frank. "In fact, you haven't been out since Arthur's funeral. Maybe we can pop down to the shops later. It'll do you good to get out."

"I'll decide what's good for me, Bonnie Prince Charlie. Has she spoken to you?"

"Briefly, yes," he says.

"How is she?"

"She's not doing so well. She's just lost her husband."

"People keep saying that as if I've forgotten. People die, Frank. You say goodbye, get back on yer bike and ride off into the sunset. In fact, losing that miserable bastard might be the best thing that's ever happened to her. But don't get any ideas, Frank. If you lay one finger on me sister, I'll have you killed."

I cock me hand as if it's a pistol. I aim at Frank, smile,

and put me gun back in its imaginary holster. I'll break that Scottish moron if it's the last thing I do.

"That's enough, Alan," says Philippa, firmly. "Frank and Dr Beiger are only trying to help."

"I'm not getting the care I need in here, Philippa. You lot have thrown me to the dogs. I want to come back to Murton Croft. I want Barry up here and I want to talk to Advocacy."

"You agreed to a six-week trial," says Philippa calmly. "You have to give it time like we agreed."

"It's not a trial though, is it? I shout. "You know as well as I do that I haven't got much of a say in the matter. Dr Bell made it quite clear I can't go back to Murton Croft even if I don't like it here so what's the point?" I stand up, "This meeting's over. I'm off for a smoke."

"Alan, please," says Philippa. But I'm already halfway out of the door.

*

Yes, okay, hands up. I can be a bit of a drama queen. But I have to say, when you consistently follow certain patterns of behaviour throughout your life, there are often reasons for it. That's one thing people never understand about the mad. We are just like everyone else; we're human. The trouble is we're more human, if you catch me drift. We're too fuckin' human for our own good.

I have to admit, I fully expected Philippa to come charging after me to sort things out. But she's no fool. She knows me as well as anyone and today she just doesn't feel like playing me game. I don't blame her. I'm getting a bit tired of me game meself.

It's Frank who eventually joins me under me willow tree.

"What do you want?" I say.

"Let's get out of here, Alan."

"Sorry?"

"Me and you are going out for the day."

"Sod off."

"No. I won't bloody sod off. Get off your jacksy when

174

you've finished your smoke. We are going to town. I might
even buy you a pint if you're lucky. Deal?"

"Why?"

"I spoke to Philippa. That woman thinks a lot about
you. She told me what a sweetheart you can be once we've got
to know you. So, this is me trying to get to know you. Sound
fair?"

"The difference is, they had to get to know me. You
have a choice. You can send me back to Murton Croft and
have a much easier life."

"See, that's one thing you've yet to find out about
me."

"What's that?"

"I'm one stubborn bastard, Alan. I never give up on
people. I've been doing this a long time. I know you're having
trouble settling in with us but to be honest, you're a pussycat
compared to some of the people I've... got to know over the
years."

"I'm too wild to tame, Frank. The best you can hope
for is that I won't try and tear you to shreds every time you
step into me cage."

"That's more like it, Tiger. That sounds like a
challenge. And I do like a challenge."

"Let battle commence," I say.

"Come on, then. Would you like to freshen up? I can
get Julie to run you a bath."

I've been wondering when Julie was going to run me a
bath. I usually get stuck with Keith, a mute orderly. But
despite all me piss and wind, they don't see me as any kind of
threat. I'm just another old timer who can't get into the bath
on his own because one fall will make me brittle bones snap
like twigs, just like every other fucker in here.

But you've really got to hand it to Frank. He is fuckin'
good, I'll give him that. He is very fuckin' good at what he
does. He's still in for a rough ride though. I'm pretty good at
what I do too.

*

If there's one thing to look forward to in here it's when I'm no

175

longer able to bathe mesen properly and I can get me nuts soaped by the lovely Julie. I bet Harry gets the special treatment.

"Take off your clothes and give me a shout when you're ready, I'll just be outside," says Julie.

"Don't worry, love. I'm sure you've seen it all before."

I undress and she keeps her eyes averted anyway. Before I take off me trousers, I try to summon a semi so I don't embarrass mesen when she helps me into the bath. In order to do this, I imagine we've swapped roles and it's Julie getting undressed for bath time. I get a bit carried away when me imagination starts running away with me so I think about Josie to calm mesen down. I pull down me boxers and I'm satisfied with me present appearance.

"Ready when you are, love."

She smiles, registering the irony without looking at me tackle.

"Are you leaving your sunglasses on?"

"Never take them off, love, not even for me ablutions."

"Well, that's... fine. Erm... let me take your arms." She puts her arms under me armpits. She helps me into the bath and me semi keeps its form but I feel me blood pumping and I want to get beneath the bubbles in case I get a full bonk-on. Julie's hands are so warm under me pits and I don't know if it's my imagination but I feel her eyes on me cock and it hasn't felt as big as this since me al fresco wank in Hyde Park under the watchful eyes of an old bloke and a Highland terrier. I feel I have to say something.

"Sorry," I say, "it won't happen again."

"Never mind. At least you can still get one, Alan. That's something to be cheerful about. I'll leave you to it. I'll be just outside, love." She supports me arms and I slip beneath the bubbles. But me cock is reaching for the stars and it soon pokes its head back up like a pink periscope. Julie is behind me and she sniggers. She actually sniggers. She walks to the door. She doesn't wiggle, look back or give me any reason to

176

think for one moment that she is even remotely interested, but her indifference makes the whole scene more erotic. She shuts the door behind her.

I'm as hard as a rock. I give the little fella a few tugs and I come in seconds, biting me lip so I don't scream from the intensity of me meagre ejaculation. I let out a long, low moan. I swirl the water around a bit to cover me tracks. But Julie knows anyway. And Julie doesn't give a toss. Maybe I've been a bit hasty about wanting to leave Willowbeck Gardens after all.

*

It's nice to get out of the morgue for a change and even though I do me best to give Frank the silent treatment, me mood has lifted with a bit of sun on me face. He's a persistent bastard.

After a trip to the supermarket to stock up on a few soft drinks, biscuits and fags, we dump the stuff in Frank's car and go for a beer. We sit in the beer garden with our pints, soaking up the late spring sunshine like a couple of regular fellas. I let mesen forget that we're metaphorically shackled together and enjoy me beer. It's a lovely pale ale and it slides down me throat like nobody's business. I make a note to pace meself so I can savour this treat.

"Crackin' day," says Frank.

"Aye. It's lovely."

"We can do this more often you know. Just say the word, Alan."

"What are you after, Frank?"

"I'm not after anything. I'm looking after you. That's my job and I try to do my job to the best of my abilities."

"Well, that just makes me feel all fuzzy inside," I say with a healthy slathering of sarcasm.

"You know, Alan, you're not getting any younger and you'd enjoy living with us much more if you let your guard down a bit and try and grow old gracefully."

He says this in a pally way that makes me cringe. I've always detested over-familiarity from people who pretend they know you much better than they do, particularly from

177

fuckin' power-trippers like Frank. They work with the vulnerable because they love to be needed and admired. People like Frank end up in this profession because their own lives are so unsatisfying and they get a chance to exert some kind of control over crazy fuckers like yours truly. He's nothing but a sanctimonious Scottish prick who suffers from the delusion that he's an important member of society. He may be a major figure in the realm of the undead that is Willowbeck Gardens, and he is good at his job, I'll give him that. But outside of those walls, he's just an ageing Scottish loner who hugs himself to sleep at night. I'll be telling him all this at some point. But for now, I'll play nice.

"You might be right there, Frank. Now go get me another beer. In fact, let's go mad. I'll have a packet of pork scratchings, an' all."

"Better make it a half, mate, with the pills."

"Righty-o. A half it is. Thanks for bringing me into town. I appreciate it. You're right. It has done me good."

"Anytime, mate. Anytime at all."

Frank does have a point. Maybe I should just relax and accept me fate. Not fuckin' likely. Yer see, this is me whole problem. I'm torn. I'm always fuckin' torn. I've never known what's best for me. That's why I've been happy enough to let other people decide, until I ended up at Willowbeck. And that's the fucked-up thing: the same people who put me here are the same people who've done such a good job looking after me for the last few years. Makes yer think. But I've got time to think things through. I've got nothing but fuckin' time.

Frank comes back from the bar with two pints and packet of pork scratchings hanging from his gob. He's looking a bit too fuckin' pleased with himself and it snaps me out of me magnanimous trance.

"To growing old gracefully," he toasts, with a grin.

"To shutting the fuck up and letting me enjoy me beer," I reply.

His smile doesn't leave his face but it palpably loses its warmth. Just when he thinks he's got me, I let him know he hasn't. Fuck you, Frank. Fuck you very much indeed.

21. I'm So Sorry

It's a beautiful morning. I can't help but feel a bit excited about getting out of here for the day.

I put me best Black Sabbath T-shirt on, spray me pits and I'm ready to roll.

We all congregate in the dining room. Julie tells me I smell nice. I give her a big grin. I get a sudden impulse to just grab hold of her and kiss her, but if I acted on every impulse, I'd be on a life stretch in Broadmoor by now.

Maybe I'm being too harsh on mesen. I'm not a violent man. I'm just a mad old randy bastard who hasn't had enough sex in his life. I'd do anything to be inside a woman again. If Cassandra ever gets around to ringing me, I might have a shot with her. I'd pay for it if necessary. I might order one in. You can order anything online these days. I'll get our Alison to send a wad of cash up and I'll get mesen sorted out by some blonde, big-titted nymphomaniac, who'll fuck me senseless for fifty quid.

The last time I paid for it was about eighteen years ago. She was hanging around outside the Mucky Duck one night. She was in her early forties. She wasn't bad looking though. I can still remember exactly what she looked like. She was deposited in me old wank bank the moment I'd shot me muck into her. She had bleached blonde hair down to her shoulders, a pleasant, round face, a nice smile and a chin dimple, like Kirk Douglas. She was wearing a short skirt, stockings and suspenders and a red blouse with the top three buttons undone to give her ample cleavage a good airing.

We went underneath the arches. I even sang that old Flanagan and Alan classic as she led me by the hand through rubble, past drunks warming their hands over burnt-out dustbins, me boots crunching on broken glass and used needles, spunk-filled condoms strewn hither and thither. She found us a secluded spot. She sucked me off to get me ready. Then she hitched up her skirt, pulled down her knickers, flegged into her hand to prepare the way in and backed onto me. It was over before you could say shiver me timbers. It was the quickest fifty quid I've ever spent, I can tell you that. Still. Like I said, it's in the wank bank now. It's not as if I haven't fucked that woman a thousand times over in me head so I've had me money's worth over the years.

Harry comes over to me.

"I wasn't sure you'd make it after last night," he says, with a chuckle.

I had a run-in with that giant Scouse bastard on the night shift. There was a documentary about Hendrix on BBC 4. They played a couple of tracks from his famous Isle of Wight set. I cranked up the volume on the TV and started rocking away on me air guitar, lit fag hanging from me gob, like Jimmy Page on speed.

Alfred, Doug and the woman with the look of constant surprise were soon yelling at me to turn it down. But I was lost in Hendrix, soloing on me imaginary Strat, rubbing it against me imaginary Marshall amp to get me feedback. Pointing at me imaginary crowd (well, that bit was real – I had an audience of a sort). The big Scouse bastard (or Kenny for short) soon dragged me back to the land of the still-alive-but-not-for-long.

Harry watched the whole scene with a look of savage amusement written across his face, gummy giggling like he does, while Kenny turned down the music and escorted me to me room. I didn't want to go at first but he persuaded me, as did the big black fella who turned up to see what all the fuss was about. We had a bit of a disagreement. It was then I decided that if me fat sister ever gets her fat fuckin' arse up here again, I want her to be carrying a portable telly under her arm or she needn't fuckin' bother.

When Kenny and the black fella had fucked off, I put some Sabbath on and they were soon back upstairs, responding to the several panic button rings that began reverberating around the walls of Willowbeck when I had cranked "Symptom of the Universe" by Sabbath up to an unbearable volume. No one fucks with Siddall when he's been captivated by a genius like Hendrix.

"Symptom of the Universe" took me back to another scene from me wank bank, backscuttling Babs against the wall of an old bikers' club in Bradford one March night in the distant past.

Kenny and the black fella showed up again, like a couple of nightclub bouncers ready to crack a few skulls. This time they meant business. The fuckers confiscated me ghetto blaster and put me to bed. If you've never been put to bed by a giant Scouser and a black bloke the size of Frank Bruno on steroids, I recommend you just leave them to it. Resistance is pointless. They didn't so much tuck me in; they trapped the covers under me so tightly that I felt like I'd been wrapped in cling film. It was quite a struggle to get out of bed for me morning slash when I woke up. I nearly rang me panic bell.

Frank sees me and comes over.

"Can I have a word?"

"Course you can, mate. You can have two if you like. Only joking, big man. What can I do for you?"

He takes me to the side of the rest of the day-trippers.

"I understand there was a bit of trouble last night."

"You know me, Frank. It's me middle name."

"I thought we'd sorted a few things out over that pint. Alan, I need you on your best behaviour today. We're going to have our hands full with this lot. Can I rely on you to behave yourself?"

I think about telling him to go fuck himself but I do like to be beside the seaside.

"Listen, I just got a bit carried away. Hendrix has that effect on me. I was only having fun. You want me to have fun, don't you, Frank?"

"Alan, you caused total mayhem. I've never seen anyone get to Kenny like that. Are you feeling a bit high again?"

Letting me know I'm getting to someone is not the right play for Frankie boy, the silly man.

"I've never felt better," I say, grinning.

"That's not what I asked."

"Listen, I didn't get much sleep the night before. I feel

better today. I'm looking forward to it, to be honest. Since you took me into town, I've started to realise I've got to make the most of it in here. I'll be a good lad. Scout's honour."

"Okay, but don't let me down, Alan. After an episode like we had last night, I shouldn't really be... you know... taking the risk?"

"I know. I've been a bad lad. I won't let you down, mate. I'll even give you a hand with some of the chronics. You could do with a spare pair of hands, by the looks of it."

I look over at Elsie and the woman with the look of constant surprise. They're both walking around in circles, grunting and gibbering. You could take them to fuckin' Disneyland for the day and they wouldn't know it.

"I don't know, Alan. I don't know whether I can risk it."

He's not joking and he's not on a power trip either. He's genuinely having second thoughts about taking me. This calls for drastic action.

"Please take me, Frank. You can't leave me here while everyone else gets to go to Blackpool. It's not fair."

I sound like a fuckin' ten-year old and this begging business is leaving a nasty taste in me gob.

Okay," he says. "But I mean it. Any shenanigans and..."

And what, you stupid Scottish cunt!

"I know. I'm going to try and change me ways, Frank. That little talk we had made me realise that you're a friend, not a foe."

"Okay. But..."

"Frank, show you have a bit of faith in me. Give me a chance." I don't want to sound desperate but I get the feeling he's going against his better judgement. If I was him, I wouldn't take me. "Please, Frank? I need this. I need to get out of this place for a day. It'll do me the world of good."

"Right, then. We'll see how it goes."

It's the first time I've seen Frank unsure of himself. He could get into a shitload of trouble if I kick off. It might almost be worth it to stitch that fucker up. But the truth is, I want to enjoy the day. I feel like a kid. I'm going to fuckin' Blackpool! I'm actually looking forward to something for a fuckin' change. I'm going to fuckin' Blackpool!

*

I stupidly assumed that Harry would want to sit next to me but he tells me he's saving a place for Julie when I plonk mesen next to him in the seat behind the driver.

"She'll be sitting with one of the dementia lot, Harry. What did you think? Were you expecting a posh hand job with a velvet glove as soon as we hit the motorway?"

He grins at the thought. He's brightened up a bit since his brother's funeral. I'm not bigging mesen up, but I'd like to think I'd played me own part in helping him get over his loss. Julie's told me I've made a big difference in Harry's life. In fact, the lovely Julie is the only Willowbeck screw that's said anything remotely positive to me during me incarceration.

"Listen, if I don't sit next to you, someone else will. Do you want to be stuck next to Doug for three hours?"

Harry still doesn't yield so I hover over the seat until he finally realises that Julie will be otherwise engaged. She gets on with Elsie, gives me and Harry a wink, before ushering her dependant to the next available seat a few rows back.

"Looks like I'm stuck with you," says Harry.

Frank still doesn't look sure he's made the right decision when I clock him getting on the bus with the woman with the look of constant surprise. I give him the thumbs up to let him know he can trust me but his weak smile lets me know he'd trust a second-hand-car salesman more than yours truly. Our Frank is vulnerable. This is the perfect time for me to let him know who's boss but it might prove more useful to gain his trust a bit more before I finish the fucker off. He's on the ropes now and he knows it. He's not stupid. He knows I'm as high as a fuckin' hot air balloon over the Alps and he doesn't know any more than I do how this will play out. He's rattled and it's me that done the rattling.

Me phone lets me know I've got a text. It's from our

183

Alison.

Hi Alan. Thanks for your lovely text. It meant a lot. I just need a bit of time to myself. I've lost the love of my life and I'm heartbroken to be honest. I know you understand. I hope you have a lovely day today. Enjoy yourself and behave. Frank is one of the good guys Alan. Give him a chance. He's a good man. Love Alison.

I sent our Alison a heartfelt text message this morning. I thought it might get her arse up to Willowbeck but it clearly hasn't worked. She's taking some time out, like I'm a fuckin' job that she can take a couple of weeks off from on compassionate grounds. It's a fuckin' liberty. And her mentioning Frank has got me blood right up. He's getting to her. That Scottish cunt is working his magic on me sister. Over me dead, rotting corpse he is. In me text, I told her how much I'd missed her. I told her I was sorry for giving her such a hard time. I told her that without her I'd be totally lost. I told her that I loved her, for fuck's sake! I won't be doing that again in a hurry. I don't know. You let your guard down and let someone in and they spit it back into your face. This is just not on.

"What's up with you?" asks Harry. "Bad news?"

"You could say that," I say. "Frank's trying to get in me sister's knickers."

Harry finds this hilarious of course.

"Well, she'll be lonely now her husband's snuffed it," he says, with his smiling eyes and his gormless, gummy grin.

"Show some fuckin' respect," I snap. I know that's a bit rich coming from me but just because I'm an ignorant selfish bastard without a kind thought for me grieving sister doesn't mean any old fucker can get in on me act. I give Harry the silent treatment as the bus rolls on through unremarkable countryside. Me mood's gone tits up and I sense darkness coming.

*

I must have nodded off. The coach has stopped and I wake up to see Frank at the front of the bus organising the toilet break. I'm creasing for a piss meself but I'd hazard a guess that many

184

of me fellow detainees will have already filled their respective pads. Harry's looking a bit desperate. The coach already smells like the main lounge at Willowbeck, just without the nasty food odours that help to mask the rank smell of the combined bodily fluids of age.

We shuffle off the bus and head for the toilets *en masse.* I end up standing next to Frank in the urinals. I sneak a peek. His prick is twice the size of mine.

"Have you spoken to our Alison recently?" I ask, while I give me knob a shake. I recall one of Arthur's famous quips. *Five shakes and it's a felony!*

"Once or twice, yes. She's in a bad way. It's hit her hard."

"She told me you're one of the good guys, Frank. Are you one of the good guys?"

"I don't know what you mean?"

"I think you know exactly what I mean."

"Don't make me regret bringing you, Alan. Today will be trying enough as it is. Please don't make a scene today. You gave me your word."

"That's the thing about nutters like me, mate. Our word doesn't mean shit," I say. I grin at him and dry me hands. It's one of those super-fast driers that nearly strips the skin of your mitts. It frightens the shit out of me.

We have tea and sandwiches in the seated area outside. Harry talks about Julie. I pretend to listen. Frank fires the odd glance me way to check if I'm behaving mesen. I am, for now. To be honest, the breakfast smarties are starting to take effect, as per usual. I was given a new one today. I didn't bother to ask what it was. I'm past fuckin' caring, but me moods are swinging like a lap dancer's tit-tassels.

Back on the bus, Harry is trying to make conversation. He's run out of things to say about Julie and he's done the weather, a couple of Blackpool memories, and I'm still not engaged.

"You miss her, don't you?" he says.

"Who?"

"Your sister." I didn't see that one coming. Harry is

attempting to have a meaningful conversation with me for a change. The trouble is, he couldn't have picked a worse fuckin' time.

"I'd rather not talk about me sister, if it's all the same to you, Harry. She doesn't give a fuck about me and it's as simple as that. She made her bed a long time ago."

"I wish I had someone like her. You're lucky, Alan. You should appreciate her. You don't fool me. She's a diamond, that woman, and you know it."

Harry's right of course but I really don't want to continue this conversation so I get up out of me seat. Frank looks up, wondering what I'm up to. I take the only available seat next to Doug, who looks about as pleased to see me as he would if Harold Shipman had come to check his blood pressure.

"Do you mind, Doug? Harry's getting on me nerves and I want a bit of peace and quiet."

He grunts and turns to look out of the window. Doug is not me biggest fan. I think it's safe to say Doug wouldn't give a flying fuck if I decided to chuck mesen off Blackpool Tower. He knows what everyone else knows. I've upset the applecart at Willowbeck. Apart from Harry and Julie, I am despised at Guantanamo Gardens.

I lean over to Doug and whisper "You're a miserable old cunt" in his ear and head back to sit next to Harry.

Doug shoots up from his chair as if he's sat on a drawing-pin. "Keep that bloody lunatic away from me! He's just called me a miserable old cunt!" he screams.

Harry is grinning like a cat that's just been at the double cream when I regain me seat.

"That's more like it," he says. I put out me hand for him to shake.

"All in day's work," I say.

The noise levels have suddenly risen. I hear footsteps down the bus aisle and Frank is suddenly in me face.

"For God's sake, Alan. That man is eighty-eight years old. Show some bloody respect, man. I can't have you upsetting everyone. Can you see the chaos you've caused?

186

Listen!"

The catatonic who grunts a lot is now grunting for England and she's not alone in expressing her distress. Some are crying, other are shouting, another screams, "Where's Donald? Has anyone seen my husband? I want my Donald. I don't want to be here. I want my Donald."

"I don't know what to say, Frank. He gets me back up, that Doug. I only went to say hello."

"You said a bit more than that, Alan. The man's in a rage. I've never seen him so worked up." He comes in close to me face and whispers, "If he fuckin' keels over... I'll..."

"You'll do what?" I say, quietly. "You're all talk, Frank. Piss off back to your seat and leave us alone. I was only havin' a bit of fun."

"You call that fun?" he whispers, trying to keep a lid on that Scottish temper that seems to be boiling over. His face his red with anger now. To be honest, I'm beginning to regret this little drama and I'm beginning to wish I could take it back.

"I'm sorry, alright? I've lost an old friend and me brother-in-law in less than a month. Forgive me if I'm not feeling meself."

"That crap might work with your sister, Alan, but I'm not buying it. I know you, mate. I know exactly what you are," he says. He knows he's crossed a line now. He knows that I know I've got to him. I try not to smile. I really do. It's not a good time to smile. But I smile anyway. I smile right in that Scottish cunt's face.

I watch the blood drain from his cheeks. He sighs deeply. He looks back down the aisle and back at me. The clamour has died down now as if nothing happened. But something did happen. And I made it happen.

He tuts and walks back to his seat.

"Jesus Christ," I hear the coach driver say.

I look at Harry. He's staring out of the window. I close me eyes and reflect on me behaviour. I feel something I haven't felt in a long time.

*

Harry's right. I do miss her. I miss me sister. I really miss her. I take out me phone and text her. I really miss you, I say. I'm sorry I've treated you so badly, I say. You are me world Alison, I say. Take all the time you need, I say. I understand, I say. And I mean it. I really do. But she knows me too well and she'll know what I'm up to. She knew it the other day. Emotional blackmail is the only weapon I have. I text her again. I'm okay for money, I say. Look after yourself for a change, I say. I'll be fine, I say. And I know, I just know the effect this will have, but for once I hope it doesn't. For once, I'm genuinely sorry. But she'll come anyway. She always comes. She's always there and she always will be.

And now I'm crying. Tears are rolling down me face. Harry's asleep. Frank's back in his seat. No one is here to witness this. I'm crying because I know what a fuckin' wanker I really am. I'm crying because I treat the only family I have left like a fuckin' skivvy and I'm sorry about it. Of course, I feel more sorry for meself. I always will. I've got a lot to feel sorry about. Me life has been one long fuckin' mess and I've got no one to blame but me. And Babs. Babs has got a lot to answer for as well. And me dad. Me dad was a cunt, God rest his soul. But not our Alison. Not me lovely sister. She's a fuckin' saint. I text her again. You're a saint, I say, and I'm so sorry, I say.

I get a text back straight away.

Are you okay? Thanks for your lovely messages but I'm really struggling Alan. Give me a bit of time. Please? I love you. You're my brother. I'll always love you no matter what. But I need some time. See you soon. X

I text right back.

No worries. Take care Sis. I mean everything I said. Take good care.

Now I know she'll be shitting herself that I'm going to try and top mesen again and that's not what I want her to think. But I can't help it if she doesn't see this for what it is. I'm saying sorry. I am sorry. I'm so fuckin' sorry.

I've got no doubt in me mind that she'll be up to Willowbeck like a shot tomorrow. She'll be there first thing in the morning. I know her. And I know how big her heart is. She's got such a big fuckin' heart.

22. For He's a Jolly Good Fellow

I defy anyone's little heart not to leap when you get a first glimpse of Blackpool Tower, rising up in the distance over the flat Lancashire landscape, as if it was the only thing for miles. Me little heart does leap but then I nod off again.

I wake up when we arrive at the Pleasure Beach. I was not expecting this. I want to walk on the sea front. I want to smell the sea. I want to eat fish and chips. I want to wear me hanky on me head. I look up at this giant metal structure through the window. It's like something out of an HG Wells book I read as a kid. What the fuck are we doing here?

Me and Harry get off first. I'm creasing for a fag and I spark up instantly. It's lovely and warm with a slight breeze. I hope Frank's remembered the suntan lotion.

Those that can walk, walk. Those that can't are plonked in their wheelchairs. It takes an age to get moving. I go back and talk to Frank.

"What we doing here? Aren't we going to the beach?"

"We come here every year, Alan. The residents love it. Can we just enjoy the day, please, without any more drama?"

"Love what?" I say, genuinely confused.

"The rides."

I look up at the massive rollercoaster and I just can't picture Elsie and the woman with the look of constant surprise with their hands in the air, whooping like some teenage thugs from Liverpool.

"What rides?"

"We go on Alice in Wonderland and a water ride in Beaver Creek."

I wondered why they got all the waterproof coveralls out of the back of the bus. This could actually be fun.

"Lead the way, Frank. I won't be any trouble." I grin at him again. This is getting so fuckin' easy.

We head for the valley of Beaver Creek. The noise around us is deafening and some of the chronics are getting a bit emotional again. The woman who misses Donald screams

190

for Donald; the woman who grunts a lot grunts a lot; the woman with the look of constant surprise looks more surprised than usual. We all look up as a carriage full of screeching fun-lovers whizzes by over our heads. The woman who misses Donald screams.

I slow down and wait for Harry and Frank to catch up.

"Well, this is a barrel of laughs," I say to Frank, while the rest of the staff try and calm down a few of me fellow lifers. Frank goes over to help Julie deal with Elsie. Elsie's not in a good way. She's trying to get out of her wheelchair. She's trying to let them know she wants to get the fuck out of here. Doug is giving me the evils. I say "Cooey" and he looks away sharpish.

Things calm down a bit as we join a little queue for one of the water rides. I quite fancy the log flume mesen but Frank has opted for the less excitable option that will be marginally less hazardous for our merry little troop.

Julie and the Chinese nurse hand out waterproof coveralls from a big laundry bag. I decline the offer. "I want to get wet, love. I'm all hot and bothered," I say to the Chinese nurse. Harry lets the nurse put his on for him.

"Not good idea, Alan. It's wet," she says.

"If the man wants to go commando, let the man go commando," says Frank with fake jollity.

"Wha?" says the Chinese woman.

"Those who dare, win, love," I add. She still doesn't have a fuckin' clue what we're talking about. "I don't want to put one on, love," I say to clear things up. "Comprende?"

"Okay. Get wet then," she says, clearly agitated. She might not understand everything she hears but she knows when she's being patronised.

"Sorry, love," I say, genuinely. "I didn't mean to..."

She's already turned around to put a waterproof on Doug.

There's eight to each raft. The rafts are circular, with rubber tyres fitted to the sides. Some of the chronics don't fancy it. They stay on dry land with the Polish bird. The rest of us get in two of the rafts and there's a member of staff for every two patients. I'm on a raft with Harry, Doug, the woman with the look of constant surprise and the woman who misses Donald. I should really find out their names. Who knows – we could be friends. I might even get me leg over and give the woman with the look of constant surprise something to look surprised about.

I have to say I'm actually enjoying meself. When our rafts get going, after our seatbelts have been fastened and checked by a big tattooed gorilla with a caring disposition, an eerie calm settles over us all. And when we gently hit one of the wooden jetties as we descend our first little rapid, the raft does a gentle spin like a painfully slow waltzer at some fairground for geriatrics. The woman who misses Donald whoops with delight and starts laughing her tits off. The Chinese woman says something to her and she stops laughing and looks at the Chinese woman as if she's just let rip with a stinker. The Chinese woman doesn't take it to heart. She'll have had her fair share of racist abuse in her time. I'm sure it's all in a day's work.

Things get lively as we descend into another part of the canyon. We spin around faster this time when one of the tyres hits the side again. The face of the woman with the look of constant surprise lights up with a huge smile as our raft dips into a deeper section of water, creating a freak wave that soaks us all from head to foot. The woman who misses Donald screams and then starts whooping with joy again.

Frank and his fellow passengers on the other raft look like they're having a great time as well, from what I can see. Even Elsie's smiling. I look over at Harry and Doug across from me. Harry's grinning from ear to ear; Doug's expression is a mirror opposite, mouth turned down, brow furrowed. I don't help his mood when I shout, "Cheer up, you miserable old..." Another wave snatches "cunt" from me mouth and gives us all another good soaking. I'm beginning to regret not wearing a waterproof. At least it's nice and warm but this ride is a little wetter than expected. Me jeans are already soaked. Not that I mind. At least we're all having some fuckin' fun for a change.

I look ahead at Frank's boat, ignoring Doug, who's shouting something at me while the Chinese woman tries to calm him down above the roar of the water. I wave at Frank. Frank waves back. Suddenly, I'm totally fuckin' drenched and when I get me wet hair out of me eyes, I see that both boats are having a right old laugh at this silly old cunt without a waterproof and I feel anger rising from me boots. But then it goes. It goes as fast as it came and I'm laughing with the rest of them. But I haven't laughed like this in a long time. It feels really fuckin' good.

While everyone is distracted with pointing and laughing at me, I catch a glimpse of the woman who misses Donald. She has somehow unclipped her seatbelt and when another little wave comes crashing over, no one has noticed that she's actually attempting to climb out of the raft. She's surprisingly agile. The Chinese woman who's still laughing her tits off with Doug is looking the other way, as are both the nurses on the opposite side of the raft, who are busy gassing. Nobody has noticed this imminent tragedy but me. The noise is deafening now because we have two whooshing waterfalls on either side of the raft. I have to act and act now. I notice a family above the canyon walls pointing down at us but only I can see them. The woman who misses Donald tries to heave herself out of the raft. I spring up out of me seat and lunge for her as she tries to slide over the edge. I dive for her legs but lose me footing, narrowly avoiding smashing me face on her seat, but I land head first onto the back of her legs and I cling on to them for dear life. Everyone is in a panic now, trying to assess the situation, but the Chinese woman acts fast and scrambles to help me and we both then haul the woman who misses Donald back to safety. We both try and turn her around so we can get her safety belt back on. It would be easier to just give the silly old bitch a knock-out punch to stop her struggling but that only happens in films. We finally manage it. A big cheer erupts around us from above. Our little drama has attracted a small audience. A foul smell is coming off the woman who misses Donald. She must have shat herself in all the excitement.

I stand up and take a bow then slump back into me seat. The raft flows into calmer waters.

*

We're all sunning ourselves, taking up an entire stretch of benches on the promenade near the central pier. Everyone seems to be full of good spirits after our little drama. Me own mood has darkened a bit but I blame that on the whacky smarties Frank force-fed me this morning.

Frank comes and sits between me and Harry. "I have something to show you," he says, laughing. "Julie went back to the photo kiosk at Beaver Creek when we all got back on the coach. It seems that your heroics were captured on celluloid."

Frank hands me the picture. Most of it looks normal: the Chinese woman is talking to Doug, Harry is looking into the water, the two nurses are talking into each other's face, but the woman with the look of constant surprise has never looked so surprised; she's pointing at some silly old cunt with long, wet, greying hair and shades, with his arms wrapped around the legs of an even sillier old cunt trying to dive out of a raft into a whirlpool. I guess the woman who misses Donald was pretty keen to join him.

"You're a hero, Alan. Thank you," says Frank, and pats me on the back.

"I should have let the silly old cunt drown," I say. I've never been good at accepting compliments.

"Now, now, Alan. Be nice," says Frank.

"I just hope you've learnt your lesson, that's all. That woman could be dead now. You need to take your job more seriously, mate. People's lives are in your hands. You should be fuckin' sacked, if you asked me."

Frank's lost for words. He nods and heads back to the others.

"That was a bit much," says Harry.

"You can shut the fuck up an' all," I snap.

I get off the bench and walk over to the railings. I stare out to sea. I wish Alison was here.

*

We're sitting down to our fish and chip dinners. I sit on me own opposite the rest of them. Harry sits next to Julie of course. I'm not attention-seeking. Despite popular belief, it's not in me nature. I am feeling pretty miserable but eating solo is just a part of me plan. Nobody gives a fuck that I'm sitting on me own, despite me heroics. I'm just being the cranky old bastard they all know and hate.

The woman who misses Donald is in distress and so are those who are sitting with her. She's just knocked over a huge jug of squash and everyone around her has been given a good soaking. She's screaming for Donald again. She's obviously either suffering from post-traumatic-stress disorder after me brave rescue or she's beside herself because she didn't join her Donald in hell. Like I said, I should have let the old cunt drown.

I see me chance. All the Willowbeck staff are fussing around the soaked table cloth. Even the woman with the look of constant surprise is shouting at the top of her voice. "She's missing Donald, aren't you, love? I miss my Alf. I really miss him. I want to see my Alf." Elsie is expressing her distress with a hideous sound that is half squeal and half grunt. A couple of the waitresses have joined in the fun. I head for the door and then I'm out in the sunshine again.

I don't have a penny to scratch me sack with but I don't need money. I've got eleven fags and a packet of Extra Strong Mints. Whatever else I need, I can steal or borrow.

I cross over to the sea side of the road and head for the Tower. The sun is still beaming down and me pits are soaking so I take off me leather, hook me finger through the peg loop and throw it over me right shoulder. To anyone looking, I'm just a regular rocking pensioner strolling along the prom prom prom. I'm under no illusions though; as soon as Frank notices I've fucked off, the plods will be searching for me and I'll be back with the wrinklies where I don't belong. I decide to cross back over when there's a break in the tram tracks. I'll be too easily spotted on the front.

I make it as far as the Tower before me phone starts ringing. If I had the entrance fee I'd be up it like a shot but it's probably a good thing I haven't. I'm feeling pretty impulsive and it would be as good as place as any to chuck mesen off. I wouldn't be the first person to check out here. Mind you, they've probably made it difficult by now, with high fences and barbed wire. This little Eiffel Tower has been a magnet for nutters who've had enough of this charade we call life since the fuckin' thing was built.

I walk up a side street next to the Tower. I take a seat at the next available bench and spark up a fag.

Memories of me honeymoon with Babs come flooding back but I make an effort to stop them breaching the levee so it won't ruin the little time I have to feel like a free man.

An old lady sits next to me.

"Lovely day," she says.

I smile and nod. This makes her uncomfortable but I figure if I can keep me mouth shut for a change, I just might blend in with the rest of humanity for a little while.

Unfortunately, she doesn't see it that way and she stands up and heads for the next bench up the street.

I walk into a rock shop. Man, have things changed in novelty rock. They still have the usual stuff: walking-sticks, sugar dummies, rock shaped like fruit, glass jars full of rock sweets; but there's a whole section devoted to rock genitalia. There are huge rock dildos, complete with veins, red bellends and jap's-eyes; there are rock breasts, even rock vaginas, for fuck's sake.

I notice the woman behind the counter is giving me the evils. "Do you feel comfortable selling this filth?" I snap. "Children shouldn't have to look at all this. It's immoral."

"They're for the stag and hen parties, love. We sell more willie lollies than owt else these days."

"Well, it's disgusting. I should complain to the authorities."

Still, if I had any money on me, I'd have bought a pair of rock tits for Harry and a cock apiece for Julie and our Alison.

I leave, shaking me head at the woman behind the counter, who is whispering to her colleague who's just come

196

back from the chippy with their dinner.

"Mind how you go," she says, feeling brave now she has backup. I flip her the finger and fuck off out of there.

Me phone rings again so I decide I best make a move. I need to be amongst crowds but not in an obvious place. I see a shopping centre. That'll do.

Me phone rings again. You'd think they'd realise I'm not available right now like me voice mail message says, but someone seems awfully keen to get hold of me.

I walk through the shopping centre looking in windows, sidestepping women with prams and teenagers in huddles. I'm soon bored. Shopping centres are no fun unless you've got a pocketful of brass.

People are beginning to stare. It's the shades. Unless I'm blind, I shouldn't be wearing shades inside a shopping centre. Best act blind. But I don't have a stick. Best get a stick. This is getting complicated.

When I head back outside I'm beginning to realise that me great escape was pretty fuckin' futile. All I've done is label mesen a flight risk. There'll be no more solo smokes in the grounds of Willowbeck for me for a while.

I sit back down on the bench where I tried to be normal and wait for the inevitable. I get out another smoke.

I'm only a few drags in when the plods turn up.

"Excuse me, sir," says a policewoman, with a geezer plod behind her who looks about three foot taller. "Can we have a word?" They sit on either side of me.

"You can have two," I say, but even I'm bored of this quip so I don't expect a laugh.

"I think we need to be getting you back to your friends, Mr Siddall," says the geezer plod, his voice a couple of octaves lower than his sexy counterpart. I say sexy but you could put Elsie in a police uniform and I'd probably want to fuck her.

"They're no friends of mine, mate. I'd much rather go for a pint with PC Whatsherface here. I promise I'll be gentle."

I get nothing. Another couple of officers turn up and I

realise if I don't go of me own accord then this will get ugly.

I get a ride in a police car though. That's always fun. It's something I never get bored of. It'll be the most fun I have for a while. When Dr Beiger hears of this, I'll be so full of pills I'll be rattling like a pair of fuckin' maracas.

We pull into the car park. Everyone's on the bus apart from Frank and Harry. Frank looks well pissed off. Harry on the other hand looks tickled pink. He gets on the bus as the big copper helps me out of the car. Frank comes over and thanks the officers.

"Do you need a hand getting him on the bus?" says the copper to Frank.

"I can take it from here," says Frank.

They wait anyway. We get on the bus. I put me hands up in the air and say, "Don't worry, folks. I'm safe and sound." I hear Elsie do that half grunt and half squeal thing but that's all I get. Even the woman with the look of constant surprise doesn't look surprised anymore. That's progress in my book.

"You're with me, Alan," says Frank. "You can have the window seat."

"That's very kind of you, Frank, but I might want to circulate."

"Please, Alan. Take a seat," he says, firmly.

I do as I'm told. I glance at Harry a few rows back before sitting down. He's sitting next to Julie.

"You behave yourself, young man," I say.

"I'll do me best," he says, with a big grin.

Julie doesn't meet me eyes. I'll never get me nuts soaped now.

The bus sets off.

"Where to next?" I ask Frank.

"We're going back to Willowbeck. You've ruined it for everybody," he says, miserably.

"Fuckin' hell. From hero to zero in a couple of hours. I should be getting a commendation for bravery. You could've lost your job if it wasn't for me heroics." He doesn't answer. "I'll be making out a report about today, Frank, and you won't come up smelling of roses. I'm calling a meeting. I want you in front of the board. You're a disgrace to the profession." I can't get a rise out of him. "They might give you early retirement if you're lucky. Personally, I think you should do time for negligence. You take too many risks, Frank. When the families of these good people hear about today, you're finished, Frank, finished. Have you got anything to say for yourself?"

He closes his eyes to compose himself. He must be boiling with rage inside but he knows how to keep a lid on all that anger. We have a long drive back home. I'll let him simmer for a while before bringing him back to the boil. I know me way around this kitchen.

23. Murder, He Wrote

I'm on mute today. Harry's been picked up by his daughter and I'm on close obs with a new bloke called Bryn. I think he's been brought in especially for me. He's Welsh. He's built like a scrum-half. Bryn is also on mute for the time being. Just as well. He's boring as fuck.

It seems Harry and I have traded places. He gets a visit every week now, and Alison's playing hard to get. After me little chat with Harry's daughter she's been making more of an effort but yet another good deed of mine has gone unnoticed. I don't know why I fuckin' bother. I really thought Alison would've come up this morning. I'd have put me fuckin' flat on it. That reminds me. I must get me flat on the market. I could remortgage it and get a full-time nurse to look after me. She might even throw in the odd blow job if I pay her enough. Who am I kidding? I'm going nowhere. If our Alison thinks she's going to let it out and live off the spoils, she's... she can... she can have the fuckin' thing, for all I care. I just want to see her.

I tried to ring her when I woke up this morning but me hands aren't working too well. I decided against leaving her a voice message. Me mouth's not working too well either.

Me and Kenny had words last night. I wanted me ghetto blaster back. He didn't think it was a good idea. I called him a thieving Scouse bastard and asked him how much he'd got for it. Kenny didn't like that. At smartie time I was given something extra to help me sleep. It worked. I slept well, a little too well for me liking. And I've been drifting in and out of sleep all fuckin' day. Still, it beats listening to Bryn.

There's just me, Doug and Bryn in the smoke lounge and it's been just the three of us all day. The woman with the look of constant surprise hasn't been in today. She's either dead, decided to stop smoking or can't stand to be in the same room as me. I'd guess it's the latter. Another woman who used to sit in here only comes in now when I'm not around. So that just leaves Doug and Harry. Harry can stay for now but I'm working on Doug. But Harry's days are numbered as well. One day this will all be mine.

Murder, She Wrote's on but I can't keep me eyes open. It's sleepy time again. I'd ask Bryn to sing me a lullaby but you know what the Welsh are like at rugby matches. Bryn belting out "Bread of Heaven" just won't cut the mustard. Still, Angela Lansbury seems to be doing quite well on her own.

Doug never misses an episode. I want to call Doug a cunt but I don't think it's going to make it out of me mouth. I just can't seem to get anything out of me mouth.

*

I can't make it down to the dining room so Bryn brings me a tray in. I manage a bit of mash but it's clap-cold and they should fuckin' know I don't do sausages by now.

"I don't eat... I can't... Julie?" Julie has come in to spark up Harry's half-five fag.

"Yes, love?"

"Sausages?" I sound like that fuckin' dog off *That's Life.*

"I know. You enjoy them, love."

"No, I don't... I can't..."

"He won't eat real ones," Harry says, grinning. "Are they vegetarian?"

"I don't know, to be honest," says me new Welsh friend.

I manage another bit of mash and tip me dinner off me plate and onto the floor.

"There's no need for that, Alan. Look at this. You've made a right mess," says Julie.

"Sausages," I say again.

"You sound like that bloody dog off *That's Life,*" says Harry, telling me something I already know for a fuckin' change. Julie tries not to laugh when she notices me watching her. She leaves the room quickly. I think about trying to call Harry a cunt but I can't. I just can't. It's not because he's not a cunt. He is a cunt. He's a total cunt. Me mouth just won't do what me brain is telling it to do. Me brain is telling me to call everyone a cunt, even Julie.

Doug comes back from dinner. Julie follows him in with a cloth and a dust pan and brush. He looks down at me and shakes his head as he passes.

"Cunt," I shout, triumphantly. I should thank him really. He stops before sitting down and turns around to face me. He wants to say something to me but his mouth's not working too well either. But it's not for want of effort. I think his rage is holding him up a tad.

"Cunt," I shout.

"Now, there's no need for that, Alan," says Bryn.

"Cunt," I manage again, but at Bryn this time. But Bryn is a bit too close and is soon wiping off a bit of mash I've just spat at him.

"You..." says Bryn.

"Cunt?" says Harry, and then he's laughing like the jolly old fucker he is.

"Harry!" shouts Julie, looking a little shocked.

"Can somebody get this lunatic out of here? I want to watch *The Weakest Link* in peace," screams Doug.

"Doug, why don't you go watch it in your room?" suggests Julie. "It'll be nice and peaceful in there for you."

"I don't see why I should have to go. Send him to his fuckin' room."

"Doug," shouts Julie. Doug doesn't usually swear either. He fuckin' does now. I've got them all at it.

I manage to flip Doug the finger. I manage to laugh. Doug goes to his room. Who's the Daddy? Even when I can't fuckin' speak, I'm the Daddy of this fuckin' manor. Like I said, one day this will all be mine.

We watch *The Weakest Link.* One of the contestants looks a bit like Cassandra.

I try telling this to Harry and Bryn but I sound like I've had a stroke. Then I'm drifting off again. I haven't even had me pudding. I am the weakest link. Goodbye.

*

It takes me a while to get out of bed and make it to me door. I'm glad they left me light on. I open me door. The big black

202

fella from the night shift is sitting on a chair, reading a book outside me room. I try to tell him about me little accident but I just can't put the words together.

He gets up. He can smell me.

"Let's get you cleaned up and get you back to your bed."

He takes me into me bathroom, wipes me arse and legs and gives me a good wash while I lean against the sink. Then he lays a towel on me armchair and I sit down while he sorts the bed out. It's everywhere. He takes off all the bedding and puts it in a pile on the floor.

"I'm just going to the laundry room. You stay right there, Alan, and I'll have you sorted in a minute."

I nod.

He comes back with bedding in a trolley and swaps the dirty sheets for clean ones.

But I won't make it back to bed. I'm going back to Kansas. I can hear Toto barking. We're going back to Kansas. I'm Dorothy. I'm wearing a little white dress. I have pigtails in me hair. I'm going back to Kansas.

*

I wake up. It's light. I try and get out of bed. I can't.

*

I think I'm dreaming but I'm not. I don't remember getting here. I try and remember how I got here. I can't.

Murder, She Wrote is on. Bryn is next to me. Harry and Doug are there. I try to call Doug a cunt. I try to call Harry a cunt. I try to call Bryn a cunt.

"Hungry?" Bryn says.

"Cunt," I say.

*

The Weakest Link is on. Doug is watching it. I try to call Doug a cunt. Bryn says, "Hungry?"

I nod.

He sets up me tray. He puts a little bib on me. He starts spooning soup into me mouth. Then our Alison walks in. She's not alone. Philippa is with her. And then Barry walks in.

"Cunts," I say. "You're... you're all just... you're all in

on it. You're just a bunch of..."

Doug gets up and walks out. I want to put me leg out to trip him up but I can't get it to move. I try to call him a cunt. Alison has gone. I can hear her crying outside.

"Cunts," I shout. "Ice cream," I say to Bryn. He puts the soup on the side. He peels off the lid. He puts some ice cream in me mouth. "That's lovely," I say. "Alison," I say. "Go get our Alison," I say. Then I'm crying.

"She'll be back soon, mate," says Bryn softly. "She's a bit upset, that's all. Have some more ice cream," he says.

"I'm upset," I say. "I'm upset, Bryn."

He puts the spoon in the ice cream and I watch it coming towards me. I close me eyes and open me mouth. I swallow. "It's lovely," I say.

After the ice cream, he gives me a little carton with a straw in it.

"Drink this, mate. It'll keep your strength up." I suck on the straw. It tastes fuckin' horrible. "Have another go. It's magic stuff, this. You need it, mate. You haven't been eating much."

I take another sip. Philippa comes back in.

"Hello, Alan. I'll take it from here," she says to Bryn.

"Get me out of here," I say to Philippa.

Our Alison walks back in.

"Alison... thanks for coming," I say, and I'm crying. She sits down next to Philippa. I want to ask her how she is. I really do. I try to smile at her. It works. She smiles back. I ask for a cigarette. Philippa goes to get me one. Alison sits right next to me. She takes me hand. I want to tell her I've missed her. I just smile. She smiles. She's missed me.

"Sorry I missed... sorry I couldn't come," I say.

"That's okay," she says. She knows I never liked him. She knows I won't shed too many tears over him. I know she wouldn't have let me go even if I'd wanted to.

"Did you... give him... was it..."

"Sshh," she says.

Philippa comes back.

"Hello, love," I say.

204

"Hello again," she says, smiling.

She gives me a cig. She lights it.

"Lovely," I say. I offer both of them what's left of me ice cream. They don't want it. "I'll have it later," I say. They're both smiling at me. "I'm sorry," I say to our Alison. "It's okay," she says. "Everything's going to be okay," she says.

It's not going to be okay. Everything is not going to be okay.

Then Barry walks in.

"Fuck off," I shout, "just fuck off," and everything is not okay. Alison is crying. They all go outside. Bryn comes back in.

"Where've they all gone? Get them back, Bryn. Get them back in here!"

They don't come back.

I finish me ice cream. Then I finish watching *The Weakest Link.*

24. Time Travel

Cassandra looks like an angel. Babs looks like a whore. Our Alison looks like our Alison. Me dad looks like a rotting corpse. He should be a skeleton by rights and I didn't expect him for dinner. But here we all are, sitting around a table in the Willowbeck dining room. It's silver service. Frank is dressed in a white waiter's suit and a black dickey bow. He looks like a right tool. But I can't fault his service. He knows how to lay a table. He whispers in me ear to let me know to start from the outside when I'm selecting me cutlery.

Madame Butterfly is playing too loudly and then I spot Arthur conducting the orchestra and a fat opera singer in the corner of the room. I shout over to Arthur to ask if he knows any Sabbath and he stops the God awful racket and starts playing "Changes", which is just fine and dandy until the opera singer comes in after the first few bars. If only Ozzy was here.

Harry is sitting with Julie and they're gazing into each other's eyes over candlelight. Harry's got a dickey bow on as well but he forgot to put his shirt on first. Julie is naked like it's the most normal thing in the world.

Then I open me eyes.

Cassandra's in front of me and she doesn't look like an angel anymore. She looks like she did the day I stopped her buying the sausages in Mrs Patel's shop. She smiles. "Hello Alan," she says. But then I hear Arthur laughing and I'm back at the table and Frank is pouring the wine. I watch me dad dissolve to dust, like he's a vampire that's just been staked. Cassandra smiles at me. Babs is cackling about something or other, and Arthur has keeled over into the string section. The music stops. The paramedics rush in and cart Arthur off in a body bag. But Frank's a real pro and serves us our soup from a silver pot, with a silver ladle. The soup is white and viscous and Frank is smiling, knowingly. I tell him I think I'll skip the soup and wait for the fish course. He pours me a glass of wine that's a little too red and a little too thick. You can't fool a butcher. I know pig's blood when I see it.

Me dad's alive and well again and at the window. He's dressing it nicely, placing big sprigs of parsley between each head of me previous co-habitees. He's drawing a crowd as well. He knows how to entice a customer.

Before he places the last head to complete his window display, he holds it up by the hair and points at it, seeking me approval. Elsie looks smashing with her head roasted to a healthy dark pink, her eyes wide with terror and an apple in her gob for good measure.

Then I'm back in the smoke room and Cassandra is there in front of me but when I close me eyes and open them again, she's gone. I try and focus on the box. I can hear her voice but Cassandra has no business talking to Angela Lansbury but I know this can't be happening because it's Nelson Mandela and he has no business talking to Angela Lansbury either. But then the face morphs from Mandela into Cassandra's. She looks into the camera and winks at me. Then I'm back in the market lavs well before the 70s re-fit and I'm washing all this blood off me hands. There's so much blood on me hands that me soap that I used to keep in a plastic bag in me pocket has dissolved to a wafer-thin slither. Then someone is shaking me by the shoulders and I want to throw a punch so I can just wash me fuckin' hands but me arms feel like lead. I give up trying and then there's nothing but darkness. I'm blind. I'm totally blind and that's just fine for now. I can still hear Angela Lansbury but the darkness is just fine for now.

*

Someone is trying to feed me but me mouth won't work. I try speaking but nothing comes out. Then I feel something warm sliding down me throat and I can't quite identify the taste but it tastes okay. I try to speak again and I get more. I try opening me eyes and I see Julie with a dish under me chin, doing the choo choo train with her spoon from the dish to me mush, but she's out of focus and it makes me feel a bit sick so I close me eyes and wait for the choo choo train to come back. I'm creasing for a piss but I can't even move so I just let the warmth spread around me and it's like getting into a bath with me trousers on. She's wiping me chin and now there's something else on the little train and it's sweet and unmistakable. Apple pie and custard. This is the life.

*

I open me eyes but I close them again. Frank is talking to Cassandra. He's chatting her up, the fucker, and I can't bear it. I know this is down to the smarties but I can't bear it. I can't hear what they're saying.

"Go away," I shout, but I don't hear it. Either I've gone fuckin' deaf or I've lost me voice. "Leave me alone," I shout. I open me eyes again. They're both still there. They won't go away. Frank's after the love of me life and there's fuck all I can do about it. I close me eyes again. I hear a door close. I open me eyes again but it's just Frank. He's trying to tell me something but I just want to go back to sleep or wake up. "Go away," I say. Then I'm drifting back to sleep or waking up. I don't know which. But then there's nothing. Just darkness. I like it. I feel it wash over me like warm water.

*

I wake up and I know I'm awake this time. I just know it. And I'm glad I know it. I get out of bed. I go for a slash. Me aim is poor but I get most of it in the pot. I'm starving but I feel dizzy. I go back to bed. It's light but I haven't got a clue what time it is. I want to listen to some music. I want to listen to some Sabbath. I ring me bell.

Kenny walks in about five minutes later.

"You look better," he says.

"Can you get me some tea and toast? I want me ghetto blaster back as well, and me CDs."

"Tea and toast I can do but your ghetto blaster's under lock and key for now. You'll have to talk to Frank about that."

"I want some music," I say. "I need some music."

"I'll let you in on a little secret, Alan. It's 5.30 in the morning. It's no time for Sabbath or Freddie and the bleedin' Dreamers, for that matter. Tea and toast coming up. It's good to see you're feeling better," he says.

"Thanks," I say. I don't know where that came from.

208

I've got fuck all to thank that Scouse twat for.

He brings me some tea and toast. The tea comes in a baby cup with a little spout. He's done me four slices, slathered with butter. I wolf them down. He helps me with me tea and wipes me mouth a couple of times. Kenny's got a soft side. But he's still a cunt.

"Can we go outside for a bit? I want to feel the sun on me face," I say.

"It's only been up half an hour, mate. I'm not sure it's a good idea."

"Please?" I say. "I want a cig under me willow tree."

He smiles. "Come on, then. Let's get you dressed first, though. You don't want to be flashing your dick to all and sundry."

Kenny wants to talk. I want to think. He's trying to bond with me. I want me ghetto blaster back so I let him witter on. I need an ally. So I even laugh at regular intervals but he knows as well as I do that he's not funny. He's about as funny as Alzheimer's.

We go back in. I've got the whole day room to mesen. Kenny's still talking. I'm still not listening. I ask Kenny for some more toast. He says he thinks I've had enough. I ask him for me ghetto blaster. He ignores me and just keeps talking. I call him a cunt. He stops talking. He fucks off.

I feel pretty chipper for a change but there's no one to talk to. I wish our Alison was here. We haven't had a proper chat for ages.

The black fella turns up with a smartie and a big thimble of water. It's one of the new ones. It's one of the time travellers. I refuse. He insists. I refuse again. He insists again.

I go back to me room. It takes me forever but I feel good about it. I sit in me chair and do some thinking but me mind's starting to race and I'm getting mesen worked up. I need to talk to our Alison. I look for me phone. I look everywhere. I look in me chest of drawers. I look in me wardrobe. I check me leather. I check me jeans. I check in me bathroom. It's not here. It's been confiscated like me ghetto blaster. I feel me blood rising. I ring me bell.

*

Dr Beiger is in no mood for nonsense. She stops me mid-rant and makes it perfectly clear that the new tablets they've put me on are for me own good. I disagree. She doesn't give a fuck. I tell her I'm losing time. She tells me that things will get better. I tell her to fuck off. She tells me to calm meself down. I tell her that's her job. She smiles. She actually fuckin' smiles.

Frank says that I should show Dr Beiger some respect. I tell Frank to fuck off. Then Kenny the Scouse giant puts his oar in. He should have gone home by now, unless I've just lost a whole fuckin' day again he should have gone home by now. I tell him to fuck off and I get out of me chair and go for him. Frank helps Kenny restrain me until I've calmed down and then they put me back in me chair. Frank is stronger than he looks. Kenny is as strong as I remember from when he tucked me in after the Hendrix episode.

Dr Beiger starts again. This time, she asks me to try and keep regular hours. I tell her I haven't kept regular hours since 1978. She smiles again. I tell her I want to go back to Murton Croft. She says I need to try and settle in. Barry hasn't said a fuckin' word. I tell him to get me out of here or I'll top meself. He says I'm being silly. I tell him to fuck off. He shakes his head. I tell him to fuck off again. He doesn't move. I tell Frank that I'm going back to me room if Barry doesn't fuck off. I say I'll go on fuckin' hunger strike if I have to, like those Irish blokes did in the 80s when Thatcher was trying to make them wear prison uniforms. I get out of me chair again and ask nicely. Please just go, Barry. I want another social worker, I say. I have that right. You are no fucking good and you never have been, I say. You've been on the sick because you're probably not that far from topping yourself too. That seems to do the trick. The truth hurts. Barry fucks off.

Nothing is resolved. I've probably just talked meself into another bottle of time-travelling smarties.

Dr Beiger says if I keep acting this way they will have to send me to an acute ward in Bradford. I tell her to send me back to Murton Croft. She says that I am a Bradford patient now and that I will be sent to Bradford. I've heard some bad things about the acute wards in Bradford. Some very bad things. I tell her I hate Bradford. She tells me if I don't get too excitable there'll be no need to go. I try to calm down. I need to try to settle in and behave or it will be bedlam in Bradford for me.

I tell Dr Beiger I will try and settle in. I say sorry to Dr Beiger, Frank and Kenny. I say sorry for smashing me chest of drawers to pieces because Kenny wouldn't answer me bell. Kenny says apology accepted and I call him a cunt just for being from Liverpool.

Dr Beiger tells me she's going to give me something a little extra to calm me down. I tell her I feel much calmer already. She smiles again. She says she hopes that I can settle in here. She says I can't go back to Murton Croft. She reminds me I will end up in Bradford if things don't improve. She says I really don't want to go there because it's much nicer here.

I tell her I want to go back to Murton Croft. We've just gone around in a big circle. She shakes her head at me as she gets up to leave the room. Nazi bitch, I say but it's like no one has heard me. Evil Nazi bitch, I say again but it's all falling on deaf ears. Did I actually say it or did it stay in me head? I say it again but realise me lips aren't moving. I haven't felt this weird since I dropped acid with Deaf Jeff back in the late 60s. Are they feeding me fuckin' acid now? No wonder I'm off me tits.

*

Dr Beiger walks into me room in full Gestapo uniform. Now I know I'm in trouble. I'm in big fuckin' trouble because this is all a bit too fuckin' real. I want the darkness to come. Then it does come and I relax a bit. But then the light is back and it's very bright, even with me sunglasses on. It's very bright. She's laughing. I can't see her but her laughter is so loud, me ears are buzzing. Then it stops and the lights go out.

I sink into the darkness. I'm sinking into it but the light is on again and even though I've got me sunglasses on and me eyes are closed tightly, the light is still getting through. I can smell something bad. Really bad. Something rotten and dead. Someone is breathing in me face. I open me eyes to Dr Beiger's face an inch in front of me. I scream. I wake up.

I ring me bell. I've shat me bed again. I'm covered in me own shit again.

25. The Tea Trolley Incident

Cassandra looks like an angel. Babs looks like a whore. Our Alison looks like our Alison. Me dad looks like a rotting corpse. He should be a skeleton by rights and I didn't expect him for dinner. But here we all are, sitting around a table in the Willowbeck dining room. It's silver service. Frank is dressed in a white waiter's suit and a black dickey bow. He looks like a right tool. But I can't fault his service. He knows how to lay a table. He whispers in me ear to let me know to start from the outside when I'm selecting me cutlery.

Madame Butterfly is playing too loudly and then I spot Arthur conducting the orchestra and a fat opera singer in the corner of the room. I shout over to Arthur to ask if he knows any Sabbath and he stops the God awful racket and starts playing "Changes", which is just fine and dandy until the opera singer comes in after the first few bars. If only Ozzy was here.

Harry is sitting with Julie and they're gazing into each other's eyes over candlelight. Harry's got a dickey bow on as well but he forgot to put his shirt on first. Julie is naked like it's the most normal thing in the world.

Then I open me eyes.

Cassandra's in front of me and she doesn't look like an angel anymore. She looks like she did the day I stopped her buying the sausages in Mrs Patel's shop. She smiles. "Hello Alan," she says. But then I hear Arthur laughing and I'm back at the table and Frank is pouring the wine. I watch me dad dissolve to dust, like he's a vampire that's just been staked. Cassandra smiles at me. Babs is cackling about something or other, and Arthur has keeled over into the string section. The music stops. The paramedics rush in and cart Arthur off in a body bag. But Frank's a real pro and serves us our soup from a silver pot, with a silver ladle. The soup is white and viscous and Frank is smiling, knowingly. I tell him I think I'll skip the soup and wait for the fish course. He pours me a glass of wine that's a little too red and a little too thick. You can't fool a butcher. I know pig's blood when I see it.

Me dad's alive and well again and at the window. He's dressing it nicely, placing big sprigs of parsley between each head of me previous co-habitees. He's drawing a crowd as well. He knows how to entice a customer.

Before he places the last head to complete his window display, he holds it up by the hair and points at it, seeking me approval. Elsie looks smashing with her head roasted to a healthy dark pink, her eyes wide with terror and an apple in her gob for good measure.

Then I'm back in the smoke room and Cassandra is there in front of me but when I close me eyes and open them again, she's gone. I try and focus on the box. I can hear her voice but Cassandra has no business talking to Angela Lansbury but I know this can't be happening because it's Nelson Mandela and he has no business talking to Angela Lansbury either. But then the face morphs from Mandela into Cassandra's. She looks into the camera and winks at me. Then I'm back in the market lavs well before the 70s re-fit and I'm washing all this blood off me hands. There's so much blood on me hands that me soap that I used to keep in a plastic bag in me pocket has dissolved to a wafer-thin slither. Then someone is shaking me by the shoulders and I want to throw a punch so I can just wash me fuckin' hands but me arms feel like lead. I give up trying and then there's nothing but darkness. I'm blind. I'm totally blind and that's just fine for now. I can still hear Angela Lansbury but the darkness is just fine for now.

*

Someone is trying to feed me but me mouth won't work. I try speaking but nothing comes out. Then I feel something warm sliding down me throat and I can't quite identify the taste but it tastes okay. I try to speak again and I get more. I try opening me eyes and I see Julie with a dish under me chin, doing the choo choo train with her spoon from the dish to me mush, but she's out of focus and it makes me feel a bit sick so I close me eyes and wait for the choo choo train to come back. I'm creasing for a piss but I can't even move so I just let the

214

warmth spread around me and it's like getting into a bath with me trousers on. She's wiping me chin and now there's something else on the little train and it's sweet and unmistakable. Apple pie and custard. This is the life.

*

I open me eyes but I close them again. Frank is talking to Cassandra. He's chatting her up, the fucker, and I can't bear it. I know this is down to the smarties but I can't bear it. I can't hear what they're saying.

"Go away," I shout, but I don't hear it. Either I've gone fuckin' deaf or I've lost me voice. "Leave me alone," I shout. I open me eyes again. They're both still there. They won't go away. Frank's after the love of me life and there's fuck all I can do about it. I close me eyes again. I hear a door close. I open me eyes again but it's just Frank. He's trying to tell me something but I just want to go back to sleep or wake up. "Go away," I say. Then I'm drifting back to sleep or waking up. I don't know which. But then there's nothing. Just darkness. I like it. I feel it wash over me like warm water.

*

I wake up and I know I'm awake this time. I just know it. And I'm glad I know it. I get out of bed. I go for a slash. Me aim is poor but I get most of it in the pot. I'm starving but I feel dizzy. I go back to bed. It's light but I haven't got a clue what time it is. I want to listen to some music. I want to listen to some Sabbath. I ring me bell.

Kenny walks in about five minutes later.

"You look better," he says.

"Can you get me some tea and toast? I want me ghetto blaster back as well, and me CDs."

"Tea and toast I can do but your ghetto blaster's under lock and key for now. You'll have to talk to Frank about that."

"I want some music," I say. "I need some music."

"I'll let you in on a little secret, Alan. It's 5.30 in the morning. It's no time for Sabbath or Freddie and the bleedin' Dreamers, for that matter. Tea and toast coming up. It's good to see you're feeling better," he says.

"Thanks," I say. I don't know where that came from.

I've got fuck all to thank that Scouse twat for.

He brings me some tea and toast. The tea comes in a baby cup with a little spout. He's done me four slices, slathered with butter. I wolf them down. He helps me with me tea and wipes me mouth a couple of times. Kenny's got a soft side. But he's still a cunt.

"Can we go outside for a bit? I want to feel the sun on me face," I say.

"It's only been up half an hour, mate. I'm not sure it's a good idea."

"Please?" I say. "I want a cig under me willow tree."

He smiles. "Come on, then. Let's get you dressed first, though. You don't want to be flashing your dick to all and sundry."

Kenny wants to talk. I want to think. He's trying to bond with me. I want me ghetto blaster back so I let him witter on. I need an ally. So I even laugh at regular intervals but he knows as well as I do that he's not funny. He's about as funny as Alzheimer's.

We go back in. I've got the whole day room to mesen. Kenny's still talking. I'm still not listening. I ask Kenny for some more toast. He says he thinks I've had enough. I ask him for me ghetto blaster. He ignores me and just keeps talking. I call him a cunt. He stops talking. He fucks off.

I feel pretty chipper for a change but there's no one to talk to. I wish our Alison was here. We haven't had a proper chat for ages.

The black fella turns up with a smartie and a big thimble of water. It's one of the new ones. It's one of the time travellers. I refuse. He insists. I refuse again. He insists again.

I go back to me room. It takes me forever but I feel good about it. I sit in me chair and do some thinking but me mind's starting to race and I'm getting mesen worked up. I need to talk to our Alison. I look for me phone. I look everywhere. I look in me chest of drawers. I look in me wardrobe. I check me leather. I check me jeans. I check in me bathroom. It's not here. It's been confiscated like me ghetto blaster. I feel me blood rising. I ring me bell.

*

Dr Beiger is in no mood for nonsense. She stops me mid-rant and makes it perfectly clear that the new tablets they've put me on are for me own good. I disagree. She doesn't give a fuck. I tell her I'm losing time. She tells me that things will get better. I tell her to fuck off. She tells me to calm meself down. I tell her that's her job. She smiles. She actually fuckin' smiles.

Frank says that I should show Dr Beiger some respect. I tell Frank to fuck off. Then Kenny the Scouse giant puts his oar in. He should have gone home by now, unless I've just lost a whole fuckin' day again he should have gone home by now. I tell him to fuck off and I get out of me chair and go for him. Frank helps Kenny restrain me until I've calmed down and then they put me back in me chair. Frank is stronger than he looks. Kenny is as strong as I remember from when he tucked me in after the Hendrix episode.

Dr Beiger starts again. This time, she asks me to try and keep regular hours. I tell her I haven't kept regular hours since 1978. She smiles again. I tell her I want to go back to Murton Croft. She says I need to try and settle in. Barry hasn't said a fuckin' word. I tell him to get me out of here or I'll top meself. He says I'm being silly. I tell him to fuck off. He shakes his head. I tell him to fuck off again. He doesn't move. I tell Frank that I'm going back to me room if Barry doesn't fuck off. I say I'll go on fuckin' hunger strike if I have to, like those Irish blokes did in the 80s when Thatcher was trying to make them wear prison uniforms. I get out of me chair again and ask nicely. Please just go, Barry. I want another social worker, I say. I have that right. You are no fucking good and you never have been, I say. You've been on the sick because you're probably not that far from topping yourself too. That seems to do the trick. The truth hurts. Barry fucks off.

Nothing is resolved. I've probably just talked meself into another bottle of time-travelling smarties.

Dr Beiger says if I keep acting this way they will have to send me to an acute ward in Bradford. I tell her to send me back to Murton Croft. She says that I am a Bradford patient now and that I will be sent to Bradford. I've heard some bad things about the acute wards in Bradford. Some very bad things. I tell her I hate Bradford. She tells me if I don't get too excitable there'll be no need to go. I try to calm down. I need to try to settle in and behave or it will be bedlam in Bradford for me.

I tell Dr Beiger I will try and settle in. I say sorry to Dr Beiger, Frank and Kenny. I say sorry for smashing me chest of drawers to pieces because Kenny wouldn't answer me bell. Kenny says apology accepted and I call him a cunt just for being from Liverpool.

Dr Beiger tells me she's going to give me something a little extra to calm me down. I tell her I feel much calmer already. She smiles again. She says she hopes that I can settle in here. She says I can't go back to Murton Croft. She reminds me I will end up in Bradford if things don't improve. She says I really don't want to go there because it's much nicer here.

I tell her I want to go back to Murton Croft. We've just gone around in a big circle. She shakes her head at me as she gets up to leave the room. Nazi bitch, I say but it's like no one has heard me. Evil Nazi bitch, I say again but it's all falling on deaf ears. Did I actually say it or did it stay in me head? I say it again but realise me lips aren't moving. I haven't felt this weird since I dropped acid with Deaf Jeff back in the late 60s. Are they feeding me fuckin' acid now? No wonder I'm off me tits.

*

Dr Beiger walks into me room in full Gestapo uniform. Now I know I'm in trouble. I'm in big fuckin' trouble because this is all a bit too fuckin' real. I want the darkness to come. Then it does come and I relax a bit. But then the light is back and it's very bright, even with me sunglasses on. It's very bright. She's laughing. I can't see her but her laughter is so loud, me ears are buzzing. Then it stops and the lights go out.

I sink into the darkness. I'm sinking into it but the light is on again and even though I've got me sunglasses on and me eyes are closed tightly, the light is still getting through. I can smell something bad. Really bad. Something rotten and dead. Someone is breathing in me face. I open me eyes to Dr Beiger's face an inch in front of me. I scream. I wake up.

I ring me bell. I've shat me bed again. I'm covered in me own shit again.

Part 3

Me Mam's Magic Vase

26. Underneath Me Willow Tree

I never thought I'd say it but I'm looking forward to Esme's Sunday roast. After the pig swill they dished up at Airedale General, Esme's dishes are like something you'd tuck into at Claridge's.

When I got back to Willowbeck on Friday night, I had a fag and a cup of tea under me willow tree and watched the sun go down over Bingley. Julie kept me company and filled me in on what I'd missed during me short sabbatical. It didn't take long. The Chinese bloke has snuffed it and there's a new inmate ready to take over his cell. That's about it. Hopefully the new boy won't smell so bad.

Frank has been away for a long weekend so I haven't had the pleasure of his company since he came to visit me in Airedale with our Alison. I haven't seen her yet either. I put two and two together. You can call me a paranoid old fart but I don't believe in coincidences. She might be still grieving, but that doesn't mean that Frank isn't slipping her one to keep her spirits up.

I asked for me ghetto blaster back, and me phone, but that's Frank's call so I won't get a decision until he comes back on Monday morning. I've been a good lad since I got back though. They've kept me off the smarties and although they had their benefits (visits from the dead and the lovely Cassandra Bekker) I prefer reality right now, at least me own version of it anyhow. Reality might be a bit dull but at least I know what the fuck's going on and what fuckin' day it is. It's about time I stuck Cassandra in the old memory fish tank and faced up to the fact that I'll never see her again, unless they put me back on the smarties, at any rate. I can always kick off if I want her to pay a visit. It's the uninvited guests I worry about.

I need me painkillers though. Me arm's still fuckin' killing me and I've never been a lover of pain. Well, I used to like it when Babs drew blood on me arse cheeks when I was on the vinegar strokes but those days are long gone. Mind you,

I've just felt a stirring down below so perhaps there's life in the old trouser trout yet. Not that I can do much with it in here, unless I could tempt Julie with a fistful of tenners. On her meagre wage, a hundred quid might just get me a soapy tit wank the next time she gives me a bath, if I ask nicely.

I have to admit, I was glad to get back to Willowbeck. Maybe I should just get used to the idea that there's nowhere else for me to go. This is it. This is the last stop before I collect me belongings and leave the station.

At least I've got Harry. I walk into the smoke room and ask Harry if he wants to sit outside. There's fuck all on TV on Sunday afternoons.

"Come on, Harry. The sky's blue, the birds are singing, Julie's in her bikini."

"If that were true, I'd race yer there."

"Come on, you old git. It'll do yer good."

"Go on, then. Beats looking at Doug all day."

"Do you want to join us, Doug?" I ask, knowing what response I'll get. "Come on, mate. We're stuck with each other so we might as well try to get along. How about it? Three likely lads setting the world to rights over a cuppa and a fag or two?" I get nothing. Not a sausage. "No? Come on, Doug. Last chance."

I want to push it but I decide not to. Like I say, I'm stuck with the old cunt so I'll put some ground work in to get to know him but I won't hold out the hand of friendship for long. If he wants to be in my gang, he'll have to meet me halfway. Who am I kidding? He wouldn't piss on me if me hair caught fire.

So it's just me and Harry under the willow tree. Harry's got his hanky on his head. Fuck knows why. We're sitting in the shade.

We talk about Julie. We talk about his daughter. We talk about me heroics at the Pleasure Beach. Then we're done. We've run dry.

"I think it's about time you told me about this wife of yours," I say. Harry does his Houdini thing again, leaving himself behind under the tree while he floats away to get away from me probing enquiries.

So I sit there, wishing I hadn't bothered, bringing the conversation back to Julie's tits and what fun it would be to dress them in Esme's trifle, when he comes out with it.

"She was knocked down by a hit-and-run driver," he says. "The bastard just left her there. They never caught him, if it was a him. Could have been a woman for all I know. She'd been to bingo. She won an' all. She had the winnings in her purse. Full house. Two hundred quid. She'd been going to the same club every Wednesday night for twenty years. Never had a full house. I never went. I hate bingo. Always have and I always will now. She'd won a couple of quid here and there, four corners and a couple of lines over the years, but she'd never had a full house. It was her lucky night." His eyes are filling up. I put me arm around him but he tenses up so I take it away. "So now you know. Happy now?"

"What was she like, Harry, your missus? That's what I wanted to know. Not how she died, mate. I was asking about her."

"What's the point? She's gone. You've got to move on in life."

"But you don't, mate. Those are just words. You can never move on, not really. Not people like us. I've been living in the past for the best part of forty years. The past is the only place I know. There's fuck all to look forward to so the past is where it's at. It's where everything is for me, Harry. You too, by the sounds of it. You've got to let the pain go, mate, and look back on who she was, what you had, not how she died. You know that Cassandra I told you about? I kept seeing her when I was out of it. She'd just appear in me dreams. But it was good to see her. I'll probably never see her again but it was good to see her, even if it was all in me head."

"She'll come again, Alan. My Gladys won't. At least that Cassandra's alive and well. Gladys won't come back. I don't even dream about her anymore. You saw Cassandra last week. She's a nice lady. Very nice."

"What? What did you fuckin' say?"

"She's nice. Bloody 'ell. Don't go off on one. I just

said she was nice, that's all. My Gladys..."

"You saw Cassandra?"

"Yeah. You were out of it. She came into the smoke room. She stayed for a bit but you kept nodding off. She'll come again, mate. She'll be back. You're lucky. My Gladys..."

I get up and leave Harry talking about Gladys. I can't fuckin' believe it. Cassandra was here, at Willowbeck. Why didn't anybody tell me? Some bastard's got some explaining to do.

*

I'm awake most of Sunday night, running it all through me head, hopping mad and ready for Frank when he drags his hairy arse back to work. Kenny's not pleased to get summoned by me bell in the wee small hours. He comes in and I'm pacing around me room like the Ghost of Christmas Past. I felt okay yesterday. I was in one of me lucid periods after four days out of this god-forsaken shithole. It's hardly rocket science. I had a holiday from all that shit they like to pump into me – just me lithium, and haloperidol on standby in case I got out of control. But I didn't. I was alright. And now this. The Cassandra controversy. A night without sleep and I'm high as a fuckin' eagle over Everest and they'll be putting me back on the smarties again when I kick off. It's inevitable. It's all so fuckin' predictable. One little trigger and I'm barking mad again. I try to look on the bright side. Cassandra came to see me. She must have got me number from Mrs P's window. She might have tried calling. Me phone. Where's me fuckin' phone? I haven't seen it since... I can't remember.

"I need me phone, Kenny."

"It's three in the bloody morning. Try and get some shut-eye and you can ring whoever it is when it's more appropriate."

"I just need to check something. I won't call anyone."

"Mate, you're exhausted. Look at yourself. Try and get some sleep. Do you want something to help?"

"I don't want fuckin' pills, Kenny. I've had enough pills to last me a lifetime. I just want me phone."

225

"It's not gonna happen, mate, so just get yourself back to bed. Come on."

"Get your hands off me, you Scouse twat! I want me fuckin' phone!"

Kenny puts me to bed. I've got no fight in me. I'm knackered. I try to look on the bright side but I'm too worked up and I need a fag.

"I need a fag, Kenny," I whimper. "I'll sit in the smoke room. I can't sleep. Just let me sit in the smoke room."

"Come on, then. But I don't want any hassle. And keep your voice down."

Kenny makes me a cup of tea and gives me a fag. I smoke it. He puts the telly on quiet. There's a documentary on about birds in Africa. We watch it.

*

I open me eyes. Doug's up and in his chair already, waiting for Carol Kirkwood to give him a sexy weather forecast. He mutters something to himself when he sees that I'm awake. Frank'll be in soon. Then we'll get to the bottom of all this nonsense. I shut me eyes. I need me strength.

*

"Why didn't you tell me?"

"Tell you what?" says Frank. He hasn't even taken his coat off yet.

"About Cassandra?"

"I did tell you. But you haven't been... coherent for a while."

"And whose fault's that? Mine? You pump me so full of crap that I'm shitting the bed and you tell me I haven't been coherent. Did she leave her number?"

"No. Alan, she took the trouble to come all this way. She'll be back, mate. Don't worry."

"I'm not your fuckin' mate and I never will be. I want me ghetto blaster and I want me phone."

"Alan, please. Let's not get this out of proportion. I haven't seen your phone. When did you last have it?"

Then I go off on one. I go off on one big time and before I know it an alarm is ringing and I'm being wrestled to

226

the floor by Bryn and Frank. Even the Chinese nurse with the nice arse has joined in on the scrap. She's sitting on me legs. I think I caught Frank a good 'un though. But this has gone too far. They'll be sending me to the Bradford ward now. I've struck a member of staff. I'm in deep shit now. Bring on the smarties. Bring out the straightjacket. It's bedlam in Bradford for Siddall.

27. The Déjà Vu Express

Murder, She Wrote's on.

*

The Weakest Link's on.

*

Murder, She Wrote's on.

*

The Weakest Link's on. I call Doug a cunt. I call Harry a cunt. I call Bryn a cunt. Bryn lights me fag. I cough. I probably turn purple. I call Bryn a cunt again. Frank walks in. I call Frank a cunt.

*

I'm in a car.
    "Where are we going?"
    No one answers.
    "Where are you taking me?"
    No one answers.
    It's dark. It's really dark. There's a hand on me hand. The hand is soft. I try and see who it is but I can't move me neck. The soft hand is stroking me left hand.
    "It's okay," says some woman. I know the voice. I know the back of the head in front of me. There's someone else at the side of Frank.
    "Where are we going?" I say.
    "Sshh," says the woman stroking me hand. "It's okay. Everything's okay."
    Everything's not okay. I'm in a car. It's night. I should be in bed at Willowbeck Gardens. Everything's not okay.

*

I open me eyes. I'm in a bed. I'm in a room. I've been in a room like this before. But it's a different room. Dreams do that to you. They put you back in a familiar place where you think you've been before but something's not quite right so you know it's a dream. The sink is in a different place. So is the door. The room's a slightly different shape. There's a

228

sandwich, a couple of biscuits and a beaker of juice on the bedside table. The beaker is green. I've drunk out of beakers like this hundreds of times. It's a dream. It must be a dream. It's just not quite right. Something's not quite right.

Someone's turning the door handle. The dead are coming to see me. Me dad's coming to dress me new window with his best cuts. Alfie Turner's coming to show me his new dance routine. Arthur's back and he's pissed off. I haven't played his *Madame Butterfly* CD.

The door opens slowly. The dead are coming for me. I close me eyes. I don't want to see who's just walked in. I'm in smartie land. I don't want be in smartie land anymore. It could be anybody if I'm in smartie land. I'm terrified. The door closes again.

When I feel safe, I open me eyes again. It doesn't feel like a dream. I sit up. I prop up me pillows behind me back. I take a sip of the juice from me beaker. It's weak. There's too much water in it. There's always been too much water in it. But I'm not complaining. I take a bite of me sandwich. It's ham with a bit of mustard on. It's me favourite sandwich. This definitely doesn't feel like a dream. I take another sip of me juice.

I put me pillows back and lie down again. I close me eyes.

*

I open me eyes.

"Hello, sleepyhead."

"Hello, love. What...? Where?"

"Hungry?" says Jenny. There's a sandwich, a couple of biscuits and a green beaker full of juice that'll be too weak on me bedside table.

I close me eyes.

This is definitely a dream. This is just too fuckin' good to be true. This is definitely too good to be true.

A soft hand is stroking me hand. I open me eyes again and Jenny's still there. She's smiling.

"Welcome back," she says.

*

It's the morning of me Care Programme Approach meeting, CPA for short (or, for those who speak English, the "What shall we do with this mad old fucker?" discussion), and I am in one of me more flamboyant moods. I ask Pat, me old fellow lifer, to crash me a fag.

"Buy yer own," she croaks.

I'm in the TV lounge, finishing me cuppa after breakfast. A few of the service users are watching a programme about tracking down will beneficiaries.

It's as dull as Esme's leek and potato soup but it beats *Murder, She Wrote* any fuckin' day of the week. Geoff still has most of his brekkie on his chin. He's saving it for later. No change there. It's like I never left Murton Croft.

Do you remember that time in *Dallas* when Bobby Ewing walked out of the shower and a whole series was part of his dream? Well, I'm Bobby Ewing. What a fuckin' shower that was.

Beth comes in to remind me of me date with Dofuckall and his foot soldiers. You can always rely on the staff to be predictable. I'm on the déjà vu train this morning and it's running off the tracks.

"Hi, Alan. Dr Bell should be in about half-ten, if that's okay."

"That's fine, love, but I've run out of smokes and nobody's crashin', are they, Pat?"

"Yer what?" Pat wakes up from her power nap.

"Never mind, love. You pop off back to sleep." I put me leather on.

"Alan? Please?" says Beth.

"Sorry, love. No baccy, no CPA meeting. If they hadn't closed down the hospital shop we wouldn't be having this conversation. Take it up with management."

Beth smiles. She's just got on the déjà vu train herself.

"Just be back by half-ten, okay?"

"Don't you worry, love. I'll be back before you can say Frank Hendrie's a wanker. Scout's honour. Dib dib dib, dob dob dob." I give her me old scout salute. Like I said, this is déjà vu fuckin' central.

When I get down to Mrs P's, me ad for Cassandra is still in the window between Naughty Norman the children's entertainer and the ad for Fred and Alice's rodent retreat. I walk in. Mrs P looks surprised to see me.

"Now then, love. How's business?"

"Fine, thank you."

"Thanks for keepin' me ad in your window. I must owe you a fortune by now."

"It's fine. You have been good customer. The lady saw it, you know. I spoke to her. She said you were old friends."

"We were, love. She's the love of me life, to be honest. She's the one that got away."

Mrs P looks uncomfortable now so I take out me tenner.

"Twenty Richmond, love, and you can keep the change for what I owe for the window. I've lost me phone anyway. I think a bloke called Doug nicked it. Somebody nicked it, any road. I'd bet me life it was that miserable old sod."

She gets me fags and gives me change and takes nothing for the window advert.

"Have you seen her?" says Mrs P.

"Only in me dreams, Mrs P. Only in me dreams."

I hang around outside for a bit just in case Cassandra shows, but me déjà vu train is sleeping in a siding now.

I look at me new watch that our Alison bought me. Dr Dofuckall will be heading across town for our meeting. Best not disappoint him.

*

Me CPA meeting feels more like a welcome home party. Me future was decided while I was in smartie land after me recent and final ruck with Frank and Kenny. Philippa, Dofuckall and our Alison were summoned up to Willowbeck to discuss me future. They decided between themselves that I wasn't quite fitting in at Willowbeck. Despite all Frank's assurances that he could cope with the likes of me due to his vast experience in mental health, all those years at High Royds and all that, I was just too much for the poor bastard. I won. I fuckin' won – the battles and the war. Mind you, I don't think Frank will have thrown in the towel. I get the feeling our Alison and Philippa played a part in getting me back to where I belong.

Dofuckall tells me in his own subtle way not to get too comfortable but as Barry told me the other day (I've reinstated the useless sod as me social worker) there are very few places that can handle the likes of me. There's a place in York apparently but our Alison won't agree to that, not now she's on her own without a husband to ferry her about. It's too far to be traipsing up on a bus or train, so unless she learns to drive pretty fuckin' sharpish, York's out of the question. It's full at the moment anyway. So here I'll stay for now.

Frank will take it on the chin. I hope he doesn't press charges. That punch I threw was a long time coming. *I plead diminished responsibility your honour! Bonnie Prince Charlie had been force-feeding me time-travelling smarties for the best part of a fuckin' month! Is it any wonder I chinned the cunt?*

*

After the ward round, I go back to me room with a cup of tea. I turn on me ghetto blaster. I know what I want to listen to. Well, I know what I have to listen to. It's time. Rain has started to thrash against me window. I prop up me pillows, put me hands behind me head and try to enjoy *Madame Butterfly.*

I get lost in it. I get so lost in it that I nearly fill me boxers when there's a knock on me door. It's a new nurse called Cheryl. Nice arse, nice tits, but she's got a face like a bull terrier. She's got the portable phone in her hand.

"There's a call for you."

Me heart leaps. I don't ask who it is.

"Hello. Alan Siddall speaking?" I say, like some fuckin' spiv in an estate agents.

"Hello, Alan."

"What the fuck do you want?"

"How are you?"

"I'm fine and dandy now I'm not getting poisoned with your fuckin' pills. You'll have to be quick. I'm listening to *Madame Butterfly* and I'm only halfway through the first

232

act."

"You had a visitor this morning," says Frank. "It was your lady friend, Cassandra. I gave her the number for Murton Croft."

"Good. Thanks." I try to avoid sounding totally over the fuckin' moon.

"Harry says hello. You should pay him a visit sometime."

"No offence, mate, but you won't be seeing me again in your little house of horrors. Tell Harry I'll send him a postcard. Farewell, Frank. Please don't call here again."

I hang up.

I need to get meself spruced up. I need some new clobber and some nice aftershave. Cassandra's coming. It's time to write a list for our Alison.

*

I've listened to *Madame Butterfly* three times now, the whole fuckin' lot of it. I have to say, it makes a refreshing change from Sabbath. I might get our Alison to get me some more opera. It's just a shame I haven't got Arthur to point me in the right direction. Maybe I could take Cassandra to the Grand. I bet she likes opera. I might just surprise her and get our Alison to get us a couple of tickets. I'll need a suit though, maybe a tux. I can hardly roll up to the theatre in me leather and Sabbath Bloody Sabbath tour shirt. We could have dinner afterwards at some posh gaff. I might need to pop out for a fag at some point. These fuckin' operas drag on a bit.

I look at me watch. It's time for a bath. It's time to blow dry me hair and talc me ball bag. Cassandra's coming to town. I've had a good night's sleep and I'm not talking shite for a change. I need to think before I speak. Me new life starts today. Second-hand Siddall, who does fuck all and knows jack shit, is back in the game. It's time to play.

*

I'm sitting in reception, in me old spot. Jenny and Beth are behind the nurses' station. Janet comes and says hello.

"Now then, you old crow. How's tricks?"

"Bloody terrible," says Janet. "I've had the

threepennies for three days."

"That's nice. You should eat more fibre, love."

"You expecting someone?" Janet sniffs the air around me. "You smell like a poor Omar Sharif. Did you drop a bottle of toilet duck on your leather?"

"Sod off. This is good stuff this. Our Alison got it from Boots."

"She's always been a useless sod, your Alison."

"Watch yer mouth, Janet. That's me sister you're talking about it."

"Since when did you give a monkey's arsehole about your sister?" I get up. "You've never cared about anyone but yerself!" she screams, as I go tell Jenny that I'll be waiting outside for Cassandra. Janet's not doing too well at the moment and she's cramping me style. Fancy, making a scene like that. She's got no social graces, that one. I still have a soft spot for the sour old bag but I can't cope with her right now. She'll be on the good stuff tonight, before she gets violent. When Janet goes off, she makes Vesuvius look like a party-popper.

28. Cassandra's Return

When Cassandra turns up, it's a bit of an anti-climax to be honest. I think she's put on a few pounds since I last saw her in Mrs P's. I did tell her to pack in the sausages. She's wearing a white blouse that her huge tits are screaming to get out of and her vast navy-blue skirt is hanging off her hips like canvas over a tent frame. But fuck, is it good to see her.

I go in for a hug. She has other ideas. She takes a step back and gives me her hand. I don't know whether to shake it, kiss it or force it down me pants. I shake it.

"You're looking a lot better. I can't believe it."

"Thanks, love. You're not looking bad yourself. Shall we go for a walk in the park?"

"Is that okay with... are you...?"

"I've got time out for good behaviour. Come on. It's a lovely day."

We walk around the park. I fill Cassandra in on me trial period at the house of horrors and explain a few things about me recent traumas. We talk about Mrs P and how she let Cassandra know that I was a patient at Murton Croft. When Cassandra turned up, it was Bev who told Cassandra I'd been shipped off to Guantanamo Gardens. I'd never thought that sackless, nasty bitch would end up playing Cupid. I'll have to thank her. I'd get her some flowers but I think she'd prefer a pound of best bacon.

Cassandra doesn't have long. We walk back from the park and she promises she'll visit me again soon and take me out for the day.

*

She comes to see me the next day. She asks me what I want to do for a couple of hours.

"How about a hotel? My treat," I say.

"I think we're a bit old for that," says Cassandra, letting me down gently.

"Speak for yerself, love," I say. "I haven't been inside a woman since I visited the Statue of Liberty."

"You've been to New York?"

"Don't sound so surprised, love. Nutters can travel too. No, I've never been to New York. It's an old Woody Allen gag."

There's a silence. We're not on the same wavelength. I'm beginning to think this is all a bad idea. I'm beginning to think I wished I'd never bumped into her again. I feel me mood darkening but she suggests she could drive us up to Saltaire and we could have a spot of lunch, visit some gallery and go for a walk.

We chat on the way there and I lighten up. We talk about our night in the Duck 'n' Drake and our walk home in the snow all those years ago.

The main street is lined with double-parked cars bumper to bumper and the village is full of families, pensioners and young lovers, living life as it should be lived.

It's drizzling a bit but no one else gives a fuck so we don't let it bother us either. Cassandra has an art satchel over her shoulder, as if it's some prop or other to link us back to our past. I ask her what's in it and she says she'll tell me later.

Cassandra looks a bit uneasy when I say I want to walk by the canal rather than going into the big mill. I tell her I feel a bit overwhelmed by all the people and I fancy a bit of fresh air first. She lets me have me own way.

"We could do a spot of fishing," I say. She looks uneasy again. "All we need is a kiddies' fishing net and a little bucket."

We walk into a gift shop. I buy a toy bucket and spade and a kiddies' fishing net from an old lady who looks like she's ready for Willowbeck herself. She looks a little shocked when I tell her she can keep the little spade. Maybe she thinks I'm suggesting she could dig her own grave.

We walk along the canal and stop now and again so I can dip me net in. Within a few minutes, we have a couple of sticklebacks in the bucket that I've half filled with canal water.

We sit down on a bench for a bit. Cassandra asks me what it feels like. Here it comes, I think. I'm just a fuckin' curiosity, a project for a nice lady to sink her teeth into, to make her feel good about herself for helping out an old freak like me.

I tell her about fishing with Dad down at the canal for sticklebacks. I tell her about me mam's magic vase with the thickened glass and what it did to the fish.

"The vase wasn't really a vase, it was more like a square glass container. Me mam never used it. It was a bit short to put flowers in so it just stayed in the cupboard most of the time. Anyway, me and me dad came back from the canal one day with a few sticklebacks in a bucket. I'd carried it all the way home and didn't spill a drop of water. I asked me mam for something to put them in and she got out this square bowl. I put some water in it and gently tipped the canal water and the fish into the bowl. I watched them swim around for a bit and then went to the sink to get a glass of water to drink. I turned around and when all the fish caught me eye, I dropped me glass and it shattered all over the floor. The fish had grown to five times their size. It shit me up sommat chronic. The detail on the fish was amazing. You could see all their features so clearly. I'll never forget it. It was the thick glass on the other side of the vase. It had magnified them so much. That's what it feels like some of the time."

"I don't understand," says Cassandra.

"Well, some days I feel like a grotty little stickleback swimming around in some huge bowl, and on other days I'm magnified, I'm exaggerated. I'm too big for the bowl I'm swimming in. I'm like a pike in a fuckin' bath."

She nods as if she understands but I can sense she wants more.

"What is it you have?" she asks.

"It's not a disease, love. It's not catching."

"Sorry. I mean..."

"I've had every label stuck on me over the years and a thousand different pills to treat me. I've been called a manic depressive, a schizophrenic and a lot fuckin' worse. Now they call me a bi-polar bear. But labels and names don't mean a thing. They've been pumping lithium into me since kipper ties were in fashion, and a whole host of other shit besides. They've given me electric shocks, they've had me in restraints – they've done every fuckin' thing but cover me in leeches."

"I saw a programme with Stephen Fry," she says cheerfully. "He suffers from bi-polar disorder."

"Does he now?" I say, trying to sound like I give a fuck.

"He said when he was high he felt brilliant but when he was low he had... how did he put it? Yes, a Tourette's view of himself; he said when he was low he felt like a C-U-N-T. Is that how it works with you?"

"The truth is, love, I never think about it, neither do most of the mad people I know. We're too busy being crazy. But no, since you ask. I never feel like a cunt. It's everyone else that's a cunt."

She laughs. It's the first time I've made her laugh since that day in Mrs P's.

"I've got something to show you," she says.

"Not your cu..."

"Alan, please. Don't be crude. I won't have it. And I really don't like all this swearing. I know you're not well but..."

"You started with the cunt talk, love, not me. Okay," I hold me hands up. "No more swearing. Well, I'll try. I've always been a foul-mouthed bastard."

She laughs again.

"Before I show you, there's something I need to ask."

"Fire away, love."

She looks at the sticklebacks in the bucket for a few seconds before looking directly into me sunglasses.

"Why didn't you meet me at the parish church that Saturday night?"

I wasn't expecting this.

"I was engaged to be married, love. Besides, you were far too good for me. Back in those days, I did feel like a cunt."

She smiles. I think she'll get used to me swearing. She has no fuckin' choice and she knows it.

"Anyway, I still don't know anything about you," I

238

say, trying to lighten the mood, before I realise that this is where me bubble will get burst or not. "Married? Kids?"

"I've been married for thirty years."

"I'm sorry to hear that," I said. "Any kids?"

"Yes. A boy. I say a boy, he's a man now. You?"

"You've got to be kiddin'. I'd hate to meet anything that me and Babs had spawned."

Cassandra goes quiet for a little while and almost does that disappearing trick of Harry's. I notice her gaze follow a young couple who are riding their bikes side by side along the tow path.

Suddenly, she opens her art satchel and pulls out a large envelope. She must have been waiting for the drizzle to stop. She opens it and carefully eases out a frayed, nicotine-brown painting.

The colours have faded over time, but there I am, beardless, short hair, me face lit up by the amber fire and flushed with the glow of good ale and good company. There's a pint in me hand and I'm smiling. There's a group of old geezers behind me, swanning pints at the bar, painted just out of focus. She hands it to me.

I take off me sunglasses.

If you enjoyed *Stickleback*, why not try our other Armley Press titles available from Amazon and through UK bookshops?

Mick McCann: *Coming Out as a Bowie Fan*
ISBN 0-9554699-0-2
Mick McCann: *Nailed*
ISBN 0-9554699-2-9
Mick McCann: *How Leeds Changed the World*
ISBN 0-9554699-3-0
John Lake: *Hot Knife*
ISBN 0-9554699-1-6
John Lake: *Blowback*
ISBN 0-9554699-4-7
John Lake: *Speedbomb*
ISBN 0-9554699-5-4
John Lake: *Amy and the Fox*
ISBN 0-9934811-0-8
Ray Brown: *In All Beginnings*
ISBN 0-9554699-6-1
Samantha Priestley: *Reliability of Rope*
ISBN 0-9554699-8-5
Chris Nickson: *Leeds, the Biography*
ISBN 0-9554699-7-X
Nathan O'Hagan: *The World is (Not) a Cold Dead Place*
ISBN 0-9554699-9-6
David Siddall: *Breaking Even*
ISBN 0-9934811-1-6
K.D. Thomas: *Fogbow and Glory*
ISBN 0-9934811-3-0
M.W. Leeming : *Justice is Served*
ISBN 0-9934811-4-7

Visit *armleypress.com*

Lightning Source UK Ltd.
Milton Keynes UK
UKOW01f0205160218
317979UK00002B/89/P